The Animals Praise the Antichrist

The Animals Praise the Antichrist

Alex Older

Crashed Moon Press

Crashed Moon Press

crashedmoonpress@gmail.com

Published in the UK by Crashed Moon Press in 2020

The rights of Alex Older to be identified as author of this work have been asserted in accordance with Copyright Designs and Patents Act.

The moral right of the author is asserted.

© Alex Older 2020
Cover illustration and design © Boots of Cherry Red

All rights reserved.

This book is sold subject to the condition that it shall not, by way of trade or otherwise, be lent, re-sold, hired out or otherwise circulated without the publisher's prior consent in any form of binding or cover other than that in which it is published and without a similar condition including this condition being imposed on the subsequent purchaser. Nor shall any part of this publication be reproduced, stored in a retrieval system or transmitted in any form or by any means without the prior permission in writing of the publisher. Permission can be obtained through Crashed Moon Press

ISBN 978-1-8380387-0-0 (2020 ebook)
ISBN 978-1-8380387-1-7 (2020 paperback)

A CIP catalogue record for this book is available from the British Library

Printed and bound by Ingram Spark
Set in Georgia

1

Dear Christa,

I'm writing this in my cell. Not, I should explain right away, a prison cell, although even now I'm surprised I've never been tracked down and locked up on some charge or other: *crimes against the species*. I won't say "humanity". I don't like that word.

In fact, I'm a monk now. It's my monk's cell in which I write. Of course, I haven't become a *Christian* monk. Can you imagine? No, we're one of the new religions that's sprung up. And our monastery is actually a squat in London, and I'm still a novice. But they think I show "enormous promise" and possess "extraordinary insight". Actually, I'm silent much of the time, which only adds to my mystique and encourages the brothers to leave me to my meditations. It's probably due to my imagined profundity that I've ended up with such a decent room. It's at the top of the building, directly beneath the roof. I have a chair, a desk, a couple of wonky shelves for books. There's a skylight, the timbers are painted white and the mattress I've been given is reasonably clean and comfortable. It's fine for what I need. Which is to spend as much of my time as possible in seclusion, thinking about you.

After you left, I never really went home – not to stay anyway. I spent a couple of nights at Jay's and I even went back to the cottage for a little while, but it wasn't safe. There was a confused scene in the village and too many people around. I was questioned, but it was easy to lie because, at that early stage, they had no idea what kind of questions they should be asking. They were utterly perplexed.

Eventually, I ended up staying with my grandma. But that didn't work out so I ran away. I took some of your money (I hope you don't mind) when I visited Svea for the last time and she let me, after quite a bit of persuasion, into your room. She'd never reported you as missing and that told me a great deal. So did the photograph I found tucked between the pages of *Doctor Glas*. Svea had some questions of her own, but I was evasive. I didn't feel bad, she was the same. About the events leading up to Easter Sunday, I told her as little as possible; as for where you'd gone, you left me no clue. Only one thing was certain: you'd gone off in a terrible rush. If I had to guess, I'd say you were out of the country just hours after you crept from that bedroom, up at the farmhouse.

And so, because it was hopeless, I came to London, hitch-hiking down. The money soon ran out, but I've got by one way or another and for some time now I've been here in the monastery. Of course, there's tumult all around us, but seeing as we are men of faith and ascetics (with nothing much to nick) we are mostly left alone.

It's time to write it all down. I don't know how much longer I'm going to stay. I'm writing it for me and I'm writing it for you, even though you'll probably never see it. I'm talking to you, Christa, and to no one else. Just as I used to talk to you before we'd ever exchanged a word, just as I've talked to you every day these past seven years, inside my head and under my breath. They think I'm in here communing with their deity. I have a feeling that would make you laugh.

As I often told you, for the first three and a half years of high school you didn't make that much impact on me. I was struck by your name, Christa Marlisa Gardner, I knew that your mother was Swedish, and that your father had died suddenly when you were twelve. They said that your family was well off. You seemed serious. I thought you must be sad, but I couldn't really tell, perhaps because you were so aloof, or that's how I found you anyway. Had I been asked, I might've said that you were someone I could never imagine speaking to, not properly. And that, Christa, was pretty much it. Well, almost it anyway. Now and then I had the strange idea – this happened only sometimes – that you made your immediate surroundings go sort of *hazy*. It seemed that the world about you lost its colour, that things went dim and indistinct. Misty. And there you were in the middle of this mist looking terribly sombre. But it was always fleeting and I was used to my mind matching up people with objects or colours or associating them with certain impressions and so it was hardly anything to get excited about.

But then one damp Saturday afternoon, with nothing else to do and no one to hang out with, I caught the bus into town. I remember I went to buy *Surfer Rosa*. As usual, the whole market area reeked of fish and rotisserie chicken. Crowds of shoppers were shuffling about, eating steaming black puddings with ketchup or mustard. I was feeling hungry myself, despite the deathly smells, but all of my money had gone on the album.

To my surprise, I spotted you. You were standing behind a table near an entrance to the food hall. The table had a banner and posters fixed to its front. You were wearing a long coat and a broad-brimmed hat and your hair was down. As I watched, you bent to tidy a small pile of leaflets. I don't think it's an exaggeration to say that I was amazed by the sight of you there, fifteen years of age, but looking older, running that stall, solo. And I couldn't move away.

I saw you catch a woman's eye and she paused and you offered her your literature. She turned it over in her hands, listened and nodded as you gestured and spoke, and then she signed something that you passed to her on a clipboard. A petition, surely. The woman moved on and again you checked that everything was in its place and then raised your head and looked for another sympathetic passerby. The next one you tried blanked you and the next, a lone older man, raised his voice and said something blunt and angry. You didn't flinch, you didn't flush, you just looked away, looked down, patted your stuff, and then searched for yet another person to stop.

In a different mood, I might have walked off after a time, and then sat on the bus and brooded all the way home about my failure to talk to you. But I was full of curiosity, and on that day feeling confident enough to do something about it. So, after a few more minutes of watching, I idled up to your table.

I mistimed my arrival. You had just become involved in conversation with a very tall vicar. He was "full of admiration for your courage and your principled stance". He would gladly sign the petition, he was no stranger to protest himself ... And on he talked. I looked at your leaflets. On the cover of one of them a rabbit was having something horrible done to its eye. I started to read. You were campaigning for an end to the testing of cosmetics on animals.

Eventually the vicar left. Your turned to me with a small smile. Quizzical is the word I would use to describe it.

"Hello, Alex," you said, and I really think this was the first time you had ever used my name. "I don't suppose *you* want to sign my petition. So what can I do for you?"

"I'll sign," I said, and you looked surprised. I took up the clipboard and signed and printed my name.

"Oh," you said as I handed it back. "Thanks."

"That's okay." I was proud of the way I was holding your gaze. I felt bold.

And sure enough, your demeanour changed. You became more friendly, leaning in my direction. "Listen," you said, touching my arm, "you couldn't watch the stall for a few minutes, could you? Jill, who I was supposed to be doing this with, was called away and won't be back until nearly five. I've been here on my own for ages and I really need the loo and to get some food. I'm starving."

My confidence faltered, but I don't think I let it show. "Sure," I said, "no problem at all."

"Oh God, thanks. I'll be quick, I promise. You don't have to do anything. Just stand behind the table so it doesn't look abandoned. Thanks again." And you dashed away.

True to your word, you weren't away long. When you returned you were carrying a paper bag from the expensive delicatessen round the corner.

"I got two signatures," I said.

"Really? Great! That's great. Oh, and I got you this to say thanks." And from out of the bag you pulled a large roll with what looked like several layers of filling.

I took it and opened it, a little doubtful. "Thanks. Can I ask what's on it? Only that place is sausage central and I don't eat meat."

You were already chewing hungrily, but you paused mid-munch. You were really looking at me now. And then you said, with your mouth full, fluttering your hand in front of it to be polite, "But someone told me that your dad is a butcher."

"He is. Well, he was. He's changed jobs now."

"But you don't eat meat?"

"No. Not for nearly two years now."

"Wow. How did he take it? I mean ..." And then you added quickly, "It's just got cheese and peppers and artichokes and stuff."

"Okay," I said. "Thanks. I am hungry." I took a bite and we stood there while we ate our sandwiches. And I told you about how furious my dad had been at first, how he'd been angry for weeks, but how he was mostly fine about it now, unless he'd had too much to drink. And then I went a little further and admitted that my dad had had too much to drink most of the time. This was more than I usually revealed when talking about my home life. You didn't even try to hide it: "I'm impressed," you said.

"Thanks," I replied. "He *is* a scary man, my dad. So yeah, I really had to stand up for myself, through all the yelling."

On the bus back home there was no need for me to brood about shyness and failure. I'd stayed with you for the rest of the afternoon, helping on the stall, learning fast, until Jill had shown up with her Docs, her long jumper, and her green crimped hair. And you'd seemed genuinely grateful. You were just so nice to me as I was leaving, beaming in a way I'd never seen before, giving me a hug. "See you on Monday," you'd said like we were good friends. As I rode home, I felt I was moving though a world transformed, but it was accompanied by the vexing thought that by Tuesday or Wednesday everything would be sliding back to normal again.

And maybe, Christa, normality would have prevailed. Back at school, I struggled to think of things to say, struggled to figure out how to approach you, and once again you seemed remote, although now in a wholly different way.

But then, a month or so after that weekend, Mrs Gee (Gee for Geography) decided she didn't like the level of chatting in her class and moved everyone around. I ended up sat directly in front of you and that made all the difference. Talking, when it's what we both wanted to do, was hard, floating around at break, waving and trying to be witty as we passed each other by. It didn't work. And it was all too public. But squeezed together in class, talking when we weren't supposed to – now we had a chance.

I was partly excited and partly numb. It's like I was trying to block out what was happening, just to keep myself from messing it up, and to spare myself the disappointment when it all went wrong.

You gave me shoulder massages and we exchanged notes. We invented the Sphagnum Moss game and you produced your "Study of the Language of Mrs Gee". Willowy Wendy preened at the front of classroom and when I said that she was "all stem and no flower" you laughed too loudly and she turned and glared at us, assuming, rightly this time, that it was all about her. We made faces and flirted so much that even Jay with his distractions, his digital watches, his tangle of headphones, his ceaseless drumming with a pair of biros, began to notice.

At last, in early June, at the end of our Tuesday afternoon double, you said, "My mum's going out on Saturday night." You were looking mainly at Jay when you spoke. "Would you two like to come down to my house? A few other people are coming too. We can have the living room to ourselves, with music and food. Perhaps Jay could buy the booze?"

Jay nodded and said "Sure." I just smiled.

When Jay called at mine that Saturday evening he was empty handed. Crouching in the porch, tying my boot laces, I looked him up and down. His denim jacket had, as usual, various bulges, but none of them were bottle shaped. As we left I was about to ask him if we needed to call at the corner shop on the way. The problem being that they knew he was a school boy there. They'd seen him in his uniform often enough, so his great height wouldn't fool the regular staff. But, before I had the chance to say anything, he walked behind my dad's XR3, parked on the driveway, stooped and pulled a plain white carrier bag from underneath the car. He adjusted the contents then held the bag open to show me: cans of beer and a bottle of vodka stood upright inside.

It was a fine and warm early summer evening. There were kids out on their bikes or playing a game of curby. Skinny Hayley Peel walked on her hands across her parents' lawn and ignored her mother's voice calling her inside. The sounds of Saturday night TV escaped through open windows and traces of barbecue smoke hung in the air. Jay was talking, already, about the latest video releases. He'd seen *Fatal Attraction*, *Prince of Darkness* was due in July. And I listened, saying little, not feeling my usual need to keep up with every film that was coming out. I became aware that above us, on the hills, the sheep were bleating strangely. Their calls seemed almost like a song. I'd no memory of the sound reaching so far down into the valley before.

I'd never visited your village, three miles from my own, and had to rely on Jay who, for some reason, knew the quickest route. He took us up by the back of the high school and then down Inkle Lane. Soon the open fields that lay on either side of us disappeared from view and the hedgerows grew high and thick. No traffic came our way. Jay and I walked swiftly, the pace set by Jay's long legs. Inside the carrier bag, the cans and the bottle jostled. I could hear robins and redstarts singing in the hawthorn.

It plays out in my mind so often, that evening walk. I think I know why. I think it's because it was the last time that it was just me, just me alone in this life. Innocent, in a way. Free of love. Afterwards, ever more so, it was Alex and Christa. Alex and Christa. For the world, against everybody else.

And that's how I still think of it, though it's seven years since you vanished.

Inkle Lane is long. Yet I came to know every turn, every section of it. I came to resent it because it was between us, and to delight in it because it led me to you. I ran down it in sun and rain and pummelling winds. I ran down it chanting your name. I trudged down it in falling snow, hands plunged into my pockets and the hood of my parka more or less covering my eyes. Running down it in the dark, with that same hood up, I almost died, not noticing an approaching car until it was nearly too late, hurling myself into the hedge just in time.

And, of course, there was the time I ran down it with nothing on my feet.

At the end of Inkle Lane is a right turn and suddenly the land changes. The road leading down to your village widens and to one side is a high and lengthy embankment. Once this embankment was heavily wooded. Now the trees had all been cut down. The slope was littered with branchwood, but otherwise barren and bleak. Clearfelling you said it was later. The trees had been felled so that native species could be planted in their place. But those new trees never appeared, the embankment remained bare the whole time we were together. It always made you angry, whenever we walked by.

There was no birdsong now. Jay was trying to persuade me that U2 is actually a good band. God knows why. My favourite album at the time, as I'd no doubt told him, was *Zen Arcade*. He was always besotted by the mainstream was Jay.

We reached the abandoned textile mill, set back in overgrown grounds, the paint peeling from the iron railings that ran along the side of the road, and I began to wonder what your house would be like. As we came around the bend, I could see neat cottages and hear the rush of the river. But at the humpback bridge, I think I just knew that you couldn't possibly live in the old part of the village.

Even during that first encounter, I detected something unusual about the atmosphere of the place, and noticed certain curious details. Of course, we'd arrived there from where I lived, a modern estate with people out in their gardens or playing on the pavements, enjoying the late Saturday sun. Wasn't this the reason for my sudden unease, simply a lack of kids riding their bikes? We both know, Christa, there was more to it than that.

Ahead of us were two utterly silent and empty streets. Each street had facing rows of workers' cottages made of stone. The cottages were perfectly kept, with fresh, white-painted doors and gleaming black windowsills. There were no front gardens, but then that was nothing unusual to me. I'd been down similar streets all over Lancashire, and in Yorkshire too, when visiting relatives. So I knew that it was odd not to see a single vehicle parked on the road. Not a single one. It all looked as it might have done fifty or sixty years ago, when hardly anyone had cars. And I'd often noticed, on these secluded streets, flowers and plants in pots and baskets out on the pavements, brightening up the front of the houses, or creepers running up beside the doors. But there were none in this place. I stepped into Clewkin Road, with Jay telling me that I was going the wrong way. I walked forward a little. There were no house plants or figurines on the inside windowsills. Again, I thought it was strange. The people that lived in these old-fashioned terraces usually had knick-knacks on display.

It was all very stark and quiet and still. I felt suddenly I shouldn't be there and jogged back towards Jay.

I only lingered there about a minute or so. But I kept hold of my first impression of those two streets. Later, when you said to me that you thought there was something weird about the place, I was able to agree immediately. And I remember thinking that you liked me all the more because of it.

The village had no pub or shop, just a small post box on the edge of the older section. We'd now turned onto your road, although I doubt I realised it at the time. Suddenly the evening seemed light and summery again. The street broadened and the houses were totally different. These were large homes and they grew larger the deeper into the modern part of the village we walked. There were bungalows and two storey houses, each one unique and set back well from the path, with big front gardens and substantial driveways. There were Audis and Mercedes, Jags and Range Rovers parked outside. The garage doors that were open revealed interiors bursting with stuff: tools and lawn mowers, extra freezers and inflatable paddling pools. All the gardens were perfectly kept, with mature plants and colourful flower beds.

Finally, Jay pointed and said, "That's where she lives. It must be, it's the last house in the village."

The river flowed close to where your house was situated, but bent away, and if you wanted to carry on following it you needed to cross a bridge and take a footpath into the woodland that rose up behind where you lived. Those woods, I was to discover, are dense and deep.

We walked up your driveway. Your house, a detached, was so much bigger than the one I lived in. I noticed a bay window, a double garage, a long wooden fence enclosing the garden at the back. And then you were standing by the open door and welcoming us inside.

I remember the shock of it, cold and warm all at once. You had this vast, unexpected existence, entirely outside of my head, beyond the reach of my imagination. I'd spent so much time thinking about you, I'd forgotten you were real. And now here you were, smiling in a large hallway I would never have pictured, with wide wooden steps sweeping upstairs, doors leading off everywhere, laughter coming from another room, and you, hostessing in a Siouxsie Sioux t-shirt and a pair of 501s, being kind to us, the awkward new arrivals. Christa, a person who had been born, and had grown up, and ate mysterious meals every day, and slept every night, and had endless thoughts and dreams and memories, none of which I knew about. Christa, a person, in truth, I'd barely any connection with, a person making me take seriously for the first time in my life the enigma of another human being.

Afterwards, when I told you how I'd felt in this moment, you said: "But you just stood there with this coy smile on your face. I thought you were being oh-so cool!"

We went into the living room, with you now carrying the drinks. You were playing *Fire of Love*. There were several people already in there, but when I think about them today I can't see their faces, even though I remember exactly who they were. I just see bodies sat in a row. I don't think I can even bring myself to write down their names. It's not necessary, is it? They were extras. What else is there to add?

Nothing. Except that at one point a guest said: "Christa, I think there's someone in your front garden."

We were on the sofa, kissing, both a little bit drunk. But drunk was the least of it. I mean, I'd kissed girls before, and I'd felt no great commotion. With you it was different. Something was up with my blood: it's like it was full of Space Dust. Such a weird mixture of weakness and strength. The terrible tenderness that arrived from nowhere. A part of me was almost alarmed. I remember that well.

The only thing in the world that mattered was your face. I kissed it, I cupped it in my hands, in and out of focus it went: lips and eyes and cheeks and hair.

And then a girl's voice said: "Christa, I think there's someone in your front garden."

It seemed to take forever to come apart, to untangle ourselves. We went to the door and I opened it and walked outside. I could hear the same voice saying: "I know I saw someone. I saw him move. A man, I think."

I hunted around for a minute or two, but no one was there.

Back inside you paid some attention to the others and I took the chance to look around. The room was long with low sofas, small tables, armchairs, lamps everywhere. There was a large, full bookcase. Nothing matched, but everything went together, and there were many interesting objects dotted about and paintings on the walls. None of my friends had a house like this and my own house, too, seemed so small and plain. My parents had no books. The walls were white woodchip and the furniture in the living room was all too big. My parents' living room existed to provide a home for the TV, whereas your TV, from where I was standing, was far away in an obscure corner.

One thing our houses did have in common: there were no family photos on the walls, or out in frames.

You came and stood beside me and took my hand. "Are you hungry?" you asked and I had no idea, but I realised you wanted me to say yes, and anyway I thought I'd better eat something, so I nodded. But I desperately didn't want you disappearing off to prepare food. "Who's hungry?" you said to the room at large and there were various responses indicating that most people were.

You went into the hall and I heard you ring someone up. When you returned you announced that you'd ordered pizza. We all tried to give you money, but you refused, saying we were your guests. The music had stopped so, while we waited, we looked through the albums you'd brought downstairs. The secret thrill, I remember, of looking through a small sample of your record collection and seeing albums by Wipers, Lowlife, The Sound.

When the pizza man arrived with a pile of boxes I went with you to the door. I watched you pull several notes from your jeans pocket and pay him and add a tip. In the kitchen, I helped you grab plates and paper napkins. I was wondering whether to tell you – but in the end I didn't dare – that this would be the first time I'd ever eaten takeaway pizza. My dad would never order it. He would sometimes pretend that it was an option and produce a menu for our local pizza place along with those for the Indian and the Chinese restaurants. But in the end I would always be outnumbered by my father who had his own vote to cast and, whether she knew it or not, my mum's too.

I hadn't felt uncomfortable since those first few minutes of being in your house. Yet now I found that sitting in someone's plush living room with slices of pizza on a plate on your knee can leave you inhibited, even after a bit of vodka and beer. I sat and stared for what seemed to be ages at the pizza, as though I was more interested in committing it to memory than getting on with eating. Actually, I *can* see them now, those pizza slices, silly as it sounds. It was the second time you had given me food and I was thinking about the cash you had pulled from your pocket and how maybe I should get a Saturday job. But then weren't Saturdays in the future going to be for seeing you? I didn't know, but I certainly hoped so. Some of them at any rate.

You didn't embarrass me by asking this across the room. You came and sat on the arm of the sofa and said, "Don't you like pizza, Alex?"

For a moment, I was mortified. I'd been sat there feeling many things, feeling I was many things, and one of them was callow, which was a cliché too. And of course my brooding had turned me into the very thing I feared I might appear to be, a bumpkin from the new-build estate.

I picked up a piece of my pizza, folded it in half and took a big bite, a boy bite as you might have said. When I dared to glance at you again, you were smiling warmly. Then you whispered, "I think Jay's already eaten a whole one to himself."

A little while after pizza, things began to break up. People started leaving. Jay didn't seemed to be in any hurry to go but I wasn't sure what to do. Should we hang on until the end or get out of your way? Then you asked: "Would you two mind helping me clean up?"

You produced a black bin liner and we filled it with bottles and cans and empty pizza boxes. This went in a skip as Jay and I walked home. We gathered glasses and plates and helped you wash and dry the dishes and put them away. Part way through, Jay went to the bathroom and you placed your arms around my neck and said, "So, are we together?" And I nodded, realising that despite all my insecurities I'd been taking it as a given that we were. And then we kissed again.

When Jay returned, you opened some wet cat food and forked a portion into a bowl, saying, "Don't go just yet. Come into the garden a minute." Carrying the cat food, you led the way out onto your big back lawn. You said, "This is for the hedgehogs, if the cat doesn't find it first," and placed the bowl on the ground.

It was cooler now, the night air stirred by a summer breeze. Off to the side huge trees towered in silhouette above your garden, the edge of the ancient woodland. All was quiet and for a moment we three were silent too, staring at the sky. In the darkness of your village you could see countless stars. You slipped your arm around my waist and rested your head on my shoulder.

And then from the woods there came the sound of screaming. One scream after another, their eeriness intensifying with the growing urgency of the calls. You lifted your head, alert, your whole body rigid. Another cry and another. "Foxes," you whispered, and I felt the word in my ear. "I usually hear them shrieking like that late in the winter." There was a lull and then the fox screams started again. On and on they went. You took a step forward and raised your face in the direction of the screeching. "Sounds strange, even for them," you said, and turned back towards me. "I wonder what's going on."

2

I had to tell my parents about you, Christa. "Boy's got a *guurl friend*," scoffed my dad and my mother laughed.

Nonetheless, they agreed that you could come for dinner (or tea, I suppose we said).

"What are they like?" you wanted to know. "How should I dress?"

We'd gone to the park after school and were sitting on the swings. There was no one else about.

"They're ... kind of ghastly."

I was ready for you to remonstrate with me. I was ready for you to say, "Oh come on, they can't be that bad. I'm sure they're fine really," and all that crap. You didn't though. You just said, "In what way?"

"In every way."

"Give me an example."

I twisted on the swing a little, staring at the ground.

"Is it hard to talk about?"

"Not with you. It's more that I want to tell you everything all at once but I don't know where to start."

"I might get my hair cut for the occasion," you said.

"God, don't bother for them."

"Well, go on. Tell me what they're like."

"My dad goes to the pub three or four nights a week. This has been going on as long as I can remember. He's always drunk. He goes out on Thursdays and Sundays with his shady mates. It's sacred. And then he'll go out on Friday or Saturday as well. Sometimes both. On Fridays and Saturdays the wives are allowed out too, my mum included.

"I need you to understand, because your life is so different to mine. There's never any money. There never has been. New school shoes, a new school bag, if I need these things it causes a massive crisis. There's shouting about me wearing things out too fast. There's slamming about. He'll always try to come up with some hand-me-down if he can. Once his mum got some bizarre bag as a free gift and he made me use it for school, until the piss-taking got too much and I ripped it deliberately. Then there was more fury. But at least I got a better bag."

You were laughing a little. "Oh, no! I remember that thing. Like something a salesman would carry? I think I might have laughed at it myself. It was notorious, briefly. Sorry!"

"Yes, that was it. God, it was awful. I used to feel sick every morning!" Now we were both giggling. "Anyway, most of the furniture in my bedroom is hand-me-down too. It's all too big and dark and heavy, but that's okay, I don't mind. Except ..."

"Yes?"

"Well, the only adult in my family I've ever really liked was my grandad, my mum's dad. He was a copper engraver. He had to serve a really long apprenticeship, which was interrupted by the war. He hand engraved rolls of copper and they were used to print fabrics. It was delicate work. I used to go and watch him doing it when I was allowed. I had to be completely quiet at all times. My grandad, he was like a point of stillness in this busy, clanging factory, sitting at his desk with all his tools, calmly engraving the copper. Outside of work, he always had time for me. He took me to the park. When I was really small I had this thing about cement mixers. I loved them. It might have been because they were orange and I've always liked orange. He always knew where there was some building work being done and on Saturdays we would go out and look at the cement mixer. On the way home he'd buy me a Prize bar, those were my favourites back then. Also, he taught me to read. He did it mainly using *Pippin* comics because we didn't have any books. When I went into infants, I was way ahead of everyone else."

"He sounds nice."

"He was, yes."

I didn't speak for a moment and you said, "In Sweden grandparents on the mother's side are called mormor and morfar. On the dad's side it's farmor and farfar."

"Okay. So he would have been my morfar?"

You nodded.

"Anyhow, my grandad, my morfar, had an accident at work. He fell down this kind of well. It was full of all the run-off from the dyes and things, a sort of horrible chemical stew. He broke his hip and ingested loads of the fluid. Before too long, I don't know if it was connected, he got cancer of the kidney. Then it spread to his brain. He started doing really weird things like only shaving one side of his face. Eventually he couldn't look after himself anymore and so my grandma decided that the best thing to do would be to have a bed in their living room and look after him there. She didn't love him, she told me this not long after he died, if you can believe it. I can't even begin to imagine why she didn't love him, or why she told me. Thinking about it, though, it was obvious she didn't really care. Mainly what she said, after he died was, 'I kept him clean!' She kept saying it over and over again in this stupid high voice, like an annoying parrot. She'd give him bed baths because he would make a mess of himself. The bed had to have plastic sheets and all that. He couldn't speak at the end. He didn't know where he was. His eyes were always really wide, with this desperate expression, like there was still some part of him that understood the horror of what was happening. I used to sit and talk to him and read him the football reports from the paper, because, although I've never my grandad loved it. And then one day, there, he died."

Your face had been changing. You tried to fight it, but it crumpled. I'd been incredibly stupid and selfish. I'd ambushed you with a story about a dying relative. You hadn't expected it.

"Oh Christa, I'm sorry. I shouldn't be talking about this." That really set you off. You started sobbing hard. I had hold of you now and you pressed your face into my school shirt and soon it was soaked.

I searched my pockets for tissues, which is something even the least gallant fool can manage to do.

"I want you to go on," you said a few minutes later, and your face was held all tight like you were stopping it from screwing up again. "Finish your story."

"Are you sure?"

"Yes. Please, Alex."

"After my grandad died my parents got all cagey. I'd watched him dying for months but they wouldn't tell me about the funeral arrangements. I was nine at the time. Eventually, I realised they weren't going to let me go. 'It'll be too upsetting,' they said. They meant too upsetting for them! They didn't want me there making it worse for them and everybody else. Because I was the one who was the saddest. So I didn't get to go. I begged them to let me go to that funeral, but they just wouldn't give in. On the day itself I was looked after by some awful old neighbour. My whole family was there except me. I should have run down there anyway. I knew where the cemetery was. It's where my sister's buried."

"But you were only nine, Alex"

"And then, after he'd been buried, my grandma started to get rid of my grandad's stuff. The bed, the bed he'd died on, was still in the living room. And at the time I needed a new bed. So my dad scrounged it off my grandma, who he can't stand, and who can't stand him.

He took that bed, the bed my grandad died on, and he made me have it. I wasn't allowed to the funeral, but that was my new bed. It's the one I've still got today. You'll see it when you come."

I shook my head. "So, in answer to your question, *that's* what my parents are like."

By then I'd been down to your house a handful of times: after school once or twice and on Fridays and Saturdays. I just lied to my parents about where I was. Not that they cared much anyway.

Your brother, four years older than us and a student, was hardly ever there. He had a car and a girlfriend and a band, and he was due to go travelling in Europe later that summer. I was introduced to Svea, your mum, and Ildi, the Hungarian woman who used to look after you both when your mum was away and still came in to do some cleaning. But I don't think your mum could quite take me in. For her, I was so inoffensive, so without a character, that I didn't really register. It wasn't for want of looking. There was something humiliating about the experience of having her size me up. I had the idea that she thought I was too young for you, though we were both set to turn sixteen in the autumn. I believed she'd have understood me more if I was the kind of boy to get worried about, roaring up on a motorbike or something. There she was, multilingual, well off, a woman of the world with a business to run. What was I? Nothing much. You saw this too and tried to explain it away. She was busy on the one hand, angry and disappointed on the other. Your dad's dying had left her with too much to do. She missed being young when she'd roamed all over Europe, having adventures she'd only drop hints to you about. And I'm sure these things were true. But still, it was strange. At home I was regarded as being an oddball, while down at yours I made next to no impression.

On the upside, she placed no restrictions on our comings and goings, didn't insist on any ground rules, maybe because she'd decided I didn't have it in me to cause too much trouble.

So, in the privacy of your room, you showed me your scars, the scars on your stomach, the scars on your thighs. And I didn't have any myself so, to start, I told you about how my first love bite was given to me by a boy on holiday when I was ten. A huge one on my neck. And I kind of liked it, but my dad was apoplectic. And then I told you about how he got angry when I was much younger, just after my sister had died. I was very small then. I had a wooden headboard on my bed. Every morning when I woke up I would beat the back of my head on that headboard, over and over again, really hard. The paper and plaster on the wall behind were ruined and I developed a bald patch, which I had for months, maybe more than a year. That made my dad irate too. I suppose he found it embarrassing. He would bellow from my parents' room for me to 'Pack it in', disturbed by the ceaseless thudding. But I couldn't stop and no one tried very hard to make me.

On your thighs, the scars were in neat little lines, all along the top and on the inside, easily hidden from view. But on your stomach they were mainly on the right side in a sort of angry criss-cross. All the scars were pink or white and you promised me you'd stopped. I pressed you hard on this. I couldn't bear the thought you harming yourself again. You searched my face for something. I think you were checking to see if I really meant what I said, that I wasn't just playing a role. I must've passed the test because you pulled me close. *Head Over Heels* was on the stereo.

On one of those first Fridays, I remember getting up to go to the loo and when I returned everything had faded away leaving you looking like some kind of artwork in the middle of your room: *Girl on a Beanbag*. The view from your window, usually dense with trees, was blank and pale, and the air surrounding you was dark grey, almost smoky. It seemed to be gently in motion. One of your favourite albums, *Faith*, was playing, your hazy green eyes were on me, and I remember thinking: "Is Christa causing this or me? Or is it both of us together?" And then: "Is Christa seeing this too?" But I didn't want to ask because it would have wrecked the mood of the moment and I'd already recognised that mood was a major thing between us, an alteration in the atmosphere of the world. Memories, sadness, silence. Music, the woods, the hills. Empty lanes at night. Falling asleep together in the late afternoon. The stop-start of time. Secrets. It was these and other elements that made up the mood we shared and we both became hostile early on to anything that might spoil it.

And *rooms*, they were important too. Your room and my room, rooms without adults in them. Did we feel safe and hidden away? Your room was far better for this. My house was so small and badly built. Often, down at yours, no one knew that we were in for hours and hours at a time. Then, too, your room was fully yours, you'd done exactly what you wanted with it, with no interference from the outside, and no hand-me-downs. So you had no bed, just a mattress in the corner, and no wardrobe either, just a long rail on wheels, crammed with clothes, and a chest of drawers. Inside one of these drawers, amidst socks and underwear, was a roll of banknotes. It was more money than I'd ever seen in my life, though you always said you didn't know how much was there. It was cash you earned helping your mum out in the office downstairs.

The walls of your room were black. You warned me about this and I remember that I laughed and said something about clichés and Adrian Mole. But this was no botched adolescent protest. You'd had the paint specially made, at considerable expense, and done the work yourself with great care. The woodwork and the radiator were oxblood red. The effect, at first, was seriously shocking to someone used to white woodchip, white skirting boards, white everything. But I soon grew to love it. It made us feel enclosed. There were candles and lamps, books and albums everywhere, and possessions left over from childhood. I remember thinking how all the things I'd owned from when I was small seemed to have disappeared. I was worried my room, when you saw it, would seem pitifully stark.

You did get your dark blonde hair cut, like you said you would, to meet my parents. And you defanged my dad with the way you dressed and conducted yourself that day. I remember opening the door to you and your artful smile as my eyes went wide and I said, "Oh my God!"

You winked and did a little curtsey. You had on black ankle boots and a black broad-brimmed hat. But there was no Joy Division t-shirt and no faded 501s. They'd been replaced by a lacy white dress with floaty sleeves. You looked mature and innocent all at once. It would have tenderised even the toughest butcher's heart.

I led you into the house and my parents emerged from the kitchen, cigarettes in hand. For a moment, I thought they were going to run out the back. A parade of men, mainly, came through our house, men with moustaches and bellies and names such as Revver and Fat Jeff. Who the hell was this with her hat and her height and her alarming arms and legs? You had be-bangled your wrist so that it jingled when you extended your hand to my dad and said brightly, "Hi, I'm Christa. It's a pleasure to meet you." Then you shook my mum's hand and meanwhile the cat, who had a thing about boots, had jumped down from the sofa and begun rubbing herself against you. You bent and stroked her and tickled her behind the ears and then straightened up again and beamed. "I have a cat," you said. "Her name is Liv."

"Malnourished", my dad had said vegetarians were when I'd made my announcement. "Stunted" with "weak bones". And "miserable sods" as well. Now I had grown taller than him, and here you were, taller still – at least in your boots. You had perfume on, your voice seemed firmer than usual, and in the brightness of the early evening sun as it poured into the living room your skin was fresh and unblemished. I think if we'd declared we'd gone vegan my dad would have scurried off into the kitchen to see what he could make.

I remember the thump of your heels on the steps as we stomped upstairs. I got a weird kind of thrill out of it. Then we were in my room and I was trying not to feel embarrassed by everything, the thin carpet with the narrow stripes, the faded valance on the base of my bed, the lack of somewhere to sit, the lack of space. But you didn't seem that fazed. You unzipped your boots and turned to look at me and now I could see that underneath it all there was something wrong. I enquired what it was.

"It's my mum. She had a huge snappy on me just before I left."

"Why? What happened?"

"She says we're spending too much time together."

"What? It's only two or three nights a week. And today's Saturday!"

"I know." You sighed and now you started to look around and then lowered yourself on to the edge of the bed. "I don't know how seriously to take it. This is the thing with my mum, she's completely random. She'll be fine about something for weeks and then ... You can never be sure what she's going to do next. She's such a moody cow."

"So how did you leave it."

"We're going to have to have another talk, apparently."

"Oh, God. That sounds ominous."

You shrugged. "It probably won't happen. But I can't be certain. She might change her mind or just forget. Or she might try to split us up. You never can tell."

"Has this kind of thing happened before?"

"Oh, yes. She stopped me from seeing this boy about a year ago – James. Have I mentioned him? Not that I cared, especially."

Abruptly, I had a feeling of coldness and fear. "But you care now, right?"

Your face changed. Your troubled expression was wiped away by a slow, soft smile. "Of course! Yes! Don't worry, I won't let her break us up. Anyway, she probably won't mention it again. Don't let it spoil tonight."

It seemed you thought there was nothing more to be said and so I attempted to move us on to other things.

"I like your dress!"

"Thanks. Do you think it did the trick?"

I laughed. "I think they were suitably impressed. And surprised. As was I."

You shook your head. "Oh, I can scrub up well, when I want to."

"So I see."

You patted the duvet. "So is this the infamous bed?"

"Mm."

"Well, come here. Let's make it about something else."

But soon I had to stop. I pulled away and you said, "Hey! What's wrong?"

I'd been unsettled. By what your mum had said. By your presence in my parents' home. "Why do you like me, Christa? Why are we together."

"What? What is this?" Then sharply: "You're not going off me are you?"

I shook my head. "Quite the opposite."

You frowned. "So what's up then?"

"I'm serious. All of a sudden, I'm worried. Actually, maybe it's not all that sudden. But anyway, I don't understand why you like me."

"And I don't understand why you're asking." You sounded cross now.

"I think it's because you're here, at my house. That's what's set me off."

You looked away and kind of pouted. Then you grinned and said, "It's because you don't think my cheeks are podgy."

"I'm being serious, Christa."

"Yes, alright. Can I look through your albums while I think about it."

"Of course."

You started to flip through. "You've got so many!"

"It's where all the money goes. It's all I ever ask for at Christmas and birthdays."

"What was your first one?"

"*Eliminator* by ZZ Top."

"Ha! Amazing. 'Legs'! What's this?" You pulled out my copy of *First Utterance*.

"Ah, well I bought that at a jumble sale at the church for 50p. I didn't know what it was. It's a crazy folk thing from just before we were born. It sounds sort of evil. I really like it."

"Evil? Can we put it on?"

"Go ahead. It makes my dad foam at the mouth. He likes Queen and Miami Sound Machine."

You were laughing loudly now and then attempting to stifle it. "Miami Sound Machine! Oh God, no!"

So you put on Comus and listened intently. And I won't say you didn't smirk at first, but you soon got into it.

"This is bonkers. Can I borrow it?"
"Yeah. You can borrow anything you like."
You smiled. "That's it you see."
"What do you mean?"
"You don't normally lend out your records do you?"
"No. That's my rule. I'll tape it for you if you give me a C90, but the album doesn't leave the house. I spend a lot of time making tapes, it has to be said. I've got about eight to do in the next few days."
"But I can borrow anything I like?"
"Yes."
"Why?"
"Because you're you."

"I think the answer is trust," you said. "The first night we were alone together, I felt it. I felt I could tell you anything. I was thinking: 'I want to spend the whole night kissing. But then I want to spend the whole night talking too.' Other boys, and as you know there's been a few ... I could just sense it would've scared them off if I'd opened up. Even if I'd had the urge, which I didn't. Or they know something about me already and they think I'm just some sad girl they can use. Bastards, every one of them. But you, I wanted you to know things. I needed you to know. That it was me who found my dad when I was twelve. All because my parents were in separate rooms. How hysterical I was. How angry and miserable I've been. That I'm not a virgin. That I've tried things with a girl. You're not disgusted. You don't judge. And you've been through so much yourself. Your sister, your grandad. Your grandma smacking you about when you were small." You dropped your voice to a whisper. "Your parents being total idiots. I don't trust anyone. Not my mother. Definitely not my brother. Did I tell you that the other day he came into my room and said, for no reason: 'You know, Christa, I've never liked you'?"

"What?"

"I know. It's just like him. Prick. But Alex, I trust *you*." You had your hands on mine now. "And you trust me, it seems. With your records and with everything else. And you don't think it's all about being *happy*!" This last word you practically spat from your mouth. "You'll never say that I have to cheer up. You'll never tell me it 'might not happen'. God, I hate that phrase! You're handsome. You're the best kisser ever. You've got guts. You had the courage to say to your dad that you wouldn't eat meat anymore. And I can tell you *anything*! Do you remember what you said? 'I'll keep your problems in my pocket. But any time you want to we can take them out again.' It's that last bit that got to me."

"Plus," I said, "I did recently break the school record for the hundred metres."

"What was the time again?

"11.28."

"Amazing," you said. And pushed me over on my grandad's bed.

3

It was maybe the third or fourth time you came to my house for dinner, Christa, that you first saw my dad drunk. My parents weren't going out that Saturday night for some reason and so my dad was drinking more at home and had started earlier. The fridge was loaded with cider, there was red wine, and a bottle of blended scotch stood on the worktop.

He was cooking, making an effort I must admit, and blasting out Rod Stewart's *Greatest Hits*. If there had been any way to get out of going downstairs and eating with them I would have proposed it, but there wasn't, not without making him angry. There was no point trying to reason with my mum.

When the shouted summons came we made our appearance in a groggy state, we'd both dozed off and slept for nearly an hour. Rod had been replaced by *Bat Out of Hell*.

My dad was wearing faded red shorts and, tucked in, a white t-shirt, now pretty stained. He was in an exuberant mood, showing off, trying to impress you. I remember that we sat side by side, rigid from the waist up, kicking each other under the table. The food was good, but my dad was fixated on the wine, topping us up constantly. When the bottle on the table was finished he went to get another and when he returned he grabbed me from behind in a vicious headlock and gave my crown a burning knuckle rub. "What about you, boy?" he bellowed. "Do you want some more of this here wine?" I struggled, but his brawny arm tightened and it was pointless. I merely indicated yes.

He poured and then said, politely, "Christa?"

"I'm not sure I can drink what I've already got," you said. The food may have been nice, but the wine was ropey.

"Suit yourself!" and his arm swooped and he grabbed your glass and downed the contents in one. Even my mum was moved to make a sound of protest.

My dad was oblivious. Soon he was weaving about the kitchen, preparing pudding and singing along with Meat Loaf, though he didn't really know the words.

As soon as we could, after helping with the washing up, we left the house and headed towards the hills. There were a couple of hours of daylight left.

"How often is he like that?" you wanted to know.

"Every week, pretty much. But it's mainly when he gets home from the pub and it's different then because I can go upstairs. Anyway, he normally just falls asleep in his chair."

"Oh well, that's alright then!"

"It could have been worse. At least he didn't start calling me a pillock. That's his normal insult of choice when he's pissed. 'Pillock,' he'll say if I drop something. Or pillock if he disagrees with some point I make. Or pillock if I've forgotten to do a chore. Or once he was supposed to pick me up from somewhere and I was delayed by a few minutes. He didn't wait, he just drove back to the house. Five miles. And by the time I'd walked home, knowing full well what was in store, he'd been drinking and was in a rage. And then I had to sit and eat some food from a plate on my knee, which I hate, while he called me a pillock over and over again. The key is not to get trapped in a room with him, which unfortunately we just did."

"God, I'm so sorry."

"You've nothing to be sorry about. It's me who should be sorry. I wouldn't blame you if you never wanted to come to my house again."

We made our way higher into the valley, in the direction of the experimental farm.

"Do you have any nice memories of time spent with your dad?" you asked.

"It was better when I was smaller. He seemed to get angrier from when I was about ten. I don't know why. I remember being taken to the Pleasure Beach at Blackpool and to see the Illuminations. We had a couple of fun holidays in Spain, one when I was six and again when I was eight. He used to buy me a chocolate doughnut and an orange juice for breakfast. And he used to give me change to play on the slot machines. But I never think about any of that now."

"And do you and your dad agree on anything? Do you ever have a conversation?"

"Not really. He loves Mrs Thatcher and always refers to the Germans as Krauts. He's not joking either, he actually seems to hate them. I remember when Boris Becker won Wimbledon the first time, and I was cheering for him. I thought we were going to have a fight."

"Oh!"

"Yeah, don't worry: I'm not aware that he has a particular dislike of Swedes. Lovely Swedes!" And I gave you a kiss.

You were smiling, but you said, "I doubt he's given us much thought."

"Maybe. He did once tell me that all Finnish girls were ugly though."

"Oh, for God's sake!"

"There's one thing we do agree on. I'm not sure what you'll make of this. It's that we both saw a ghost once. At the same time. That was a father and son moment, if you like."

"No! What? You believe in ghosts?"

"Belief has nothing to do with it. It's not like we were hoping to see one. We weren't on a ghost hunt. But we saw something for sure. And I think most people would label what we saw a 'ghost'. I know I saw it and ... that's all I know. I don't know what it was."

"What happened?"

We were close to the river's edge and I indicated that we should sit. There was a small waterfall and a pool beneath full of rocks and copper coins. We dangled our feet over the side and I thought about how to explain it.

"It was actually Christmas Eve, which seems like a bit of a cliché. We were driving over the West Pennine Moors to collect my grandma for Christmas Day. It was about 7 o'clock at night, so dark, obviously, and fine and clear. It was just me and my dad in the car, with me next to him in the passenger seat. Along that road there are places where you can see certain points ahead and then you loose sight of them for a moment due to a bend or a dip or some trees or whatever."

You nodded. You knew the road, I'm sure.

"Anyway, it happened like that, but I can never remember which one it was, flakey as it sounds. It wasn't trees. It was either a bend or a dip. So before we hit the blind spot, I saw a white figure leading a white horse across the road. He was in old-fashioned clothes, a heavy, long coat and a three-cornered hat and he was holding the reins of his horse and I could see the horse's legs moving and its flank and tail and muzzle and hooves, all moving, and then we lost our view of where it was and when we could see again it was gone. All in a handful of seconds, but very clear. It wasn't just vague. All the details were there. I could tell from the way my dad touched the brakes that he'd seen it as well. And a few moments later I mentioned it. I said, 'I thought I saw something just then.' And he said immediately, 'A man with a horse.' Unlike me though, he was completely weirded out and when we got back home he started in on the spirits, the Christmas brandy. He took it very seriously. In fact, he was scared. He's very superstitious. It makes me wonder about the inside of his head. He believes in God, bizarrely. You'd think it would make him have doubts about being such a shit."

"I can't help noticing that your only father and son thing ends up with him getting drunk again. Are you absolutely certain he's your dad?"

I laughed.

"Do you think he knows he's supposed to love God, not just believe in him?"

And so we drifted on to the subject of faith.

"It makes me feel sick, Christianity," you said. "I mean it. Hymns. *Songs of Praise*. The Bible. Vicars. I hate all of it. What I can't stand is this idea that once you're born, which you didn't request, you're stuck in this trap of the Christian universe. It's like being born in a dungeon. There's no way out, you're always being watched. Judged. You have to believe in God and you have to obey him with all his ridiculous laws or else you're going to be punished forever more. At least, that's what some Christians say. But what if you don't believe in God? Is that your fault? How is it your fault? Is it a choice? I've *never* believed in God. If you don't believe, you don't believe. I don't see what you can do about it. But still you have to suffer, or you would if any of it was true. Imagine all the people in history who actually had to worry about this stuff, who had to wonder if they were destined for heaven or hell, or if their faith was strong enough. Not allowed to doubt, especially not aloud. Even though there isn't the slightest evidence of God's power or love anywhere. Everlasting life? But only on his terms, of course. And who wants it anyway? It's a sick idea. If I was going to worship a god it would have to be a god of death."

"You're such a goth."

"Ha! I know. I should just get on with it and dye my hair."

You were impassioned now: "I think I'd hate Christianity even if I did believe in God. You're dragged into the world and forced to live your whole life for him and then he won't let you go even when you're dead. It's a hideous thought. No escape! Your soul being held a captive. Forever. What a *monster* he is. I had this children's Bible growing up and I used to read it all the time and look at the pictures, and that's what I used to think: 'What a monster he is.' Abraham and Isaac. The Flood. I remember a picture of all the animals drowning. What did they do wrong? When I was at primary school we used to have to sing this religious song, over and over again. 'Lord of the Dance' it's called. You must know it." And you sang part of the chorus.

I nodded.

"I used to practically have a panic attack every time it started up. I had this image of this idiot wiggling hippy Jesus figure dancing in front of me, banging a tambourine, trying to take over my body and mind. And part of me wanted to run away and part of me wanted to kick him in the balls! It's the worst song ever written."

"I can't help noticing," I said. "That you deny God exists, but you speak as though you're furious with him. Everything you're ranting about was invented by humans."

You conceded the point, wrinkling your nose. "You're right, obviously. It's all our fault. Human beings are idiots. We just tell ourselves endless lies."

You bent and reached for the river water with your fingertips. "I wouldn't mind so much if the lies were better," you said.

*

"Hello mister. There's no escape from me you know. What are you reading?"

It was lunch time and raining so I'd taken myself off to the library. Most of my mates were away on a history trip that day and I'd come prepared.

"Oh, it's this book about video nasties. It's not from here. I got it from the library in town."

"You're such a wholesome young man. That's why I like you so much."

I was sitting, in a secluded corner, on an armless easy chair. You collapsed on to the seat beside me, flinging your bag on the floor, tucking your legs under yourself and turning in my direction. You were grinning. "You're always hiding in here," you said.

"I'm not hiding! Are you here just to annoy me? I was reading."

You pouted and pretended to be offended. I just shook my head in mock disgust. "Sorry," you said. "Go on, tell me about the nasty nasties."

"You're not interested. You only like black-and-white films."

"That's not true! Anyway, I remember from the news: banned videos. *Nazi Cannibals On Heat* or whatever. Just your sort of thing."

"Funny. The book is about how politicians and busybody Christians banned a whole load of films because they thought we'd become depraved if we watched them at home." When I mentioned Christians you pulled your face. "I used to look at the boxes of these films when I was small. I remember the corner shop always seemed to have a copy of *Driller Killer* in the window."

I dropped the book into my bag. You said, "I'm feeling quite depraved now," and thrust yourself towards me and we risked a quick bit of snogging.

Just as we pulled apart Mrs Midgley rounded the corner and said sharply, "Lunchtime is almost over!" which wasn't really true.

We gathered our stuff, laughing, and left. I said, "I think she let us off lightly because I used to volunteer one lunch break a week to do shelving and stuff."

"You were so good until I corrupted you." But then you grew more serious. "Listen, you know what we were talking about the other day, how you saw a ghost once?"

"Hmm."

"Well, what would you say if I said that I thought there was something odd about the old part of our village?"

"I'd say that I didn't want to say anything, but that I sensed it right away. That first night that Jay and I came down."

"What, really? You're not just humouring me are you?"

"No. Seriously. I noticed the silence, the total lack of cars. The houses are all the same, smart, but strangely bare. No ornaments, no plants. No kids about. No signs of life anywhere. And a sort of heavy atmosphere about the place. It disappears once you get to the newer part of the village. I always run most of the way to your house anyway, but if I happen to be walking when I hit the humpback bridge then I start legging it again until I reach your house."

"That's incredible! That's exactly it. I hate going through there. If I'm just going for a walk then I'll head off into the woods, but when I'm going out or coming home I always hurry past the cottages. I even mentioned it to my mum the other day to see what she thought, but like everybody else she's always in the car. She had no idea what I was on about. She's not sensitive like we are. Why did we take so long to find each other? I knew you wouldn't just laugh at me."

We were outside now. The rain had eased to a fine drizzle. Despite the weather, there was pre-summer-holiday excitement in the air. Over by the entrance to the gym a plump red-headed girl was shouting the word "Bumchin" over and over again in some lad's face. Soon others came to join her in a chorus of "Bumchin, Bumchin, Bumchin," enclosing the boy in a circle.

"But why mention it now? Has something happened?"

"It's probably nothing. I don't know, it did seem peculiar. The other evening I was walking home. I was just passing by the old houses when I saw two men appear on the street. They came out of neighbouring front doors at almost exactly the same moment. And this is what got me: they were dressed identically. They were both tall, skinny men and they both had smart grey trousers on and paler grey shirts, tucked in. It sounds silly, but the way they were dressed made me think of Ian Curtis. Anyway, they just nodded at one another and then walked off silently in the direction of the church."

"The church? Are you sure you're not just getting angry about Bible bashers again."

"No, no, no. The church isn't in use any more. It hasn't been an actual church for a good few years. I don't know who owns it now."

"Oh, okay. I'm not sure what to think then. Maybe it was just a coincidence. Or you do get people who like to dress the same sometimes. I've noticed that quite often."

I could see you were growing frustrated with me. "No, no. It wasn't like that. Perhaps I'm not explaining it right."

"Sorry. Tell me again."

"They came out of their houses at the same time. They were dressed very neatly and *exactly* the same, all in grey. They nodded at one another, sort of formally, and then went off in silence, side by side. Do people act like that where you live?"

"No, of course they don't. I take your point."

"Thank you. So you agree it's a bit strange?"

"Yes. But I have no idea what it means. The place is just weird."

"Me neither, but I thought we could do a little snooping over the summer. I'll feel safer if it's the two of us. There's something about those streets."

"Definitely. That reminds me, with you mentioning summer. I've been meaning to ask again: did you and your mum ever have that talk, about us spending too much time together? Are we free to see each other as much as we like over the break?"

"No, we never had it. All she said was that she wants me to do some typing for her on some weekday mornings over the holidays. That's it."

"Six whole weeks to do what we want."

You raised your eyebrow at me: "I know. It's going to be amazing."

On summer weekday mornings I woke up after my parents had gone to work. While you did typing for your mum, I dusted and vacuumed upstairs and down and watered my dad's tomato plants. If it needed doing, I'd mow the lawn.

And then, if I was coming down to yours, I'd leave the house and start to run. I'd run through the estate and up towards the high school. Past the school, I'd turn onto Inkle Lane and belt along between the hedgerows. Sometimes, I'd call out your name to the big open sky. I had new jeans on, jeans that you'd bought me, and new t-shirts to wear too. I was feeling good.

Past the clearfelling, past the derelict mill, and hurry through the old part of the village. And then I would slow down and walk the rest of the way so as not to arrive at your door completely out of breath. You'd be in the kitchen preparing lunch or making up a picnic.

What a relief it was to be free of the uniform, to be free of the homework, and every other part of the dreary school routine. And to be free, too, of the boredom and vagueness that had come with being thirteen and fourteen years old. At eleven and twelve, I'd had my bike and my computer to occupy me. I still had the impulse to play games. But a year later I'd lost interest in my BMX and my computer had become obsolete – which is what my dad yelled at the man who came round to try to get him to pay for it. The past two summers I'd spent haunting the library and the video shop, filling my head with stories and wishing keenly for something to happen. At the same time, I'd developed the habit of talking to myself, alone in the house. Only it wasn't really myself I was talking to, it was someone else, someone without a face or a name, someone I didn't know yet. A confidante. Definitely a girl. Now, I realise that I was talking to you, Christa, two years early.

And here I am, alone in my cell, talking to you again.

In recent days, there's been violence on the streets near by. Men have been arriving at the door of the monastery, in greater numbers than usual, looking for a place to spend the night. On occasion, we offer them a bed. More often, they are far too agitated and we are forced to turn them away.

Hugging in the kitchen, we'd risk getting caught by your mum, though I don't remember that we ever did. Sometimes we'd eat at the breakfast bar. Sometimes we'd lie on the lawn. And sometimes we'd pack everything up and hike out into the woods or up into the hills. Apples, bread and cheese, tomatoes, chocolate and crisps. You knew so many remote and secluded spots. You said that like Alice you were a curious sort, but not many others in the village were the same. It helped us to have the world to ourselves.

I remember us with our tops off at the edge of the woods, high up on the hillside. We felt safe. The sight of your scarred skin in summer sunlight shocked and excited me, especially the mess of lines on your stomach. I thought about how calmly my grandad had engraved his copper rolls, and how angrily you'd cut yourself. I imagined fabrics, bedding and curtains, printed with the pattern of your scars. I wanted them for my room.

For a little while it was just touching and kissing. And then we had sex for the first time, and then many more times, both outdoors and in your room. And in that manner, picnics and sex, the holiday slipped away. *Sommarlek* ... It wasn't until the last week, I think, that you made your discovery in the woods.

I arrived, as usual, in time for lunch. I hadn't seen you for two days. We had a rule about keeping up our friendships. So I was dying to get together. It had been raining and I didn't expect us to be going out. But you wanted to head into the woods that afternoon. The leaves were dripping, the earth soft underfoot. It had been an educational summer. I'd had a little Collins Gem book when I was young and had tried to learn about types of trees, but I'd never done that well. Now, at last, I knew about ash, oak, and maple, hornbeam, hazel, and birch. We'd seen squirrels, foxes and, late one evening, a wood mouse. You were teaching me about the different species of birds.

Along the established trails, the people we met were never large in number. They tended to be out with their dogs. Even along well-trodden routes, the terrain could be demanding. The ground to the sides of narrow paths fell away sharply; below were deep wooded areas rich with fungus and decay. Always you would plunge from the path and run or scramble down into these damper, darker parts of the wood and we would wander through thickets and clearings, usually undisturbed. Once, however, early in the summer holiday, we encountered a pair of the men dressed in grey. Both wore grey, short-sleeved shirts and darker grey trousers. Both were thin and they were walking together in silence. These two were young. It was my first glimpse of them. We stopped and stared. They nodded curtly in our direction and proceeded on, back in the direction of the village.

You'd been attempting a little research in the local archives. Little had turned up, but one discovery you made was suggestive. It was a set of photographs of a street party held on Clewkin Road in 1977 to celebrate the Queen's Silver Jubilee. Even though the pictures were in black and white, it was clear that the houses were not all painted the same at that time. There were hanging baskets and plants in tubs out on the pavement. We could make out cars at the end of the street. The residents were ordinary families with excited children. And something new that you noticed. We could see TV aerials on the roofs of the cottages. This was no longer the case, all the aerials had been removed. This seemed to us to be a rather odd development. And why had so much changed in just over ten years? Who were these people? Jogging past the houses, along one side of the road each, we attempted to peek into dim interiors. Neither of us saw television sets or personal clutter, just sparsely furnished rooms with little in the way of comfort or ornamentation.

We were hardly obsessive, but we did a little hanging about, always in daylight. As the summer passed, though the streets were usually empty, we saw individuals dressed in grey coming and going three or four times. It was hard to know if it was the same people that we were seeing on each occasion. They were men of different ages, dressed alike, entering or leaving identical houses. Something seemed to be afoot, but we weren't truly alarmed by it, more intrigued and pleased to have our own private mystery of sorts.

And then, walking in the woods alone, you stumbled across something in a clearing. It was a campsite, a place where someone appeared to be living, not merely hanging out for a night or two to drink beer and get stoned. That humid, late-August afternoon you insisted that we both go to look at what you'd found. You were all caught up in it, feeling curious for sure, but I think you were annoyed too. You thought of the woodland as being *yours* somehow.

First we climbed, following the path, and then we tippled off the trail and descended into the heart of the wood. It was a sticky day, barely any cooler the deeper we went. No breeze stirred the branches and the two of us walked in silence, treading with far greater care than usual. I'd never felt uneasy in the woods before. I kept looking around to check if we were being watched. We approached the area slowly, more or less creeping along at the end. I caught sight of a tent and and a washing line strung between trees.

We watched and listened for what felt like ages. All was quiet and still and so at last we moved forwards. A row of wet grey shirts hung on the line, soaked from the morning rain.

"It can't be a coincidence can it?" you whispered.

I shrugged. I wasn't as interested as you, but I was on edge.

You touched the shirts and said, "No labels. No sizes. Nothing."

"Christa ... I don't think we should be here."

"I know, but just give me a minute."

Whoever was camping out had at some point been burning wood. Rocks, maybe from the river bank, had been brought to make a fire pit. A couple of metal skewers with wooden handles were lying on the ground.

The tent was a simple two man A-frame with a canvas of dark green. To my horror, you suddenly lurched towards it, as though overpowered by the desire to pry.

"What are you doing!" I hissed. "That's someone's stuff. They might even be in there. Come away!"

But you were gone, under some sort of inquisitive spell. On your knees now, you unzipped the door flaps. I got ready to run.

Very swiftly you crawled half inside, paused a moment, and then backed out, doing up the zip and getting back to your feet. The whole business took only a few seconds.

"There are books," you said, "some food, a few items of clothing. A sleeping bag. That's all I saw."

"Can we please get out of here? Now."

"Yes, okay."

But still you didn't move.

"Christa!"

"Hey! You!" Someone was shouting from above the clearing.

"Shit!" you cried and started to run.

Now it was my turn to hesitate. I hung on, just for a moment, and caught sight of a figure approaching through the trees. I saw a tall man in a grey shirt. He was different from the men in the village. I glimpsed a thick mass of hair, also grey, and a full grey beard. He was powerfully built and his head looked enormous.

"You!" he called again, speeding up, coming at an angle down the slope. I turned and fled. I was, of course, very fast and I soon caught up with you, Christa.

4

A couple of days later we returned, cautiously, to the place where the man in the woods had been camping. His tent was gone and so was the washing line. The fire pit, with its char and damp ashes, remained. We searched for any clues he might have left behind, clues as to why he'd been sleeping there and what relationship, if any, he had with the oddballs in the village, but we found nothing.

Dispirited, you kicked at the ground with the toe of your trainer: "We must have scared him off. I'm not sure if I feel glad or guilty. Perhaps a bit of both. I still want to know who he was and what he was up to."

"Why would a couple of teenagers scare off a massive bloke like that?"

"I don't know. It could be that he was worried by who else we might tell about him being here. The police. Or the people in the cottages maybe."

"Why would we speak to them? Anyway we've seen them walking in the woods too. And he had the shirts so surely he knows them."

"Good point." You frowned and paced about a while, looking thoughtful. Eventually, you said, "Do you think he watched me crawl into his tent?"

At the time this struck me as a strange question. "Wouldn't he have shouted at us a minute or two earlier if he had? He didn't appear until you were back on your feet and the flap zipped up."

You shrugged. "Yes, I suppose so. But I'm starting to think there's something funny about all this. It doesn't feel right."

"What do you mean?"

But you didn't really answer me. You seemed out of sorts and irritated, and shortly after we set off back in the direction of your house.

The Autumn term began. On the first day back we were treated to an awful speech in assembly about how this was to be the most important year of our lives so far. Our futures depended entirely on our performance in the exams that were now less than a year away.

Afterwards you said, "I can't get my mind on it all, can you?"

"You'll be okay. We both will. We're actually quite clever."

"Yeah, I guess ..." You shrugged and looked away. You were doing a lot of shrugging lately, and, as the summer holiday faded, you'd started to seem remote.

The first Saturday after we went back to school, we didn't get together at all. You'd arranged with Jill to volunteer on the animal welfare stall again and you didn't want me to help. When I suggested I could run down to yours in the evening you just shook your head and said you'd be too tired. So I attempted to stay at home, but was driven out by my father's gloating. "Given you the elbow has she, boy? Probably had enough of you pulling your face." His belly was bulging in his tucked-in t-shirt. He was smoking the umpteenth cigarette of the day. My was mother laughing in the background. I didn't feel like explaining that you were campaigning against the maiming of animals, against the ruining of rabbits' eyes. I went up to Jay's dad's farm and stayed until after midnight.

The Saturday after you were busy again, at least in the afternoon. This time, though, you wanted me to come for dinner. When I arrived, you were outside your mum's garage with a brand new bicycle. You'd bought the heavy Dutch kind, with a basket on the front.

"Isn't that the wrong type of bike for round here?" I said. "It's going to be hard work going up hills."

You were obviously annoyed. "It's got gears. I'm not aiming for speed. Besides I want to be upright when I ride, not huddled over the handle bars. I want to get about on my own a bit, and I want to be able to look around as I go." You climbed into the saddle and peddled down the driveway and then back up again. I had to admit to myself that you looked impressive riding it, stern and stylish.

That bike made me jealous. It wasn't the bike itself, but the way you rode it. You had this haughty air about you, or that's how I saw it at first. And in miserable moments I thought that you'd bought it to get away from me. I didn't understand what was really happening, that you were trying to free yourself from something else, something engulfing, heavy and black.

Your expressions started to change. You scrunched up your face and sat slumped at your desk at register, not with any great melodrama, but enough for me to notice. You complained that your joints ached. Sometimes you said all you wanted to do was go to bed, and sometimes you said you couldn't sleep. You started to miss days from school and when I rang you up you said you had a fever or a headache so Svea had let you stay at home.

In your room, you'd lie rigidly on your mattress saying odd things: "Do you ever feel like you'll start crying if you have to tie your shoe laces one more time? Just tying your laces. Do you know what I mean? Just bending down makes you want to burst into tears. You can hardly stand to do it. But you do it anyway. Then you have to straighten up again and do something else. Put on your horrible coat. And then do something else. And something else. And it's all too much. Do you ever feel like that, Alex?"

Or: "Sometimes when I can't sleep I get so sick of myself. I feel so clammy and panicky thrashing about in bed. So I lie still like this and then I imagine I'm curled up naked in a dingy floating in the North Sea at night in the rain. I imagine I'm going to drown or die of hypothermia. I imagine the fear and the darkness and the freezing water lashing and lashing against my skin. The incredible shivering! Then I feel calmer about being in bed and if I'm lucky I drift off to sleep."

You turned sixteen and then, a few days later, so did I. You just didn't care. There were no celebrations for either of us. I bought you several small gifts. The only one you showed any interest in, to the point of obsession, was a copy of *Perverted by Language*. You played it over and over again, sitting on your beanbag with your hat pulled over your eyes. I would go out of the room and come back in to find "Hotel Blöedel" playing one more time and the stirring air almost blackened. All I could see was your figure slumped there. I couldn't even see your face.

I'd noticed some time ago you were losing weight. I wanted to check your skin for fresh cuts, but you didn't want me to touch you. I misunderstood and thought you were working up to rejecting me completely. And so, one wet Saturday, I kept putting off the journey along Inkle Lane. I put it off by more than two hours, finding things to do in my room. I even did some maths homework, telling myself that, well, Christa's copying so much from me at the moment I better make sure I do it properly. For my sixteenth birthday, from my parents, I'd asked for a phone extension to be run into my room. At about half past three it rang and when I answered you were sobbing at the other end. "Why aren't you here?" you shouted. "You've chucked me, haven't you? You haven't even got the guts to tell me! The first sign of problems and you've just run away! Oh, because Christa's gone loopy again!" I tried to interject. "Bastard!" you screamed and slammed down the phone.

I ran to your house through the stubborn autumn rain. I ran like I expected the world around me to understand my emergency and yield. I was furious with the puddles, livid about overhanging tree branches, bends in the road, cars on the country lane. "GET OUT OF MY WAY!" bellowed my brain.

At the edge of the village, by the humpback bridge, I met you on your bike. You were far too lightly dressed: Allstars, jeans and a t-shirt. You were drenched and unsteady. "I was coming to your house!" you cried. "I'm so sorry, Alex!" You jumped off your bike and almost clattered onto the road after it. I caught you and held you up as you wept on my shoulder, your thin frame heaving. You clutched at me so fiercely. I realised I'd been stupid and self-absorbed.

The rain was unrelenting and growing heavier. I was about to suggest that we head for home when I saw three figures standing behind you on the bridge. Each wore a long dark coat and they were holding up black umbrellas. I had no doubt that they were from the houses just behind, that they were men in grey. They stood in a line, appearing to stare directly at us for a moment. One of the men turned his head and spoke and all three turned and retreated, vanishing round the corner. It was only then that I suggested to you that we move ourselves.

Back at your house, I made tea while you dried yourself and changed. We took the tea to your room and you sat, with your back to the red radiator, talking and talking. After all the muted afternoons and evenings of recent weeks, you seemed desperate to communicate. Eventually, you started talking about the morning you found your dad's body. You'd never told me about it in anything like this kind of detail before. You just kept going, wiping away the tears as though they were nothing more than an annoyance.

"It was the start of summer, early June. I was up quite early that morning. It was a Saturday. If it'd been a Friday I wouldn't have found him. But no, it was a Saturday. I went down into the kitchen and mum was making toast and hot drinks. 'Your father's still in bed,' she said. 'Would you take him some tea?' They'd been sleeping in separate rooms for about two years by then. Of course, I agreed. I loved him. It would be nice to do something for him. He was always doing kind and thoughtful things for me. I remember thinking I would pretend it was my idea, the tea. I remember thinking my mum didn't deserve the credit. I knocked on his door. There was no answer. I tried again. No answer. So I opened the door really softly, just a crack. It was very warm that day. He was on his back in bed with the duvet thrown off. He was a big snorer. We teased him about it, my brother and me. My brother and I got on much better back then. Wow! That's a strange thought, isn't it? Mats and I actually being friends. Anyhow, when they started sleeping apart mum tried to pretend that was the reason: dad's snoring. I wasn't fooled. I wasn't stupid just because I was ten. The room was completely silent. That's how I knew something wasn't right. Except I didn't know, not really. That's just how it seems now. But I definitely listened more carefully, waiting to hear him make waking-up sounds. Nothing. And yet he was on his back. He should have been snoring. I pushed the door open some more and walked into the room, listening, waiting to hear him breathing, snoring. Waiting for him to turn his head. It didn't happen, but I didn't drop the tea or anything. I put the cup down in slow motion on his bedside table. That's how I see it in my mind now, like I'm outside, looking in. No movement. No snoring. No breathing. Nothing. Everything still and quiet. I must have put the light on. He was all the wrong colours: ashen, blue. His earlobes were purple. I can never forget that. The expression on his face didn't belong to him. It didn't belong to anyone alive. I was rooted to the spot, but I started to wail. I remember a sound like a siren coming out of me from somewhere. Then mum was behind me, dragging me out of the room. I made it hard for her, trying to fight her off, until I collapsed on the landing. And there I stayed, a screaming heap, until the ambulance came."

Later, while we were lying on your bed together, you said of your mother: "She never goes to his grave, you know. Not so as I can tell."

"How far away is it?"

"About five or six miles. That's one of the reasons I wanted a new bike. So I could go by myself. We used to go together. I suppose she'd still take me if I asked her. But I don't want to go with mum anymore. I want to go alone."

Your mum was out until late. When you were tired, at last, of talking we went downstairs and made some dinner. You took a bottle of red wine from the rack in the annexe. Shrugging, you said, "She might notice, she might not. I don't care."

We ate in the kitchen, sitting on stools at the breakfast bar.

"Imagine," you said, "how much I would hate God if I actually believed in him."

"I thought we'd worked out that you *do* hate God, even though you deny he exists."

"Oh – yeah." And we both laughed.

"Sometimes I think it would be easier if there was someone to blame. Of course, that's not how it is, is it. God being to blame. Instead you get all that crap about God's love. Or God *is* love. Why do they fill kids' heads with it? It's a pretty evil thing to do when you think about what life is really like. What do you think animals would make of the idea of a loving God? Rats can laugh, you know. Just think, some vicar faced with pews full of rats, all laughing at him.

"But actually there's no one to blame, apart from humans being to blame for killing billions of animals every year. There's just nothing. Things happen for no reason and life can be snuffed out any old time. Meanwhile, get on with your homework. How do people stay sane?"

Back in your room you opened a drawer, rummaged, and pulled out a key.

"My mum used to call it 'the study' but dad just called it his 'den'. She doesn't know I've got a key. Ildi knows, but not my mum. It's never been touched, not since the day he died. Well, I think Ildi dusts from time to time. But it's been preserved. Do you want to see?"

I'd often noticed this door upstairs with its dead lock. There were several rooms in your house I knew nothing about. You opened it, we went inside, and you switched on a pair of floor lamps. It was a large room, filled with your dad's stuff. A long row of LPs leant against a cabinet of separates. In one corner, on a wooden stand, were a TV and a VCR. Against the back wall was a sofa covered with a burgundy throw. You dropped onto the sofa with a casual air that told me you'd spent quite a bit of time in this room. I'd expected, I think, to take a quick peek and talk in whispers. Anything you touched, you'd handle with great reverence. I soon saw I was wrong.

There was a framed film poster on the wall opposite to where we were sitting. A drawing depicted a woman cradling a man in her arms. Above this image were the words: "Ingmar Bergman's *Nattvardsgästerna*". We both gazed at it for a moment and then you said: "My dad loved the films of Ingmar Bergman. And the plays of Strindberg. He went to Sweden on a sort of pilgrimage, which is how he met my mum."

There were shelves of books and hand-labelled video cassettes. I remember the line of Bergmans: *Summer Interlude*, *Persona*, *Hour of the Wolf*, more besides. I said, "Have you watched any of these films?"

"The Bergman films? Yes, because they were his favourites. I've watched them all. I even taped a couple recently and added them to the collection. I liked *Persona* best. But there are loads more he didn't have on tape."

I wanted to look through his records or pull things down from the shelves but I didn't know if it was appropriate. You seemed to guess what I was thinking and clambered off the sofa and went over to the row of LPs. On your knees on the floor you said, "Come on, let's have a look through."

As I joined you, you said, "He was mainly into rock and prog, jazz and blues." You began to flip through the albums. "I'm looking for things you might not know. What about this?" You pulled out a copy of *Red* by King Crimson. I shook my head. "'Starless,'" you said, tapping the back of the sleeve. "Amazing. And he loved this guy, John Fahey. Do you know him? Let's see: *Blind Joe Death*, *Death Chants*, *Dance of Death*." You put them down on top of *Red*, one after another: "Death, death, death. They're not gloomy though, unless you're me. If I put any of these records on, I just cry." You jumped up abruptly and went over to a chest of drawers. From the bottom one you produced a bottle of whisky. Glengoyne, two thirds full. "Let's have some of this. It was his favourite." You had a quick glance about. "No glasses. I'll be back in second."

I sat on the sofa for the first time. There was a paperback novel on a table close by: *Doctor Glas*. I picked it up. Your dad had marked certain lines and phrases with a pencil. The only one I remember is "separate bedrooms".

You reappeared with a pair of tumblers and poured us two fingers of scotch each. "*Skål!*" you said, clinked my glass and downed your whisky in one. "Yaarrgh!" you cried and poured us more.

Soon we were laid on the floor with *Rumours* on the stereo and a good deal of the whisky inside us.

"Where's your sister buried again? She was, wasn't she? Buried, I mean."

"Yeah, she's buried." I named the cemetery.

"I thought that's what you'd said. That's where my dad's buried too. I wonder if they're close together."

I drank some more whisky. "My dad bought a family plot. They'll all be in there one day. I'll be somewhere else."

"With your family."

"I find it impossible to imagine ever having a family."

"You don't want to get married? Have kids?"

"No. Especially the second part. Definitely no kids."

You propped yourself up on your elbow and looked down at my face. "Don't you want to ... I don't know, make up for past mistakes? Do a better job than your parents did?"

I didn't like your questions. "No. Not at all."

"No, me neither," you said. "No kids. Not ever."

On your hands and knees you went over to the Hi-Fi to flip the album. When you returned you lay yourself on top of me. You were drunker than I was.

"I want to do it in here," you said.

"Really? What time is it? When will your mum be back?"

Your frown was scornful. "Fuck knows. I don't care. I want to do it now."

You rolled onto the floor and, up on your knees, took off your black jumper and your bra. You fluffed your hair and stretched up your arms. "I'm all yours," you said, twisting your hands in the air.

"I don't want to," I said.

Your arms sank and your face darkened. "What's wrong? Why the hell not? I want to. I'm making my demands." You attempted a smile.

"And I'm saying no. I'm allowed."

"Alex! This isn't funny." You pushed at my shoulder, hard.

"Do I look like I'm laughing? What's your problem, Christa?"

"What the hell's that supposed to mean? Why are you being such a shit?"

I reared up off the floor with such fury that you flinched away. "A shit! Because I don't want to take part in your latest bit of black magic? You only want to do it now because it's got some weird meaning in your head. It don't know what it is, but I know it's got nothing to do with me!"

You turned away from me. I didn't know whether it was in rage or shame. The music played, but for several seconds we were silent. I saw that you were beginning to shake. I reached out and touched your pale, bare shoulder and you fell back against me and howled. Our row on the phone, everything to do with your dad, the wine and the whisky: your sobbing was like a fit. I began to get frightened. I didn't know how to calm you down. I stroked your hair, made soothing noises, and held you tightly. I didn't believe it for a minute, but I told you everything would be okay. It seemed to go on forever.

When at last your sobbing did subside, I said, "No one else interests me, Christa. I want to be with you all the time. But I think you might need some help. Help that I can't give."

You didn't speak for a moment. Then you said, "I don't know why you just said that. You know I've had so-called help already, and it didn't help at all."

I went with you to the bathroom, cleaned up your face, and watched you brush your teeth. I took the whisky glasses downstairs, washed them, and brought you water. You insisted that I borrow the records you'd selected, the King Crimson and the Fahey. I knew it was a big deal, you lending me your dad's albums. I promised to take the utmost care of them and we locked your dad's den. I returned the key to its place in your drawer and stayed with you until you were under the covers and growing sleepy. I slipped out of your house just in time. I'd barely begun the run home when your mum passed me in her Audi.

The next morning I woke up flooded with guilt, a feeling I wasn't used to. I was angry with myself for rejecting you and for saying you needed help. I could still feel you lying on top of me and would have given anything to have you there in bed with me then. It was a struggle for me to understand what I'd done. I felt I'd stepped outside the circle we'd drawn around ourselves. I'd had, I think, a moment of claustrophobic panic, or something like it. I swore to myself that I wouldn't let it happen again.

Which goes to show what my promises are worth, Christa.

We'd made no plans to meet the next day. I was supposed to be going to my grandparents' bungalow for Sunday lunch. So I was surprised when my dad bellowed up the stairs: "Boy! Your girlfriend's outside on her bike."

You were standing astride the frame of your Dutchie at the top of the drive. You seemed so out of place on our estate. BMXs, Raleighs and racers were what everyone had round my way. And then, too, you didn't really look like yourself. It was wet again. You were soaked, sickly pale, and shadowy under the eyes. Neither of us, it was obvious, were feeling good.

I held my palm to your cheek as we stood in the damp and you tipped your head to the side and let the weight of it press into my hand. We stood like that for a moment and then you said, "Your dad's watching us out of the window."

"I couldn't care less. The man's a total arse."

"I had to see you, just for a minute. Sorry to turn up like this. I was just trying to pluck up the courage to come to the door when your dad saw me loitering."

"You should come in and get dry."

"No, no. You're going out soon aren't you?"

"I'm not going now. We'll stay here while they go."

"I don't want to cause problems."

"It'll be fine. They won't be bothered this one time."

"Okay. If you're sure."

We went inside and I was hideously aware of the lack of privacy, so different to your house. Up the open-plan stairs we thumped and I bundled you into the tiny bathroom at the top of them with a towel. Then, without giving myself time to think about what I was going to say, I darted back downstairs and went into the kitchen where my parents were now sitting. They had a look on their faces that said: "We don't mind you having a girlfriend, but we do mind any outbreak of oddness or disorder." It was obvious this counted as both.

I closed the door between the kitchen and the living room, a door that was only ever closed during arguments.

"Christa's upset. I'm not coming to grandma's today. I'm going to stay here with her."

My dad, a mummy's boy underneath it all, said, "Oh no! Oh no you're not! Your grandma's expecting you. You're coming with us and that's that."

"No, I'm staying. Christa is upset. She needs to talk."

My dad sneered. "Not my problem. I'm not making your excuses for you. You're not letting your grandma down and that's final." Then he added, "What's she so upset about?"

"That's private," I said, and I could see that he hated it. "She's having a rough time. That's all I can say."

"You know, Alex," said my mother, "this isn't fair on us, your dad and I. Christa shouldn't just turn up here in this state. This is our Sunday too."

I looked at the glass ashtray sat between them on the kitchen table. I felt like scooping it up and hurling it at the patio doors.

"Only a handful of years ago," I said as coldly as I could, "she unexpectedly lost her dad. The pain doesn't just vanish to a deadline. And sometimes it comes back. I'm sure that's something you can understand."

There was silence. Neither of them were looking at me now.

"What shall I tell her?"

My dad made a disgusted, dismissive gesture. "Don't make a habit of it," he said. I opened the door and left the room. "And phone your grandma later to apologise," he called out as I reached the bottom of the stairs.

I found you in my room, perched on the edge of my bed. *You're Living All Over Me* was playing on the stereo on tape. You'd turned the volume up.

"It's fine," I said. And I never did mention how difficult they'd been about it, until now, writing this in my cell.

Your hazy green eyes seemed unusually large. I think I'd often felt that we weren't really in a relationship of equals, that you were bolder, stronger, and much more clued-up than me. Even as you'd grown more and more desolate, I viewed it as a situation in which you had a kind of power, the power to withdraw, the power of self-sufficiency. Now you were looking at me with wide, grateful eyes, eyes that were seeking reassurance too. Despite my determination, when I'd woken up that morning, to never let you down again, I wasn't sure how to respond. I remember that we just held onto one another silently for a time.

My parents left. You started to cry and cried a lot. You were hungover and you'd got up at some silly hour and gone for a long bike ride in the rain. You told me that I was all the help you needed. You said you'd had a dream in which you were my sister and we'd had sex. I didn't have time to respond to this before more things came tumbling out. You hated your own brother. You felt nothing for your mother. You'd told me things you'd never told anyone else. Trust was everything. You were going to be a better girlfriend. Your dad would have liked me because I love music so much and read lots of books. You had three thousand pounds saved up in a post office account, did I know that? A few days earlier you'd sat in your father's den and cried so hard you thought you were going to tear something inside. What had set you off? A story you'd read in one of his books, "The Letter Writer" by Issac Bashevis Singer. We must never break up. We could run away to Gretna Green and put an end to our parents' control over us. You supposed that was a stupid idea. You didn't even believe in marriage. But don't let's split up. Let's look after each other. The world wants to eat us alive.

Afterwards, when it had all come out, we lay on my bed listening to *Psychedelic Jungle*. You were silent for several minutes, resting your head on my chest. Eventually you went up on one elbow and looking down at my face said, "I saw something really strange early this morning, out on my bike."

"What was that?"

"I was riding over the moor tops. There's a field that's quite flat compared to the rest of the land around there. The men in grey – I'm sure it was them – were in the field. About five of them."

"Five? What were they doing?"

"They were spread out quite evenly and they were walking forward slowly in a line, looking at the ground. I stopped to watch them, but almost immediately one of them spotted me on the road and started staring. I got nervous and cycled off. It's lonely up there, especially early on a Sunday."

"Mmm, it is. So you've no idea what they were up to?"

"They were carrying something, each grey man. Little bags I think. But I couldn't work out what they were doing."

"Hmm."

"You sound like you might have an idea."

"I don't know. Yeah, actually I do have a theory. But I want to talk to someone before I say what it is. Then we'll see."

"Very mysterious." And you smiled a heartfelt smile for what seemed like the first time in ages.

We had sex then, and you left before my parents returned.

5

When my parents came back from my grandma's late that Sunday afternoon they discovered me at the kitchen table doing some homework. After all, Christa, I had no desk in my small room.

Perhaps finding me surrounded by school books forced them to hold back a little, but, they were still determined to have a go at me over your appearance at the house that morning.

It was preposterous. Quite often a mate of my dad's would turn up, anxious and unannounced, and ask to borrow for a few days the mortgage money that my parents kept tucked away in a drawer in the living room. Presumably these mates (there were two or three who did this) needed to pay their own mortgage or rent. My dad would always oblige. Even more often, my dad would bring drunks, loud as trumpets, back to the house after a visit to the pub, including on school nights, in a house with open-plan stairs. In the summer months, my dad barbecued burgers and twenty people would turn up with armfuls of bottles and cans. The next day I would be drafted in to help clear up the mess. Now the pair of them stood in the kitchen and glared at me because you had appeared unexpectedly, looking dishevelled and distressed, *just this one time*. They used ridiculous language, accusing me of "mooning" about since you'd arrived on the scene. They complained about my always having a miserable face. They pretended to care about the effect all this was having on my school work, though neither of them had gone to the last parents' evening.

Nothing came of it, nothing was resolved. I think, mainly, my dad was furious because I had, for the first time ever, refused to go to my grandma's for Sunday lunch. He wasn't being a parent at all. He was being a soppy son.

But the amazing hypocrisy of this performance of theirs was revealed all the more starkly just a few days later. I was returning from seeing the person I needed to speak to about your early-morning encounter with the grey men out on the moors. As I came through the front door I could hear a strange noise. In the living room, on the sofa, sat my dad's friend Phil. My dad was pacing with a cigarette in hand. Beer cans were out on the side tables. Phil was weeping and rocking. From somewhere inside him was coming an extraordinary keening sound, a kind of high-pitched cry of horror and despair.

Phil's face was badly beaten: bloody, swollen, cut, with big bruises coming up. My dad jabbed his finger at the stairs without a word of explanation and I went to my room. I felt sorry for Phil, but I couldn't help remembering how angry my dad had been just because you had turned up at our house a bit wet and sad.

I'd been that evening to see Jay, and, more importantly, Jay's brother, Carl. Carl is older than us. I'm not sure by how much. I think he was about twenty four back then. (Although, perhaps Carl is no longer alive. Perhaps Jay is dead. I've no way of knowing, Christa.) Carl lived up at his father's farm some of the time, but then he would disappear off for, say, six months and return with tales of work and women in other parts of the country or, on one occasion, France. He was a sort of hippy, I suppose, but a hippy with an edge. He liked to drink, he liked girls, and he was known to be well-informed on the subject of drugs. Jay's dad's drug of choice was talk. He loved to talk. That's to say, he loved to *boom*, boom at you in a friendly manner. He was a loud, exuberant man; but I'd seen him grow grim and worried looking at the mention of Carl's name.

Jay took me down to Carl's room, which was in a part of the farmhouse I'd never seen before. Carl was sat cross-legged on his bed rolling a joint, listening to Beethoven on a set of crackly 78s. He had abundant black hair, longish, and a wiry black beard. His room was large and exceptionally neat, but full of curious objects: old smoking pipes, bits of military paraphernalia, a Bakelite radio. In one corner, there was an antique dressing screen with peacocks on the four panels.

I asked Carl about what you'd seen on the moor, leaving out all the details about it being the men in grey. I asked him in such a way as to suggest that I already knew the answer and was just looking for confirmation, which was genuinely the case.

"Oh yeah," he said, "there's no doubt in my mind at all. They were looking for mushrooms. For sure."

I described in more detail where you'd had your sighting.

"Oh aye," Carl said, "you'll get 'em by the bucketload up there. In a good year. And this has been a *magic* year, so to speak." He chuckled, dragged on his joint, and passed it to me.

"So you've been out picking them this year?"

"Yeah, some. Not where you're asking about, but other places nearer by. We get 'em on the farm, of course. But there are better spots not far off. This part of Lancashire's notorious for shrooms. We're near the end of the season now, but the conditions have been perfect this year – it's the wet autumn, you see. Yep, I've been out picking right enough. Early doors is best, like you say."

"Do you dry them?"

"I do. Then I've got myself a supply all year round. What about you? You ever taken any magic mushies? What about you, Jay?"

Jay shook his head in such a way as to indicate that not only had he not taken magic mushrooms, but that he had no interest in ever doing so. Soft rock, video games, and drumming: Jay's enthusiasms were pretty different to Carl's.

I said no too. But I said it differently to Jay. Then I said: "So I'll still be able to find a few at this time of year."

"You will, but they'll be much thinner on the ground now. Which is why those blokes your bird saw had such a rigorous system going, I expect."

Carl rose from his bed and changed the 78. Then he wandered on his thin, long legs over to his wardrobe. It was a heavy piece of furniture, well over a hundred years old. He opened the door and I saw neat lines and piles of clothing – shirts, jumpers, jeans. He reached into a part of the wardrobe with shelving and came back towards his bed with something in his hand. It was an amber plastic pill bottle.

"This should sort you out – you and your better half."

I popped the lid open. It contained a rough brown powder with quite a lot of stalky, woody-looking bits mixed in with it.

"Are you sure? Can I pay you something?"

Carl grinned and shook his head. "Nah. Trust me, I can spare it."

So when I arrived home that night to find my dad's friend sobbing on the sofa with his battered face, I had in my pocket a vial of dried magic mushrooms. In an odd way, I think it insulated me from the shock of what I saw when I went into the living room. Later, upstairs, with music on, I felt only a kind of mild disgust.

Of course, I was also a little bit stoned.

The next day, at school, I told you all about my evening.

"Is this normal," you asked sharply, "beaten-up men in your house?"

"No. But my dad does have a few shady friends. I know he visited one bloke in prison who'd been done for raping his ex-wife."

"Bloody hell!"

"Anyway, never mind about that. What about the mushrooms? I'm surprised now that you didn't know what those men were up to."

"I don't know anything about fungus, really. Flowers and trees, yes. Fungi, not so much. But there's a big book on the subject at home, so ..."

"We don't need a book. We've got the mushrooms. Enough for two. That's what Carl said. Are you up for trying them?"

"I ... maybe. If I'm being honest, I find the idea a bit frightening."

I was disappointed, but I don't think I let it show. "Well, they're dried so they'll keep. Have a proper think about it."

"You're keen aren't you?"

"I'm curious, it's true. Yes, I'd like to do it. But only with you, though. I won't take them on my own."

You nodded, looking a little uncertain. "There's no pressure," I said. "None at all."

At home, the mood was horrible. Ever since the attack on Phil my dad had been more than usually volatile. Perhaps you remember that it was my job every school day to come home and dust and vacuum the house, upstairs and down. Suddenly, work I'd been doing to the same standard for years wasn't good enough. One night, for instance, my father came home in an obvious rage, stomped upstairs and tore open the flimsy door of my parents' bedroom. "Alex!" he bellowed moments later. I went to face him. He was standing rigidly, staring ahead, with the canopy sunbed switched on. "Why haven't you done the hoovering?" he asked when I appeared in the doorway.

"I have. I did it when I got home."

He pointed to the carpet. In the ultraviolet glow you could see bits on the carpet invisible by the light of an ordinary bulb.

"Well, you'd better bloody do it again. Only this time do it properly. Pillock." And he pushed passed me out of the room.

So I hauled the vacuum cleaner back upstairs and ran it over the carpet by uv light. The offending bits didn't come up. The vacuum cleaner wasn't very good, the bristles on the roller were all worn away. I switched to the hose and, on my hands and knees, scraped at the fabric with an attachment until it looked a little better. After that, I always hoovered in there with the sunbed switched on. I actually heard my mum boast to one of her friends about how I kept their room "spotless".

It was maybe the following week, when cleaning beneath my parents' bed, that I made a disturbing find: a long metal cylinder, solid, but with a hole drilled at one end through which was threaded a loop of cord. It was very heavy and obviously a weapon of some kind. I stood in there room weighing this object in my hand, imagining the violence it could do to a human face, a human skull. I guessed my dad had made it at work. Alone with him in the car a few days later, I asked him what it was.

"Cosh," he replied.

Meanwhile (well, certainly it was around the same time) you had a rough encounter with your brother. Mats came home from Durham for a long weekend, chiefly to play a gig with his band, which was still together, at least part-time. The Jennet Device I remember his band was called. I imagine he thought it was a clever name. On, I think, his second night, you woke up at around three-thirty a.m. needing the loo. Out in the hallway, you noticed that the door to the bathroom the two of you shared was ajar and the light was on. There was also, you said, an undeniable stink in the air. You found Mats, in a totally out-of-it, drunken state, lying on the floor by the side of the bath. He'd shit himself.

You tried to rouse him. He wouldn't cooperate. He merely moaned and turned over so that his face was pressed into the bath panel. You shook him, swore in his ear, prodded at him hard with your foot. Nothing. At last you began to try and undress him.

"Why did you bother?" I wanted to know when you told me about this later. "You should have just left him there."

"Because when mum gets worked up, she gets worked up *generally*. Or sometimes she does, anyway. Mats behaves like an idiot and she decides that we're both out control, and that she's a terrible mother. Not that she ever says it aloud. And so she starts trying to impose a new regime on the household as a whole. It's a sort of one-size-fits-all parenting. He messes up and I have to suffer. I was trying to avoid that. The last thing I need is mum randomly noticing we're there."

You removed your brother's trainers and socks and began the disgusting business of trying to peel off his jeans. The smell, you said, was appalling. The shit was all down his legs. Suddenly, Mats opened his eyes.

"Whatthefuckyoudoin?" he said, or something to that effect.

He wanted to raise himself. He managed to sit up using the bath as an aid. You crouched in front of him ready to try and help him stand. Get him into the shower and his clothes into the machine, this is what you were thinking. Then disinfect the floor, and mum will never know.

Mats wasn't grateful, not at all. The next thing you knew, he'd made a fist and walloped you in the left eye. You screamed. Later you told me that you screamed with rage, not pain. That said, Mats was really smashed and hadn't held back. Now you were sprawled on the floor and Mats was trying to totter to his feet. This was the condition in which Svea, your mum, found you both.

Your mum started shouting. You didn't even wait to find out whether she was going to be fair. Climbing to your feet, sickened by the pair of them, you stormed out of the room, cupping your eye with your hand. Svea tried to restrain you, but you yanked your arm away. "*Dra åt helvete!*" you yelled, right in her face. "I've no idea why I shouted it in Swedish," you told me later. "It just came out that way. God, she looked so shocked, though!"

In bed, you found you were shaking. The area around your eye was throbbing badly and you couldn't get warm. After very little sleep you got up and went downstairs. Your mother was sat at the breakfast bar drinking coffee. Like you, she'd barely slept. Of course you had a spectacular black eye, swollen and purple. No one had applied a cold compress, so it was even worse than it needed to be.

Your appearance so early in the morning took your mum aback. She wasn't ready for you, that's what you felt. She hadn't finished working out what it was she wanted to say. And then your black eye took her aback still further. She was upset and flustered. Not like her at all. She examined your eye, checked your vision, and even cried a little. She apologised to you and admitted that she wasn't sure what to do about Mats. She was furious with him, but he lived in Durham now, most of the time. She felt she had limited options. You said you didn't care just as long as he stayed out of your way. Your mum was worried about what you were going to tell people about your bruises and you became angry then and said that that was all she cared about, staying respectable. But even as you said it, you knew it wasn't true. Your mum had never really minded about what other people thought. This was different, though, with evidence of violence in the home. You softened your tone. You said your priority was making sure no one thought that I had done it, that no one thought I was beating you up. Your mum said something kind about me then. You liked this and so you proposed to tell the following story: that you'd been to Manchester alone, that you'd been waiting to catch a bus back home from Chorlton Street coach station when someone had tried to snatch your bag. You'd fought back and the would-be thief, a skinny, ferret-faced type, had smacked you in the eye and legged it. So much better, you said, than: "I walked into a door." Your mum agreed and changed the subject. She started talking about Stockholm and how it was long overdue that the two of you went back there, visited family and explored the city together, properly, now that you were older. You didn't believe that this would happen any time soon, but you humoured her anyway.

Later, in your room, you found an envelope on your desk. "For Christa, with love from mum", it said on the front and there was two hundred pounds inside.

You took a note into school explaining – dishonestly, of course – the origin of your black eye. You were drawn aside and asked a few questions. They asked about your home life and they asked about me. But they were soon satisfied.

I had to endure quite a few cracks about "Beating up your bird", though not from anyone I liked. And you had to endure quite a few expressions of concern about your safety. These were mainly of the "What were you doing in Manchester on your own?" variety. There were one or two attempts to probe further, to "Check that you're okay". From these you emerged unscathed.

But then something alarming happened. It was midweek and you were very late for school. Register was done, double games had already started. You were hurrying over the humpback bridge, leaving the old part of the village, when a group of the men in grey appeared, approaching around the bend in the road that lies just beyond the derelict mill. One of the men glanced in your direction, almost shyly you thought later, but then his expression changed and he spoke in urgent undertones to the others. You knew they were talking about you, you just knew it. You were pressing on, a little uneasy now, when suddenly you felt them behind you. You felt them and you could hear them, their boots on the road. And then they overtook and more or less surrounded you, five of them, keeping you in the middle of the road, obstructing your way.

They were dressed alike: black boots, grey trousers, shirts of a lighter grey, long dark coats. Each had short hair. They were all quite young. You said they looked like they might be religious, or they could've passed for a band, a band in a black-and-white photograph.

You started moving backwards on the road, turning you head, looking for a car. One of the men, perhaps the oldest in the group, stepped forward with an outstretched arm. The gesture was meant, you saw, to reassure you. You looked at his face. There was no malice, simply a kind of seriousness, a determination. In my mind's eye, Christa, I see them standing there, standing in the road on the outskirts of the village, solicitous, but over-earnest.

"Please," the man said, "we're not going to hurt you. I appreciate that we must appear unusual and even threatening. I'm sorry for that. Let me say again: harming you is the last thing we would do. Quite the opposite in fact." And with this he raised his finger towards his left eye. "With apologies for the personal nature of the inquiry, who has done this to you? Your injury here." By now your bruise was a darkish purple and a sickly yellow, still very noticeable.

"What?" you blurted out, laughing too.

"Your black eye," he said, utterly unembarrassed and unfazed, "is it the result of violence?"

"I don't believe this." You walked forwards and then veered abruptly to the side of the road, towards the hedgerows. The men adjusted their position, deterring you from leaving, and yet staying at a distance. Once more their spokesman held up his hand.

You were more angry than frightened. "Okay, yes," you cried, "a man hit me! Punched me right in the eye. Men hit women all the time. Perhaps you know something about it. Now let me through. Because, despite what you say, you're behaving like a bunch of budding rapists!"

That last word dispersed them like you had fired a gun shot into the air, that's what you said to me later the same day. Without looking back, you were off at full pelt towards the bottom of Inkle Lane.

"Bloody hell," I said when you reached the end of your story. "I mean, I always thought that you'd end up having some kind of encounter with them. But I never imagined them behaving like that. Being so direct and prying."

"I know. And I have to say, it might sound paranoid, but I have a feeling they've been watching me, watching me for a while. I can't be sure, obviously. On one level, it does seem ridiculous. It was just something about the way they spoke to me. Like they knew perfectly well who I was. I felt it was me *in particular* they were interested in." You shrugged. "Maybe I'm getting carried away."

"No, I don't think so. We just don't know. What they did was extremely strange. They're clearly up to something. It must be religious, don't you think? The way they act and dress. And with them all being men. I can't help thinking they must have some weird ideas about girls. Religious types often do. We can't rule anything in or out. We need to find out more about them."

But you weren't really up to sleuthing. For a time the incident in the road, on top of your poor state of mind, left you living, as you put it, "like a recluse", which was only a mild exaggeration. You starting cycling to school, but abandoned cycling just for fun. And although the weather had improved, the rain giving way to cold, clear days, you didn't want to go walking in the woods and certainly not around the village at night. You took to peering out of your bedroom window in the early hours, and out of a hall window that overlooked the driveway at the front, half convinced that you would catch silent grey figures trespassing and keeping watch over your house.

A fortnight after Mats punched you, your eye was fully healed. At some point during those two weeks, sitting in your room, you told me that for a brief period you'd gone out with one of Mats' friends, a boy three or four years older than you. One night at his house, when you'd both been drinking, he'd lain with his full weight on top of you and slapped you repeatedly in the face, calling you a slag, and saying that you were his to do with as he wanted. Pulling clumsily at the buttons on your jeans, he'd tried to force you to have sex. Eventually you'd managed to roll him off his bed and he'd landed heavily on the floor. He was drunk and winded and you'd grabbed your things and left.

I wanted to know if you'd ever told anyone about what happened.

"Oh, yes. I thought about it for a few days and then I decided to do something about it. So I wrote his mother a letter."

"No way! What did it say?"

"It said something like: 'Dear Mrs Jackson, Last Saturday night, when you and your husband were out at the Royal Exchange, I visited your son Martin at your home without your knowledge.' Then I complimented her a bit on her 'lovely home', putting in some details so she knew for sure that I had been inside. Then I went on to say: 'As far as I'm concerned, Mrs Jackson, this information is strictly between you and I. What you choose to do with it is entirely up to you. I would like you to know that after several glasses of red wine your son pinned me down in his bedroom, hit me over and over, called me a slag, and tried to rape me. I am fourteen years of age. In telling you this, I should make it clear that I want nothing from you and will never contact you again. Nor will I contact the police. I cannot prove my story, but I can tell you this: if you look in the top of Martin's wardrobe you will find three video tapes marked *Moonlighting*. These tapes actually contain Swedish porn and we watched some of it together whilst sitting on his bed in his room.' And then I signed it: 'Yours sincerely, A Distressed Young Woman Determined To Get On With Her Life.'"

"God! Did anything happen?"

"Well, he never showed his face round here again, that's for sure! He and Mats were pretty good mates, but Mats stopped seeing him, as far as I can tell. At one point, Mats did mutter something about how Martin had 'gone a bit strange' or something. So it seems like there were consequences. Honestly, though, I'm glad I don't know what exactly – I like to imagine all kinds of horrible scenes with his mum." You were sat on your beanbag, half smiling, with one arm crossed against your chest.

"And were you distressed, as you said? You must have been."

"If I let myself, I could probably get more upset about it now than I ever did back then. At the time, it was like it'd happened to someone else. If you'd asked me just after I would have probably said that I was much, much more angry about factory farming or animal testing than about pathetic, pudgy Martin with his floppy blonde hair. Anyway, I got my revenge."

Revenge: you believed in hurting people back. After Mats had punched you, you had me use a Polaroid to photograph your eye several times, documenting the changes in the swelling and discolouration. You also had me photograph you sitting on a sofa holding up a sign. It read: "THIS IS WHAT MATS GARDNER DID TO HIS SIXTEEN-YEAR-OLD SISTER WHEN HE'D HAD A DRINK."

Mats was back in Durham. You sent him a letter and some sample pictures. In your letter you said: "Maybe a future employer would like to see these? Or a future wife? Don't ever hit me again."

All of which makes it sound as though you were feeling strong. But you weren't at all. You'd promised Jill that you would do a stand with her at a big animal welfare event in Manchester. Several groups were going to have stalls throughout the city one Saturday. Yours was going to be near Piccadilly Gardens. She'd warned you that it might be tough, that it wasn't anything like as easy to campaign in the city. People could get shouty, confrontational. She'd admitted that she'd been spat on and threatened in the past. Then there were those – mainly blokes, but not only – who would try it on, and those who were just plain weird. You'd said yes anyway, but now you didn't want to go.

"I don't even want to look people in the face at the moment. And then everyone probing, asking questions, getting angry. Oh no, Alex: *other human beings!*" You shuddered. "I don't want to do it. I'm not in a fit state."

But you did do it in the end. Jill picked you up early in her old banger and off the two of you went.

And then, as arranged, you and Jill came and collected me in the early evening and we called in at a ropey pub where we thought they wouldn't be too fussy about age. Jill tucked us away in a dim corner of the lounge and went to buy drinks.

In the car the two of you had offered up a more or less cheery version of events: loads of signatures, loads of literature handed out, lots of support. But you were both freezing, you'd had a bit of hassle from some drunken football fans, and a man had asked you out and become a full-on pest when you'd said no. In the end, it had taken three or four of you shouting at once to drive him away. Even then he'd hung around nearby for a while looking aggrieved.

But while Jill was getting the drinks you let me know hurriedly that something else had happened, something with a significance that none of the others on the stall could have understood.

"I can't believe it! *They* turned up. Two of them!"

I hesitated for just a moment before saying: "What, the grey ones? Really?"

"Yes. Well, I think it was them. They were dressed the same as each other and pretty much the same as the ones who stopped me in the road."

"Did you speak to them?"

"Yes. I was talking to this woman and then we finished and as she stepped away they just sort of appeared from behind her and nodded at me and we had a conversation. Well, they did most of the talking."

"What about?"

"I'm not sure I followed everything they were saying. It was noisy and they kept mumbling. Anyway, it was all about animals and suffering. They said something about animals' emotions and something about 'essences'. Needless to say, nothing like the conversations I had with anyone else today. Maybe it's best if I tell you about it later. But I did make a note of their names. Or the names they gave, which sound suspect to me." You rummaged in the pocket of your jeans. "They signed the petition and each donated twenty quid. Most people only give a pound or two, if that. I was very surprised. Anyway, yes, here it is." From a crumpled piece of paper you read two names: "Dr. McCoy and Dr. Horace. Their addresses are just scribble."

"Dr. McCoy? Isn't that from *Star Trek*?"

"I know, that's what I thought. "

Jill arrived back with the drinks. You drank yours quickly and she bought us both another. After the second round Jill drove us back to your house and dropped us off. As we went up your driveway, I said, "I see you mum's out again. That's good, I suppose."

You were opening the front door. "I know. I haven't told you this, but I think she's seeing someone. I think she's in a relationship."

"Really? What gives you that idea?"

"Oh, she's been out at night even more than usual. And then she seems kind of cheerier but also more distant and distracted all at once. But mainly it's because I walked in on her in the office and caught her laughing flirtily on the phone. Then she whispered something and hung up. Not very subtle, is she?"

"How do you feel about it?"

You were sat at the bottom of the wooden staircase, pulling off your green DMs. "I don't want to meet him. Not ever. I don't want to meet anyone she sees."

You had a bottle of red wine in your room and you opened it and poured us both a glass.

"So, go on then, what did they say to you? The two men."

"They said that it was important to take the suffering of animals seriously and they thanked me for what I was doing on a cold Saturday afternoon. I think I was just gaping madly at them at this point, but they seemed to mean it. They got quite close up to me, but, as I say, they were murmuring and it was hard to hear at times. They said a few things about animal testing, but then they started talking more generally. They said that all animals are fundamentally the same. This is what they kept coming back to. They said it several times: all animals are the same. Not in their bodies, obviously, but in their essence. That's a word they used several times: 'essence'. They said this includes humans too. So they said that a child and a monkey and a beagle and a rabbit were all examples of the same thing. They said ... what was it? Something about it's not the organism that's important, but that all animals feel the same things. Fear, joy, grief. All animals have desire." You took a big mouthful of wine and sat looking puzzled a moment.

"Go on. It's not what I would've predicted at all."

"No, I know. I'm not sure I'm telling it right. Oh, yes, so we shouldn't be kind to animals because we're better than them, we shouldn't *condescend* to be kind to them. We should be kind to them because we're the same as them. When we look into their eyes we see ourselves. We shouldn't put detergent in a rabbit's eyes, because we'd never do that to a child. We should have compassion for animals the way we have compassion for ourselves. That's about it, I think."

I pulled a face. "So, in the end, we're all animals. Is that it? Not very deep, really."

"Mmm ... No, I don't think that is quite it. Not 'we're all animals', but that all animals are essentially the same. It's different."

"Okay. I'll have to think about that. And what were they like? What was it like to talk to them?"

"They were okay. Not scary or anything. An odd vibe. Intense, but maybe nervous too. I don't think they get out much. They did seem very interested in me. They were really focusing on everything I said, which wasn't that much, admittedly."

Garlands was on the stereo. You kept topping up your glass. I recognised the mood you were in. You were determined to get drunk.

The conversation started to skip and repeat: the grey men; the unknown man your mum was with.

"I haven't eaten anything since lunch, you know. Apart from those crisps in the pub."

I know. You told me a few minutes ago."

"What do you think they're up to? What do they want?"

"I think it's some sort of religious thing. Maybe like a cult. People who don't blink enough."

"Why are we the only ones who've noticed they're here?"

"How do you know that we are?"

"I should eat something in a minute. I tell you, I can't remember the last time my mother and I ate a meal together. I suppose it doesn't help that she eats meat. Do you think it's true that sheep and pigs and cows are essentially the same? I bet he wines and dines her all the time, this new man of hers. I bet he wines and dines her like a fiend. She'd expect it. I know she would. She thinks she's hot property."

"Let's go downstairs and get some food."

"Okay. Why here though? Why in this village? What's here?"

Maybe that's the point. There's nothing here anymore. The pub, the post office, even the church, have all closed down. It's lifeless."

"My dad said it was a good place to run a business from because there were no distractions. Now he's gone and she's distracted *all the time*. It's all right for her, but I'm stuck here. It's such hard work to get anywhere, Manchester or whatever. Like you say, that's probably why they're here, away from prying eyes. Hidden. No distractions. Ha! No prospect of escape. I wonder how those two got to town today. They don't appear to have cars."

We were in the kitchen, preparing some food, when your behaviour lurched abruptly into the wild.

I remember you hunting in the annexe for another bottle you could steal without your mum noticing. Nothing seemed right so you'd come back and carried on chopping, your head down, your hair falling over your face. You'd grown quiet. Tired and talked out, I thought. And all your movements were slow and deliberate. When you left the room again I assumed you'd gone to the downstairs loo. Then I heard the front door open and the house fell silent. I waited, listened, went into the hallway. The door was ajar. A pair of your pumps were missing.

I didn't know if you even had keys. I pulled my trainers on, put the door on the catch, and hared down the driveway after you. It was cold and clear with a big, bright moon. I could see you running down the middle of the road some way ahead, making for the old part of the village. I increased my speed. I remember the feeling of power in my legs. But when I caught up with you, I had no power to persuade you to come back to the house.

"No! Get off me!" you cried. "I'm going to see what all this is about. They've got no right to follow me. To sidle up to me when I'm on the stall when I'm tying to talk to people about the hideous treatment of animals. That matters to me. It matters! Blah, blah, blah! All animals are the same! Blah, blah, blah! Stopping me in the road and asking about my black eye!"

You shook yourself loose, flailing. "It was *my* black eye," you shouted into the night.

And so we went, not quite together, with you flinching away whenever I drew near or reached for you, along to Clewkin Road, where the cottages sat in silence, with only dim light showing in some of the windows behind curtains that were drawn.

You marched halfway down the street and seemed to choose a house at random.

"Wakey wakey, weirdos!" you shouted, hammering on a white front door and then reaching sideways and rapping hard on a window pane.

Nothing visible happened within the house you'd selected. But as I looked around, standing behind you in the road, I saw curtains twitch in some of the cottages.

"Christa, you're upset. Let's go back. Now's not the time."

You weren't interested. Instead you crossed over and banged on another door. "You've been following me about, haven't you?" Your voice was so loud in the empty street. You waited, darting your head in all directions, stepping back to look at upstairs windows. Again, there was no response. And then, to my astonishment, you went to yet another door, crouched down and pushed open the letterbox. Pressing your mouth to the slot, you yelled: "Popping up in the woods! Stopping me on my way to school and being all creepy! Creepy men! Turning up in town today!"

The door at which you were crouching made a rattling sound and opened slowly.

You tottered back and straightened up. A tall, thin man with close-cropped hair stood in the doorway, only just fitting there.

"Oh!" was all you could manage to say.

Some way down the street a second cottage door opened and a man stepped out. Moments later, on the opposite side, another man appeared. Swiftly, the only sounds being those of locks and latches, the pavement began to fill. Soon most of the doors had opened and perhaps twenty individuals had emerged. At the top of Clewkin more were gathering, coming round the corner in ones and twos, forming a silent, staring group.

You'd retreated into the middle of the road and were clutching at me now and trying to look everywhere at once. "Shit!" you hissed, gripping my arm. "Alex!"

The tall man who had been the first to open his door, the one through whose letterbox you'd shouted, moved towards us, then stopped a few paces distant and held up his hand.

For a few, fast heartbeats we were all frozen there in our respective positions, figures in a nocturne. Then the man spoke:

"Miss Gardner," he began – and I heard you catch your breath – "you are by no means the only person to have noticed our presence here. There have been others who have been curious, and even one or two who have sought to intrude upon our peace. Yet you are the only one who has been ... I will not say expected, but hoped for. Yes, certainly hoped for."

I remember how shocked I was by what he was saying. But when I glanced at your face, it was rapt and clear.

"However," the tall man continued, "you have not come at the right time. And I fear now that there never will be a right time. Our group, our Brotherhood, is leaderless and in crisis. This explains, in part, why our tentative ... *approaches* to you, if that is indeed the correct word, have been so clumsy. In truth, it is worse than that, they have been entirely *unauthorised*." This last word he seemed to hurl out into the night air. He shook his head sorrowfully and added, "For this, I must apologise."

The man had a thin, sharp face, unlined, but old looking all the same. He stopped speaking and glanced around at the watching members of his "Brotherhood". Some part of him seemed to sag suddenly and he rubbed at his scalp with a bony hand. There was a pause and then he straightened up again and, more softly now, in his rich voice he continued: "You are visibly distressed, Miss Gardner, and for any role that we have played in your present disquiet I am truly sorry. Believe me, truly sorry." When he repeated his apology, I remember that you let out an enormous sigh, as though you had been holding your breath the whole time since the beginning of his speech.

"However, I must ask you to go now. We are disordered, more disordered than you can possibly understand. We may have some dealings together in the future, but, I regret to say, it is more likely that we will not. I leave you in the care of this exemplary young man." For the first time his eyes left yours and he glanced at me and nodded, though barely. Then in a ringing voice he cried, once only, "All of you, please go inside! There is nothing more to see." Within moments the onlookers had vanished and the street was filled with sounds of footsteps retreating around corners and of doors being secured. The tall man remained, smiling just a little. "Curiosity will, no doubt, have some part to play in the degree to which you respect our wishes. We ask that you do not communicate with us, nor seek to inquire into our affairs. If we need you ... well, you are, of course, our neighbour and we know where you can be found."

And with that the man turned away from us and seconds later had vanished behind the locked door of his cottage.

You sank to your knees and started to laugh. It wasn't hysteria or anything, you were really laughing.

I crouched down and put my arm around you and you leaned into me for support. "Well, there we have it," you said, still laughing. "The thing is, I'm not even that surprised." I helped you up. You seemed steady enough, and even brushed down your jeans with your hands. "I'm really not. I probably should be, but I'm not. I think I half expected it. Honestly."

We stood together in Clewkin Road and for a moment I was really feeling our aloneness in a place that just a minute ago had been full of watching men. But then I saw him, a figure far down at the end of the street, beyond the rows of houses, standing in front of the wall that enclosed the disused church. Even at a distance I could tell that he was very tall. He had a great mass of hair and a thick, full beard. His head seemed huge.

"Look!" I hissed, and pointed.

"Of course," was all you said.

6

Despite your regular complaints about how difficult it was to get there, you decided that we should go to Manchester one Saturday before Christmas. You said you needed to do some shopping. I think, too, that in the aftermath of our encounter with the greys you were trying to spend as little time as possible hanging about in the village. Curiosity, as the tall old man had predicted, was giving you trouble, and this was hardly surprising. The old man had done everything to arouse, and nothing to allay, your inquisitive spirit. He'd been so heavy-handed about this that you even worried it was deliberate, that he'd set you some kind of test. "Am I passing or failing?" you wanted to know. I'd no idea.

Quietly, I was upset and disturbed. I could hardly blame you, but you'd become fixated on "the Brotherhood", as you were calling them now. Of course, you wanted to know who they were and what they were up to. But, even more, you wanted to know why they'd been *hoping* for you – *you* in particular – and why, if you searched within yourself, you had a sense of being *expected*. What, you wondered aloud, over and over again, was your role in all of this strangeness? And would you ever get to know the answer? You said you felt you could only hold off investigating further for so long.

That Saturday I was up very early and running down to your house before it was fully light. First we had to get the bus – a lengthy, slow ride out of the valley – and then the train from town to Manchester Victoria. You were wearing a long coat and a wide-brimmed hat and as we waited on the platform you sang "London" to me by The Smiths. The train was of the slam-door kind and we had a compartment to ourselves. As we bounced along on lumpy, springy seats a smell of ancient dust rose up into the air. Pulling into the station, we took turns at leaning out of a pushed-down window, your hat staying safely inside the train.

We headed straight for Oldham Street. Records were always top of the list. This trip gave rise to a couple of musical infatuations. In Vinyl Exchange you bought *A Date With Elvis*. Before long you declared that "People Ain't No Good" was one of your favourite songs ever and you were always singing it. You especially liked the backing vocals from the children's choir. My best discovery was a mint copy of *Miami* by The Gun Club. I think you were a bit upset that I'd found it first. Even before we left the shop, you were imploring me to tape it for you. It didn't disappoint: sibling lovers, animal darkness, a violent man dead on his lawn. We loved the lyrics on that album.

A hot drink in Koffee Pot – "Tea • Toast • Snacks" – and then we made our way to the other side of the street, to Affleck's, and at the arcade entrance gave the deaf punk two twenty pence pieces. He was standing just inside the covered walk, boots planted apart, his leather jacket studded, holding up his cardboard sign. "He's the Gatekeeper," you said, "but it's cheap to cross the threshold." I remember us really dashing about that day, at least in the morning: to Paramount Books – "Mags • Art • Music • Film" – past roadworks, past rickety fruit and veg stalls, past newsagents with big yellow signs for Benson and Hedges, down the broken escalator to the underground Market Centre, back up to Athena near Piccadilly, and, at last, over to the Corn Exchange.

In the Corn Exchange, we ate lunch at the veggie cafe: mushroom soup and a roll and then tea and cake. I remember that while we were sitting there we ended up talking again about the period when I was small and my grandma would hit me and send me home with bruises.

"So your parents definitely knew?"

"Oh yeah, they knew. They saw the bruises. And anyway my grandad was still alive then and he went over and had a word with my mum."

"But they *still* kept sending you to her? Even though she was hitting you hard enough to bring up marks."

"They were at work. They needed someone to look after me. That's what they said. Someone to get me off to school and then I needed somewhere to come back to at home time. She looked after me in the holidays too, at least until I was eleven."

"And how long did this knocking you about last?"

So then, for the first time, I told you about how I put an end to it, how I stopped my grandma giving me a smack.

"It was one school holiday. I was about eight at the time. She'd started hitting me when I was five or six, I think. She told me once that the wrong child had died, that it should've been my sister that lived. She was probably right, but you shouldn't say it, should you?"

As an answer, you reached across the table and grabbed my hand.

"I mentioned all this to my mum and she just said that my grandma didn't really like boys, only little girls. Anyway, we were out somewhere, waiting for the bus. A bus pulled up and I thought it was the right one so I got on first and started walking down the aisle towards the back. The seats at the front were all full, you see. But it turned out it was the wrong bus and both my grandma and the driver had to call me back. I was daydreaming. And some of the women on the bus started to laugh. Where we used to live was ruled over by frightening old women and they all seemed to hate one another bitterly. My grandma must have felt humiliated. But she didn't do anything until we arrived home. As we were coming back into the house she tripped me up. I went down onto the living room floor. Then she started hitting me over the head with the handle of her umbrella, hitting me around the eyes and the temples, shouting about her embarrassment over me getting on the wrong bus. It's bizarre, really, thinking about it now, that such a simple mistake should have set her off."

"What did you do?"

"I remember it so well. I remember realising that I wasn't that small anymore. I was getting bigger, stronger, and I didn't have to take it. I remember this moment of total calm even as she kept trying to hit my head and face. It was easy. I just grabbed the umbrella out of her hand and sprang up with it. I'd joined a gymnastics club about a year before and I was developing. And so then I hit her with her own weapon. Whack! Right in the mouth. She screamed and cowered away and I hit her with it again on her back, as hard as I could. And then again, a couple more times. She shrieked and yelled for me to stop and that was it. I threw the umbrella on the floor and she never touched me again."

"Ha!" You sat back in your chair, shaking your head and smiling. I could see you savouring the scene as you imagined it, enjoying my small victory against the cruelty of the world. *You believed in hurting people back.*

After lunch we wandered, hand in hand, around the Corn Exchange. In the second-hand bookshop, I bought some Penguin paperbacks: *La Vita Nuova*, I remember, and *First Love*. We gazed in windows and browsed the stalls, flipping through the crates of vinyl, picking up pieces of vintage jewellery. There were head shops selling idols and candles, bongs and pipes. The perfume of Patchouli oil drifted by. Posters on the walls that I recall seeing were for *Hellraiser* and the remake of *Cat*

People with Nastassja Kinski. There were band posters too: Joy Division, Big Black, Dead Can Dance. Someone was playing *Death Church* by Rudimentary Peni.

We entered the dimness of the army surplus place, its windows almost entirely covered with greatcoats and German parkas. Unlike some of the units, it actually had a ceiling. Knives and military memorabilia were laid out in cases, the walls were draped with flags.

As we were looking around, I asked you, "What did Sweden do in the war? Which side did they fight on? I've never thought about it before."

You sneered. "Neutral. But they still sold loads of iron ore to the Nazis, and allowed German transports on the railways. They did take in some Jews though. I've only recently read a bit about it myself. Just in an encyclopaedia at home."

We carried on looking at the stuff for sale, a mixture of the useful – kitbags and boots – and things that I couldn't understand anyone wanting to own. The two blokes running the place were paying no attention to us. They were used to all sorts in there.

Except, as it turned out, someone like you.

We both stood still. A mouse was running across the floor of the shop.

"Huldah," I heard you murmur.

"That bloody mouse again!" said one of the men from the shop. He was tall and dressed in a camouflage jacket. His combat boots thudded on the floorboards as he lurched forward, broom in his hand. The mouse had disappeared.

"Stop it now!" This came out as a real bellow. It was already gloomy in there, but things turned dimmer still and the air seemed to stir. Beyond the open door all sight of the Corn Exchange disappeared, leaving nothing more than a rectangle of distant, hazy light. For a few seconds we each stood silently. I went rigid inside the darkness in motion. It was cold against my skin. Just for a moment, it was hard to breathe. And then everything returned to normal, the dingy light came back. I scanned the faces of the two men. They looked waxen and confused, and that told me something I'd been wondering about since we first started going out.

Slowly, you approached the corner where they were standing together, the one with the broom having now retreated. I was watching from behind you, but it seemed, judging by their expressions, that you'd fixed them with some kind of intimidating stare.

"Leave the mouse alone. Do you understand?"

They nodded in unison, dumbly.

"The mouse is the same as you. You're the same as it."

They just blinked, bubble-eyed.

"You're mice."

You turned to go, but then turned back and slapped your palm down on the top of a glass display case. "Why do you sell all this? That's what I'd like to know. And who the hell buys it? It's utter shit!" And, without waiting for a response, you strode out of there.

Back on the main floor of the Corn Exchange, you were pretty bubble-eyed yourself.

"Something's *definitely* going on."

"Yep!"

"I'm feeling weirder and weirder in this place," you said.

"Shall we go?"

"No. I really don't want to. Not yet."

At first we weren't sure what to do next. We just stood there, laughing and glancing around.

"We've seen something like that before, haven't we? Tell me I'm not going mad." You were speaking in a whisper.

"Yeah, but never like that. And never with other people there."

"Oh well, I doubt they'll hurt the mouse now."

"They wouldn't dare."

In the end, I decided to go for a haircut at the unisex place and you sat in there and waited and watched. You were disappointed because you wanted me to grow it out. "It's such a lovely chestnutty brown. It'd look amazing long." But I decided to stick with my new-wavey do.

I've grown it now. It gives me a more spiritual air. Not that you'll ever see it, Christa.

After my haircut, I joked that you should get a palm or tarot reading from the clairvoyant in her booth and for a few moments I think you considered it seriously. But then you said, "Maybe not. I don't want to scare the poor woman to death!" Instead we went into Madimi's Corner, the occult book shop. It'd been closed for lunch when we'd gone there earlier in the afternoon.

As we entered, the owner of the shop was in conversation with another customer:

"– some say he had a house on a street since lost, buried beneath our feet, beneath this very building. Or he may have lived close by in what is now the music school."

The bookseller had long white hair, held back in a ponytail, and fluttering hands covered in silver rings. One of the rings was set with a glass eyeball.

We started to browse. The customer said something that I couldn't hear. The pine shelves were filled with books on ritual magic, demons, paganism, druidry, folklore. I was looking though a book of drawings and paintings by an artist named Spare. You had a book in your hands on mysticism, magick, and drugs. As you came over to show me a chapter about mushrooms and other hallucinogens, I heard the white-haired man say: "Well, of course, Dee was an astrologer *and* an astronomer, a magician *and* a mathematician, a Christian, an occultist *and* a scientist. This is why he's a figure the modern mind struggles to cope with." His voice was rounded and strong, like that of a Shakespearian actor.

You kept hold of the book on magick and drugs. It contained a surprising amount of practical information. Eventually the other customer went and we were left alone the proprietor. We were still looking through the prints and pamphlets, at the ceremonial items, but the owner had begun to cast glances in our direction and so you carried the book up the counter and said you'd like to buy it.

The man studied your face for a few moments. "You're a student?" he asked. "At the university?"

You nodded, your purse in your hand.

He looked over at me, looked back at you, and smiled kindly. The book was lying on the counter and he patted it. "Such matters need to be entered into with great care. You do understand that?"

"Oh, of course. I'm not sure I'll actually ... do anything anyway."

The man laughed a little. "I see." He reached down and produced a brown paper bag and slipped the book inside. You passed him a note from your purse. It was when he presented you with your change, and your fingers made contact with his, that it happened. Abruptly, clearly alarmed, the man jerked his gaze upwards to the glass roof of the Corn Exchange. In the same instant, he raised his arm and then dropped it again. After a few moments of twisting his head about, he gave a short moan and fell back into the wooden chair he kept behind the counter.

"What's the matter?" you cried, leaning forward on your toes.

"I ... I thought it was falling down on me. The great domed roof. But no, it was going in reverse. Broken masonry and shattered glass ... all mending. Quite wonderful."

"I'm sorry, I don't know what you mean."

The man was silent a moment before saying: "I barely know myself."

You walked around the side of the counter and stretched out your arm, but the man flinched. "Forgive me my dear, but I think you should keep your distance." His theatrical voice still carried, even as he hunched in his chair.

You stepped back. "What have I done? I'm so sorry! I'm having a really strange day!"

"I don't doubt it. As for what you have done: I don't believe you've done anything ... yet." He squeezed his eyes closed tightly, pressed his forefinger to his forehead, and then, after thirty seconds or so, popped his eyes open again. "I think it may come to pass that you will *prevent* something from being done. Some destructive deed will be thwarted by your actions."

You looked over at me. I moved to stand beside you, and placed my arm around your waist. "Can you tell us more?" I said.

The man shook his head. "Induction. It was not your futures I glimpsed, but my own. My future, changing. Of course, this is not a thing we are usually permitted to see. It is very rare." He peered at you with curiosity, and also as if you were his co-conspirator. "I believe what I have just experienced was something akin to a power surge. I have always been ... well ... a little psychic." He chuckled modestly. "But that, my dear, was an experience of a different order entirely."

With a slight wobble, the man got to his feet. From beneath the counter he produced a bottle of brandy and a glass. He poured himself a short drink and downed it in one.

"A confluence, you see. A coming together. This place, this extraordinary place, and you and me." He poured another drink and raised his glass. "Cheers!" He was clearly reviving, and, in fact, was looking happier and happier.

We stayed a short while longer, talking to the man, speculating about what had happened, and trying to glean whatever we could from the things he said about it. But he grew at once more jovial and more cryptic, no doubt due to him getting rapidly drunk. Towards the end, he said, "It's a curious business my lovely young things, but for once I have scant desire to enquire. I've read my James. Montague Rhodes, of course. Something has been lifted, and that's all I need to know."

On the train back, you sat with your head leaning against the window, you hat in your lap, your eyes closed. It had grown dark. Streetlamps and lighted homes flashed by.

As we approached the station, you straightened up and looked over at me, sitting opposite, and managed a wan smile. "Nearly there," you said, and began gathering your bags.

"Do you still feel weird?" I asked.

You shook your head. "That's the thing," you said, "I don't feel anything at all now. I just feel flat and empty."

"What can I do?"

You shrugged. Then you said: "I haven't quite decided about this, but maybe you could bring those mushrooms down. I think I'd like to try them. The book says they're good for low spirits."

7

At this time, if you remember, Christa, my dad was going through one his phases of being obsessed with gambling, and with horse racing in particular. Often, all excited, he would clamp my neck in the crook of his arm and bellow close to my ear, "I've got a horse!" Rubbing his knuckles fiercely against my head, he would be sure to shout it again, more than once, "I've got a horse! I've got a horse!" And this meant he was going to place a bet.

His talk was filled with the language of the "gee-gees". He spoke about places he'd never visited, racecourses around the country, as though he went there all the time: Aintree, Ascot, Chepstow, Goodwood, Haydock, Kempton Park. Actually, he was just in the bookies a lot, an awful lot, much to my mum's silent despair. Just as he didn't hide his drinking, so he was open about having a punt. Sitting at the kitchen table, early in the morning, hungover, chain smoking and drinking instant coffee from a massive mug, he'd study the racing pages of the *Express*. At this same table, at mealtimes, it would all come tumbling out: bets placed each way, doubles, trebles, accumulators, Yankees and Canadians. I had no idea what any of it meant. I just knew that there wasn't enough money to pay the bills and that the smallest extra expense would have my dad stressed and rampaging. Yet always there was enough for the pub and enough for my dad to have another horse.

In the bookies, or maybe in a nearby pub, he acquired a new group of friends. From this hideous bunch the two blokes I remember best were brothers. Both of them had moustaches and both of them worked "in security". One was more or less normal looking, apart from the weird yellow highlights in his hair, and he was called Dean. But his brother had a bizarrely long face and so he was known as "Horse Head". I never knew his real name.

For a while, Dean and Horse Head, as well as assorted other troglodytes, would appear on occasion back at the house with my dad after closing time. This would happen even on a school night.

Late one Thursday, some time after I'd gone to sleep, they all arrived, armed with cans, packets of fags, still jubilant from somebody's win on the ponies much earlier in the day. My dad put Queen on the stereo and soon my room, at the top of the open-plan stairs, filled with smoke. It was nearly Christmas and far too cold to open a window, at least according to my parents, who disapproved strongly of "letting the heat out".

I thought about putting some music of my own on to try and mask their noise, but I knew that if my mum passed my bedroom door and heard it then she would have come in and have a go at me for being awake. And so, as the minutes passed, I lay there, angry, trying, and failing, to get back to sleep. The whole thing made me feel so pathetic.

Everyone was speaking at once, raising their voices to be heard amidst the boasts and the piss-taking and the guffaws. My dad's voice was the loudest of the lot, every few moments I would hear some new exclamation of his:

"Oh, yeah – *saf*!" He said this all the time, saf. It meant 'smooth as fuck'. "Plonker!" he'd cry. "Dipstick!" And, of course, his favourite, "Pillock!"

"What am I like?" he'd demand to know. But very soon he appeared to have the answer. "Because that's what I'm like!" he'd declare, concluding another bit of bluster.

One of his oddest habits was that he'd held on to words I'd used myself briefly years before when I was a kid. That night I heard him claim, "Our Alex says it's rad." "Rad" was a word I'd favoured for a few months in 1983 when I was going through a BMXing phase. I hadn't described anything as being rad in years.

He was planning a lads' holiday to Spain with Dean and his brother, and so Horse Head had temporarily become "*Cabeza de Caballo*". They said it over and over again: "*Cabeza de Caballo*! *Cabeza de Caballo*!" I lay there wondering where the money for that holiday would come from.

More cans were cracked open, Queen was flipped over, and the quality of the air grew worse.

Gradually, the nastiness and the aggression increased. I started to hear comments about "shirtlifters" and "gypos". All I wanted to do was sleep.

There was no particular reason why I decided to go downstairs. I'd never done it before, but this time, once I'd thought of it, I couldn't resist. The more I lay there and pondered it, the more it seemed to be the only thing to do. I suppose I was just sick of the idiocy. And so, about an hour after they'd arrived, I got out of bed and wearing only pyjama bottoms and a t-shirt I opened my bedroom door and walked down into the living room.

It was as if something had escaped from the attic, as if something grotesque and shameful had lurched into view.

A kind of foggy pandemonium broke out. I was involved, I don't want to pretend I wasn't, Christa, but I don't remember exactly what it was I said. My parents started yelling at me through the cigarette smoke to go back upstairs. "Go back to your room! Go back to sleep!" Their guests stared at me like a freak had appeared on the scene.

I shouted back, something, no doubt, about it being impossible to sleep. I think I also said that it was becoming impossible to breathe. My dad didn't like that.

My sister had suffocated to death of an asthma attack. He was on his feet, standing straight in front of me, bellowing, his suntan ablaze. I screamed something back, right in his face. I have no idea what it was, but it must have had some force.

Because what I remember next is bending away, turning and twisting my middle, eluding his grip. I knew for sure I was in trouble – danger, that is – if he caught me. I was across the room at high speed, sending a side table of drinks and ashtrays flying. Then I was clawing at the porch door, the front door, and belting up the short driveway onto the street. My dad was right behind me. He was making noises like an enraged bull, so I accelerated away, down the hill. Even with nothing on my feet, he had no chance of catching me. As I neared the bottom of the road he shouted something violent sounding, but I couldn't make it out, and I really didn't care.

It was a clear December night. My feet were bare, so were my arms, and my pyjama bottoms were made of cheap, thin cotton. I knew I didn't have long before I started to freeze.

I considered, briefly, going up to Jay's. His house was nearer than yours and his father was always welcoming. But I couldn't face waking them, especially when his dad, a farmer, had to get up so early. It was asking too much of a friend.

So I set off running in the direction of your house. I expected the cold, hard surfaces of the pavements and road to be agony on the soles of my feet, but it wasn't as bad as I'd feared. I kept my eyes on the ground and thought of Zola Budd. Small stones were the biggest problem and I did find myself crying out and stopping and hobbling now and then.

Up past the high school and then down Inkle Lane. Despite the cold, despite my lack of footwear and the stabs of pain, it all seemed, in a way, so easy. I was full of adrenalin and felt strangely free. I think in my mixed-up state I believed something would be done for me, something could be arranged, and then I wouldn't have to go back home. I even had moments of euphoria and whooped ecstatically as I rushed by dark and empty fields.

It was when I crossed the humpback bridge and began passing through your village that I started to worry about what I was going to do when I reached your house. How would I attract your attention? What would we do then? The idea of knocking at the front door, of rousing the whole household, was out. Even if I could predict how your mum would react – and I certainly couldn't predict it – I knew that Mats was home for Christmas. Mats was full of grudges and couldn't be trusted. He would try to use all this against you in some way, maybe to persuade your mum that I was rough and disruptive, a pleb from the estate. Amongst his many other faults, Mats was a snob. Yet snobbery works. For the first time, I felt ashamed of my ridiculous predicament. I almost turned around.

But, even as I slowed down, your house came into view and I understood that I couldn't just go back. I was cold and sore. I wasn't even sure *how* cold and *how* sore, which I knew was a bad sign. I had no house keys on me. And in any case my dad would still be fuming and drunk. The idea of simply running back home, when looked at again, seemed pretty stupid. In fact, *everything* seemed pretty stupid, everything except the prospect of getting inside and warm. I reached your driveway and stood there and wondered how to proceed.

In the end, I clambered over the fence and into your back garden. I examined the door of your large shed, but it was padlocked. I danced about a little on the neat, damp lawn and considered those scenes in American movies where some brat tosses a stone or two at a bedroom window to attract their beloved's attention. The last thing I wanted was to crack a pane of glass, but I thought I'd better give the pebble throwing a go.

I was spared the need. I was due a little luck and, abruptly, it arrived. From the woods, rising high behind your garden, there came a glow of light. It faded away briefly before reappearing, its source having apparently moved. For a few seconds all was quiet, and then the foxes began to scream. I found myself so caught up in their excited-sounding cries that I turned my whole body in the direction of the trees. Later, you told me that for a moment you'd been terrified, that you thought you'd discovered one of the Brotherhood standing in your garden, watching the house. You'd been woken by the shrieking of the foxes and come to peer out into the darkness, mainly to see if the strange lights that you'd first noticed several nights earlier had returned. Instead you saw me standing there and it was only after several thumping heartbeats that you realised who I was.

Startled by the noise as you opened your window, I span around, and I remember how joyful I felt when I realised that it was you up there.

"Oh my God. Alex. What the hell's happened? What's going on?"

"Can I come inside? Please? I'm in my pyjamas and I'm freezing."

"Oh, no. Okay, I'm coming down now."

A few moments later you appeared at the back door and unlocked it.

You led me into the kitchen and sat me down on a chair. "What's happened, Alex?" you asked again, but before I could answer you said, "My goodness, look at the state of your feet."

They were dirty, grazed and scratched. There was blood. I'd cut them in several places. "I need to wash those right away," you said.

You vanished and I heard you dart up the stairs. Three or four minutes later you were back with a bowl, a towel, soap, cotton wool, and TCP. You began to prepare a bath for my feet.

It was just as you were lifting my feet into the warm water that your mother came into the room.

You must have heard her, but you didn't turn or even raise your head. You simply stayed kneeling down and stuck stubbornly, tenderly, to your task.

Svea stood behind you and regarded me, regarded us both. I was damp, grubby and shivering. I was wearing very little and looked, surely, rather wild. It was the middle of the night. And yet, for the first time, I felt your mum was actually registering my existence. More than that, she seemed transfixed by the whole unexpected scene.

Then I saw a spasm of anger pass across her face. I readied myself for an outburst, but instead she whirled around and said sharply: "Mats, go back to your room. Upstairs now, please." I barely caught a glimpse of a groggy Mats in the background before he disappeared. He murmured something that I missed and Svea hissed, with real fury this time, "Don't be foolish! Go to bed!"

You washed my feet carefully, lifted them out, dried them, and began to apply antiseptic to the cuts. Meanwhile you mum was making sweet tea and watching you work. She made no comment other than: "I'm afraid, Alex, that you may well develop chilblains." When she said it, her accent was unusually pronounced.

"I don't mind."

With mugs of tea in our hands we sat around the kitchen table. I was now wearing a winter coat of yours that you'd grabbed from the hall and your mum had put the heating on. Without omitting anything, and with some background information for your mum's benefit, I told both of you all that had happened in the past two hours or so.

I thought your mum was amazing that night. She wasn't angry with me for disturbing your household, she didn't try to take my parents' side. It was even her who suggested that I stay for the weekend. You didn't have to ask. Mainly, it was your mum's face that I glanced at as I recounted my story. She was beautiful, of course, in a stern way, and had been an actress for a time when she was young. All of her expressions and other responses were exactly right. You once told me that she'd let slip to you that she'd never felt comfortable being a mother, but she was perfect for the part just then. In charge and kind.

Later, though, when I praised Svea as we talked together by ourselves, you merely shrugged and said, "Oh, she's still feeling terrible about the night Mats punched me in the eye. That's what all this is about for her."

I slept in the guest room and at around eight the next morning the three of us drove, in your mum's Audi, over to my house. The driveway was empty. My parents weren't entitled to sick pay until they'd been off for several days. They'd gone to work as normal.

By now, with a calmer mind, I'd remembered the spare front door key, hidden beneath a plant pot in the greenhouse. I was wearing a jumper, jeans and trainers borrowed, whether he liked it or not, from Mats. Inside, I changed quickly into my uniform, grabbed my school bag and some extra clothes and left my parents a note: "Spending the weekend at Christa's. Home – probably – Sunday eve."

That Friday at school I was in a strange state, exhausted and elated all at once. I told several friends about what had happened, but most seemed bewildered and didn't really know what to say. I was surprised that they weren't more shocked or that they didn't grow more angry on my behalf. Their reactions were vague. I didn't much care. Your mum had been sympathetic and I was sleeping at your house for the next two nights. And my parents had no idea what I was saying and to whom I was saying it. I hoped this would cause them worry and shame. At home time, when I saw you waiting for me out on the lane, I was filled with the most intense feeling of happiness I could ever remember.

Walking to the village, enclosed by hedgerows, passing beneath bare black boughs, you told me how you'd bumped into a neighbour you used to do some babysitting for a year or two earlier.

"She asked me if I'd noticed anything strange about some of the newer people living in the village and if I'd noticed activity around the church."

"What did you say?"

"At first I tried to laugh it off. I said, 'I'm a teenager. I'm always daydreaming. I don't notice much.' But when that didn't work I admitted that I'd talked to them once or twice."

"Wow, really?"

"Yes. I said I thought they were some kind of Buddhist group. That they were into peace and meditation."

"What did she say to that?"

"She agreed that they caused no trouble and kept themselves to themselves. But she still wondered about the church. I said they'd mentioned a meditation and learning centre, running courses. She seemed a bit put out, and said something about it altering the character of the village. I said, 'I don't know what you mean. The village doesn't have any character. Everything's gone.

The post office, the pub. And now the church.' And we left it at that."

"Ouch! And what are they actually doing with it?"

"I've no idea. But I aim to find out."

That evening you made a pie with chestnuts, mushrooms and shallots, and a caramel apple cheesecake, Swedish-style. I sat at the breakfast bar amazed as you baked. Normally we lived off pasta and salads. You made enough for everyone, even Mats, and you and I ate with your mum. Svea told me how you used to follow your mormor around in her kitchen near Stockholm and ask her endless questions about food when you were a little girl. Back then, your mum thought you might grow up to be a cook. I had a glimpse, just a glimpse, of everything being different, for all of us. I heard chatter and laughter, felt warmth and contentment, and the light was soft and soothing. But then it was gone. In any case, what we had that Friday night was good enough.

Your mum went to bed early – she was due to be away for much of Saturday – and so, after dinner, we cleared and washed the dishes.

Up in your room you said, "I bet she's taken a Valium," and started to undress. I did the same. We lay on your mattress. You wanted to go on top, as always. You sat astride me and lifted your arms above your head and rotated your wrists, showing me all of yourself in the candlelight. You shook your hair out and I slipped inside you and I remember thinking, "Wow, this has all become so easy." It was hard to believe I'd ever been worried about it. And we kept at it for about an hour, with pauses while you leaned forward and whispered in my ear and asked me to say things. So I said what you wanted and you closed your eyes, gripped me hard, and smiled.

*

On Saturday morning you came into the guest room just after eight with a cup of tea and slid into bed beside me.

"Morning."

"Morning. Oo, I say."

"No, no – I need the loo."

"I bet that's not all you need though."

Afterwards you said, "How are your feet? It's a fine day. Do you think you'd be okay if we went into the woods?"

I felt at my soles and flexed my toes. "They're a bit sore. Maybe, if I put some plasters on."

"Good. And what do you reckon about taking the mushrooms today?"

"Really? Are you sure?"

"Yes, but we've got to take them early. We don't want to be tripping at, say, six o'clock, when mum's back."

We both took showers and then, as we ate toast in the kitchen, you gathered some bits and bobs of food, and stuffed them into a daysack. Mats was prowling around, but there was a point at which he went into the downstairs loo and during that minute or so you produced the plastic pill bottle from the front pocket of your bag and shook it in my direction. After swiftly tidying up the kitchen, we said goodbye to your awful brother and left the house.

We took the mushrooms, half each of the intense, earthy powder, almost as soon as we were outside. Then we headed for the bridge and, beyond, the trees.

While we waited for something to happen, we walked and, among other subjects, talked about the light I had seen in the woods two nights earlier.

"So you've seen it before?" I said.

"Yes, a couple of times now. And moving just like on Thursday. It's never before midnight and the foxes seem to be agitated by it. They always wake me up. It must be something to do with the Brotherhood."

"But what are they up to now?"

"Who knows?" And, in a deeper, plummier voice, you intoned, "They are disordered, more disordered than I can possibly understand. They ask that I do not seek to inquire into their affairs."

"Ha ha!"

"Do not laugh my exemplary young man. They are leaderless and in a bit of a tizz."

"Hee!"

And that's how it started, with big grins that wouldn't go away and lots of giggling.

You'd read in your book on magick and drugs to try to avoid fretting about whether or not the mushrooms were kicking in. "It says to try and avoid introducing anxiety into the experience. Don't worry if you're uncertain if anything's happening or not. That's normal. It says if you're with someone then it's best not to keep asking questions like, 'Are you tripping yet? What can you see?' Apparently, a moment will arrive when we both just know."

We'd been in the woods for around an hour, moving forwards some of the time, but also stopping to examine fallen leaves, fronds of fern that had survived into the very late autumn. You kept doing impressions of the tall old man from the Brotherhood and we were laughing more and more. Eventually we found ourselves, smiling like maniacs, staring at the moss on the trunk of an alder tree.

"Is it me or is the green amazing?"

"It's all amazing. Look at the texture of the bark." You began rubbing and prodding the fissures, hooking the tips of your fingers inside and then pressing the palm of your hand flat against the tree. "Look," you said. "Look."

At last, after who knows how long, you turned from the alder to me.

"Oh God, Christa. Your eyes. If anyone you knew saw you now ..."

"Yaargh!" You flapped your hands in front of my face. The effect was startling: trails –afterimages of your hands dotting the air. "Don't mention other people. It freaks me out. I can't think about anyone else. There's just you and me."

So I sang the theme to *You and Me*, the 70s kids' programme. You hugged me and jumped up and down on the spot. "I wish we could listen to music."

I started to wander off, but you grabbed me and said, very gravely, "I need to see a holly tree."

"Ha ha!"

You grinned, then frowned. "No, I mean it. I *must* find one. Come on. Quick!" And you began to march away.

"Wait!"

We weaved erratically through the woods, not managing to find what you were looking for. At first you kept starting up with a kind of lesson about holly, and then forgetting and stopping. The theme of your lesson was winter: holly as a festive decoration, birds and mice eating the berries of the holly bush in the colder months, hedgehogs hibernating in the fallen leaves. It tumbled out in fragments. But still we couldn't track down an actual tree and you were becoming upset.

Meanwhile, the wind had picked up. Beneath tumultuous clouds, the woods appeared to be flickering. One moment everything was bright, the next grey and dim. It seemed to me that a hidden hand, a gargantuan hand, was fiddling with nature's controls. And yet, still, where colour was to be found, especially green, it was the richest and most intense I'd ever seen.

I began to notice also a soft green glow. It came from within the crevices of tree trunks and emanated from the brackets of fungi that clung to oak and birch. It ran in luminescent veins down the branches waving overhead. I wanted to know if you were seeing the same thing, this foxfire all around us. When I turned to you to ask, I saw it playing through the strands of your hair, like you were some fairy of the wood.

Except that you were no such thing, at least not for yourself. You'd been silent for some time. Sitting down on the blackened trunk of a tree that'd uprooted long ago, you became totally withdrawn. You began staring at your hands, but after a time hid them away inside your coat pockets. You were ignoring me, looking anywhere but in my direction. Then you pulled your hands out again and turned them over and over, gazing now at the palms, now at the backs, flexing your fingers, your face twitching strangely.

"Christa ...?"

You flinched, then covered your face. "Don't. Don't look at me. I can't bear it. I can't stand to be seen."

I approached the dead tree trunk slowly, but you leapt up and backed away.

"What's wrong? Don't you see the foxfire? Your hair is alive with light."

"My hands!" you screamed, and held them out to me. "My hands are hideous. I'm all shrivelled up! I thought I was young, but I'm not. I'm a hag! A crone!"

"No, no. Don't be silly. You're beautiful. You're the Queen of this place. I can't tell you how gorgeous you look amongst the trees."

"I'm a witch! Is my face old too? It must be. Of course it must." You began pressing at your cheeks and chin, trying to feel the wrinkles.

"Christa ... you need to calm down." I knew there was something I needed to say. I had to grope for it. "We're on mushrooms. Remember? Magic mushrooms."

"That's not it. That doesn't explain it. Everything before wasn't true. This is real now."

This argument made me hesitate. It's hard to believe, but in the moment it seemed persuasive.

You were examining your hands again, grabbing one with the other, frantically. I watched you in a state of confusion. It'd started to spot with rain. All kinds of odd thoughts about rain coursed through my head. Then a man spoke to me. "It's not rare, when folk are on mushies, for them to think they've wet themselves." It was Carl, Jay's brother. I heard his voice so clearly, as though he was standing directly by my ear. He'd offered up this nugget whilst making coffee in the kitchen of the farmhouse during a recent visit. He'd been asking if we tried his shrooms yet.

I became convinced that if I could explain to you what Carl had said then you would understand what was happening to you, that you were trapped inside your trip and having a bad time.

It didn't work. It probably came out wrong. In any case, I couldn't make you listen. Part way through you began to take off your clothes. At first, I thought it was because you were misunderstanding what I was saying, that you were checking yourself for pee.

"No, no – " I said, but you interrupted:

"I need to see myself. I need to see who I really am. How I really look. I need to know the truth."

It didn't stop with your coat. Off came your boots, your jeans, your top layers too.

I tried to intervene, but you batted me away. "Stop it. Get off. I need to see!"

I was really struggling now. You were standing in the woods, in the December rain, dressed only in your underwear and you were sobbing and clutching at yourself, pulling at non-existent sagging bits.

"I knew it!" you shouted. You were staring at your stomach, scratching and jabbing at it with pitiless fingers, raking your scars.

"Christa, please!" The branches of the trees were swaying and leaving trails against the sky. I sensed that the woods had become watchful, hostile. The foxfire had gone, all the magic. I was starting to cry too. "Christa, please be kind to yourself. The trees are getting angry."

Your whole upper body started to shake. "I know," you hissed. "The knots have faces."

"Christa ..."

"They hate me. They think I'm evil. They're right. I've known it all along. Ever since I was a little girl."

You whirled around and ran, stumbling and catching the floor with your hands. Then upright and off again.

Something had been done to us, something wicked. A spell had been cast. That's how I felt as you reeled away from me. We'd been wrenched apart and now we were lost. The woodland was a labyrinth. For a moment all I could do was watch you go and fight to stay calm. In the wild motion of the trees I could hear a murmuring: "*She's gone. She's left you. You'll never find her. You'll never get out. You'll be here forever.*" A part of my mind knew I had to resist.

I gathered up your clothes and pushed them into the bag that you'd dropped. I picked up your coat and began to follow you at walking pace. All this was in keeping with my attempt at self-control. It didn't last. Panic tugged at me and I began to run.

I can't be certain how long we were separated. All the enchantment had turned to murk and menace. The only thing that comforted me was running. Running became the point. I was desperate to find you and I was desperate to outpace my fear. Tearing along, I called your name, again and again. I kept thinking that I saw you and went lurching after phantoms. I was soaked and gabbling to myself. I was convinced I could hear a fox laughing and that its laughter was coming out red.

I found you merely by chance. At the edge of a clearing, I saw you from behind. You were white and trembling, smeared with mud and flecked with leaves. You weren't alone. Planted in front of you, his massive hands grasping your shoulders, was the man who had been camping in the woods during the summer, the man whose tent you'd invaded. It was the same man, I believed, who had been standing at the end of Clewkin Road the night the Brotherhood had emerged from their cottages.

"Hey, you!" I called. "Leave her alone."

He didn't react. With a sense of dread, I took a few steps forwards. As I did so, I saw that the man's long arms were fully extended, as though to keep the distance between the two of you as decent as possible. And rather than holding you prisoner, he appeared to be holding you up.

He was talking to you in a low, deep voice and searching your face with his gaze. He was trying, I could see now, to get through to you about something. Several seconds later, I saw you nod your head, just once, almost as if in surrender. At this, the man lifted his hands from your body. You wobbled, but didn't fall down. The man looked in my direction.

"There is nothing to fear," he said. "Here is your girlfriend."

8

I moved towards you across the clearing and as I did so I caught myself wanting to look like I was taking over now, like it was me who was in charge. My trip was well past its peak, but the world seemed no less bizarre. With the winter solstice only four days away, you were all but naked in the woods, filthy and shivering. I'd had a terrible time alone, searching for you, certain you were going through something even worse. And yet here we were, reunited beneath the gaze of this towering stranger. I should've been thinking only of you, but of course I couldn't help wondering who he was.

You sagged against me as I reached you. You were shaking so hard. The man caught my eye and gestured at the coat I was still carrying. "We must get her warm as quickly as possible," he said.

"It's not just this," I said. "I have these too." And I began pulling the rest of your clothes out of the bag.

"Good," the man said. But mud from the soles of your boots had got over everything and I wondered how we were going to get you through the front door if your mum had come home early, or if Mats was lurking downstairs.

I glanced at the sky. The light was fading. I was supporting you as you struggled to pull on your things, guiding your arms into sleeves. There could be no disguising your condition. Your clothes were wet and dirty, your hair was tangled and streaked with mud, you were freezing and weak and obviously upset. Svea would go berserk. I couldn't bear it, not after she'd been so understanding about my own recent drama.

I looked up at the man. He had a heavy brow, dark eyes, an iron-grey beard to match his mass of iron-grey hair. He must have been six foot four. He was an intimidating stranger to ask a kindness from.

"I don't know what to do," I said. "I can't take her home like this."

"I quite agree. There was never any question of it. We must get you both dry and clean."

"But where?"

"Hm. I'm no longer living in a tent, if that's what you mean."

"Oh."

"What's your name?" you cried suddenly, staring up at the man, pushing wet hair away from your face. "I thought you were going to gobble me up before, when you came out of those trees. But you were so nice to me."

He smiled, just briefly, and then bent down towards us, capturing us entirely in his gaze. "My name – and I don't always give it out so freely – my name is Manus Ainger."

"Manus Ainger," you said wonderingly.

"Yes. And now we must head for my cottage. It's growing dark."

We were coming down fast and it's not as if mushrooms give you a hangover or anything. Your strength started to return as we walked and you warmed up a little. I realised that on top of the rain and the cold and all of the distress we'd forgotten to eat. I brought out a couple of chocolate bars from the bag you'd packed and was pleased when you said you'd like one.

Manus led the way. He had to keep adjusting his pace and waiting while we caught him up. The rain, which had eased, started to fall hard again. Manus was wearing a black waterproof of some sort and now, slowly, with a glance behind him first, he lifted his hood. It was a dreary, more or less silent trudge back to the village. I kept having the same thought over and over again: "Why the hell are we following this strange man?" It was hardly fair of me. I was the one who'd hinted to him that we needed help. Still, I was uneasy. As I watched his huge frame weaving through the trees, I had the feeling he was going to take us far further than a warm fireside, to a new place entirely.

It was a real surprise when Manus brought us to the front door of a cottage on Clewkin Road.

"You live here?" you asked, not bothering to hide your astonishment.

He turned from the business of putting his key in the lock and said, eyebrow raised, "Yes. Why?"

"Erm, nothing. It's just hard to believe you fit. These houses seem pretty small."

He tipped his head to one side and frowned. "Repeated references to my height will not win you my friendship."

"Oh, sorry." Your apology was flat, it sounded like you didn't care. What was really going on, though, was that you were deciding to just come out with it all and be honest:

"The thing is, I wasn't even being truthful. I didn't expect you to live here because we found your campsite in the woods, back in the summer. I know you saw us that day too, by your tent. And then we had a night where we met ... well, we thought we'd met everyone along here, all your neighbours. They seem to belong to some kind of organisation. And one of them, another tall man, he told us that your group – or his group – was disordered. That was the word he used. And that it was leaderless. And then we thought we saw you standing at the end of the street, the same night, I mean. So we made up a story between ourselves that *you* were the group's lost leader. But now here you are and I'm not sure what to think."

It was a funny little speech, especially coming from someone who was such a mess. Manus, obviously delighted, ran a large hand over his damp beard, tugged it, and then began to laugh. It was a real rumble from deep within. "Not bad!" he said. "Not bad!"

"What do you mean."

"I mean, Miss Gardner, that you're not far off."

"How do you all know my name? And, while we're at it, why am I *expected*, or *hoped for*, or whatever it was he said?"

"Is that what Walter told you?" Manus shook his head. "Not like him to be so ingenuous. But enough for now. Inside to get dry and warm."

Manus opened the door and ducked directly into the front room. We went in after him.

The house *was* small and made Manus look even bigger. It was quite something to be inside one of the cottages. The whole time I'd been running back and forth between my house and your village we'd been speculating about the goings on within these walls. The room in which we were standing was just as unadorned as I'd imagined. The floor was made of stone flags, the furniture was wooden and plain. There was no sofa, no cushions, no television set. Manus had allowed himself a small rug in front of the open fireplace, but it was shabby and pocked with burn marks. There was a wooden bookcase, which was full, and an old-fashioned record player in one corner, with a small collection of LPs propped beside it. There was only one picture on the walls – a dusky painting of a street in a European city. At some point later that afternoon, when Manus saw me looking at it again, he said, "That street is in Gdańsk."

"Oh," I said. I didn't even know what country Gdańsk was in.

Manus had allowed us a moment to take in our new surroundings, but now he took charge.

"This could all be very awkward." he said. "Let's not allow that to happen." He dashed up the stairs and returned with two grey shirts. They were enormous. From the kitchen he produced a wooden clothes airer. He placed it by the hearth and said, "I'll start a fire in a moment. Alex – it is Alex isn't it? – your clothes are wet but not too dirty. While I wash what Christa is wearing, we will dry your things off. Meanwhile you need to get Christa upstairs for a hot bath. There is no shower here I'm afraid, but in any case a bath will be more beneficial."

We headed upstairs to the tiny bathroom. "How does he fit in here?" you whispered. I started to run the hot water, changed out of my clothes and put on one of the grey shirts. It hung about me like a piece of Victorian nightwear. Meanwhile you were undressing too. I grabbed our tops and jeans and took it all down to Manus who was building the fire. Then I hurried back to you and slipped the little bolt to lock the bathroom door.

"Not that it would do us any good, if he wanted to bust in," you said. You were swirling your hand in the water, testing the temperature. Before too long you climbed into the bath and I crouched on the floor at your side.

For a while you lay in the steaming water in silence. When you did finally speak it was to say only, "Oh, God." Then you ducked yourself under the water and stayed there for what must have been more than a minute.

After you came back up we began to talk. We spoke in whispers. You cried a little bit, but laughed at yourself too. The whole thing was like a secret, urgent conference. We told each other what we had seen and felt during the trip and you said that your mind had played the cruelest of tricks on you by convincing you that you were old and withered. You said old age was your worst fear, especially as you were certain you wouldn't be having any children. And, of course, we talked about our bonkers situation, and about Manus and who he might be. We agreed there was something strange about his accent. It was impossible to place and seemed to suggest half a dozen nationalities all at once. There were a few tense seconds when we heard him coming up the stairs, but he was outside the bathroom door for no more than a moment and only so that he could tell us where we would find clean towels.

We lingered in there. Who could blame us? Anyway you needed to get properly warmed up after our ridiculous escapade in the wood. When at last we did go downstairs, both wearing Manus's shirts, the fire was blazing and our clothes were drying out on the airer. Manus made a pot of tea and served a plate a ginger biscuits. We each sat in wooden chairs, a short way back from the hearth, and for a brief time we focused on our refreshments and said very little.

It was Manus who started the conversation. Looking at you he said: "What – if you don't mind me asking – what precisely did Walter say to you that night? I mean, of course, the night you came to us ... seeking answers."

So you repeated, almost word for word, all that the tall old man had said. You related to Manus how you'd been stopped about your black eye and how the two men – named, supposedly, Dr. McCoy and Dr. Horace – had approached you on the stall and spoken about how all animals are essentially the same.

"Hmm. For myself, I'm going though a long phase of not being entirely in agreement." Manus murmured. Then, more loudly, "But that's for another time. Now look, I need you – both of you – to understand something. That is, if we are to get to know each other better."

You nodded eagerly.

"You are feeling better then?" Manus said, though he had asked you this once already.

You nodded again. I suspected you were still feeling pretty bad, but I said nothing.

"Good. Excellent. What I need you to understand is that we are an eccentric bunch, we who make up this 'Brotherhood', as Walter insists on calling it. In fact ..." And suddenly Manus sprung to his feet. "I'll be back in a moment," he said. With a two or three strides he was at his front door and an instant later he'd disappeared out on to the street.

We looked at one another, astonished.

"What's he doing now?"

"Haven't a clue."

"The scary thing is, I don't think he's mad. It's something else."

"I agree. Maybe we're about to find out what."

A few moments later Manus came stalking back inside the cottage. Behind him there was another member of the Brotherhood, dressed in wide grey trousers and a thick grey jumper.

"Now then, Christa, Alex, allow me to introduce you to Helen."

We both stared. The Brother was a woman. True she had short hair, a boyish cut, but there was no doubt at all. Helen was female.

She was smiling down at us on our chairs. Her smile was a mixture of friendliness and ironic amusement. It was hard to guess her age, maybe thirty five.

"Hi," you managed to say. I was grinning like a loon.

"Thank you, Helen," Manus said.

"No problem. Nice to meet you both," said Helen, her smile broadening so that she crinkled a little around the eyes. I think she'd enjoyed our obvious surprise.

Then Helen turned and left, closing the cottage door behind her.

"There is no Brotherhood you see," Manus said, seating himself beside us again. "But, for various reasons, Walter is attached to the name. It has to do with the origins of our group, I suppose. We have taken many wrong turns along the way. Walter is an old-fashioned man, and also rather theatrical. Neither of which affect his brilliance in his field. In other words, he is merely one example of that eccentricity to which I referred."

"But if he doesn't like women –"

"I didn't say he didn't like women," interrupted Manus gruffly.

"Okay, sorry. But if he has old-fashioned ideas about all of that, why did he say those things to me about my being expected or hoped for or whatever? I mean, I'm a girl."

Manus smiled. "Walter would no doubt refer to you as a *young woman*, not as a girl. If I may sidestep your question just for a moment and ask one of my own. How did you feel when Walter said those things to you?"

You looked down at the floor. Your bare legs were tucked beneath you on the chair. I suddenly felt uneasy and got up to check how your jeans were doing on the airer. They needed more time.

"I felt," you said, as I sat back down, "I felt like it was right. I felt like I *should* be hoped for. I liked it. I liked it a lot." You didn't look up after you'd spoken.

Manus nodded. "I sense you are feeling a touch of embarrassment in confessing that to me, but in fact that is precisely what I was hoping to hear. Walter should have been more guarded. But it is true that we have wondered if you would be interested in our work, and in playing a small but vital part in it, some time next year. It seems extraordinary to find someone who may be right for us so close by, but then extraordinary things are part of the mix in life."

You'd raised your head now. You were pale and looked utterly exhausted, but I could see that your mind was aflame.

Sure enough you said, "I have so many questions. What is your work? Why might I be right for it? How do you know I might be?" Then you gestured in my direction, "And how come we didn't notice there are women living here too? That's not like us."

"I don't know ... Do they all have a boy's haircut, like Helen? Maybe we saw them and didn't realise."

Manus shook his head, smiling. "Some do and some don't. Perhaps what you notice and what you do *not* notice is less predictable than you imagine."

"What do you mean?"

"I mean it's not, straightforwardly, something you can control. Awareness is, in part, a deception." He scrutinised us. I think we must have looked puzzled because next he said: "I'm not trying to baffle you. In any case, a likely explanation is that we are very busy people, and this has been especially true in recent months. Mostly we are at work or resting here in the cottages. Some of us walk in the woods, then there are those who spend their free time in other ways. It's likely that you haven't laid eyes on the majority of our group."

"Except the night you all came out on to the street," I said.

"Indeed. Most of us were there then, including several women."

"We've been wrong about everything." You sounded disgusted.

"Not at all. I doubt that very much. What else do think you know?"

"You've taken over the disused church."

"Correct," Manus said.

"You're some sort of religious group?"

"Hmm. That's a difficult one to answer. The church, I should say, is our workplace, not a place of worship. We are certainly not a religious organisation in any conventional sense."

You'd just begun to say something else when there was a rap at the cottage door. We both jumped and Manus grunted and rose from his chair. He opened the door, stepped outside and spoke softly and briefly to his visitor. When he came back inside he went over to our clothes and felt them.

"These are not entirely dry, but they are dry enough to get you back through your front door looking respectable."

"You have to go?" I said.

Manus nodded. "Yes, I'm needed now." He looked down at you. "Christa, I can see you're disappointed, but it's probably for the best. No doubt it's time you were getting home and, if you don't mind me saying so, you're looking rather pallid, despite your reassurances."

Slowly, we stood up. It was hard to think so suddenly about practical things. We plucked our clothes from the airer and went upstairs to the bathroom to change, hanging Manus's massive shirts on a hook behind the door. Back downstairs Manus had placed our boots in front of our chairs and we sat down to pull them on and do up laces.

Neither of us spoke. Both of us, I think, were feeling pretty funny about everything.

Manus was crouched by his fireplace, attending to the fire. You were hunting for your bag when he said, "And of course you were correct earlier too: I *am* the leader of this group, though for a time this year I walked away." He raised himself to his full height and held his lower back like it was painful.

"Why?" you said, turning round to face him.

He shrugged. "Disagreements. Doubts. Especially the second."

"Can we know more? I mean about all of it."

"Yes, but first you need rest. Too much running about in the woods, out of your young minds on drugs."

You did something then I'd hardly ever seen you do – you blushed.

Manus laughed. "Dear me, if you had only seen some of the states I have been in over the course of my life you would have no cause whatsoever for embarrassment."

"Really? You? You've taken stuff?"

"Monstrous amounts," Manus said. "Much of it of my own invention."

"What?"

"Enough," Manus held up a slab-like hand. "I must go. What are your plans for tomorrow? How about breakfast here at, say, ten o'clock. Is that something you both can manage?"

"Yes," you said firmly. "Alex is at mine tonight anyway." And then, "We don't eat bacon. Or any meat, actually."

Manus look pleased and gestured towards the door.

Your mum, for once, had been wondering where we were. She'd been at home a while, had asked Mats what time we'd left that morning, and couldn't understand how we could have been out for so many hours, especially in the rain.

Your lies were convincing enough. We'd set off for a walk into the woods, picked up the route of the abandoned railway line and followed it all the way to the nearest town several miles distant. Having spent some time there, and had tea and cake in a cafe to avoid the worst of the weather, we'd realised it would be too dark to take the same trail home and so we'd had to come the long way round, over the moor-top road. We were very tired and very damp, but it'd been a stimulating walk and we'd had plenty of exercise.

While we changed, and you made a fuss of Liv, your mum cooked us some pasta, the first time on any of my visits she'd made us something to eat. There was so much to ponder, so much to take in: the nightmarish trip, our meeting with Manus. But I didn't want to think about any of it. Looking out of an upstairs hallway window, I could see lights from houses in the village flecking the night. There was a rich atmosphere of an ordinary Saturday evening, at least in my head. Saturday night sitcoms were showing, to be followed by a disaster movie. It didn't matter that we weren't watching. Just knowing they were on was homely. Over on Two they were showing *À bout de souffle*, a French classic we'd both heard about and which you'd said you were taping. All of this seemed to be enough for me just then. Lamps in the dark as winter set in, a simple meal being prepared, films on TV. I felt a desperate urge to burrow into the moment. I didn't want to know about Manus in the church with his secret work, or imagine my dad getting ready for the pub, with the smell of aftershave drifting about and the sound of pinging as the sunbed cooled down. I didn't want to remember the lies we'd just told your one remaining parent or the sight of you in the woods clawing at yourself, convinced your were ancient and ugly. Everything was so screwed up and, for the first time ever, I found myself caring. Your mum's kindness had put me in a really strange mood.

You didn't feel the same way at all. After dinner, you lay lifelessly on the bed in your black and blood-coloured room and went over everything again and again. Only your mouth moved. Mushrooms, Manus, embarrassment, old age, Helen, Walter, the cottages, the church: on and on it went. I remember it as though a single light was shining on your lips and the only sound was the sound of your deep voice, deeper than ever, but that can't be right, there must have been more lights, and music playing too.

    At last it stopped. You'd drifted off. I sat on the beanbag for several minutes, hearing the filling rustle beneath me, listening to your breathing. Mats came upstairs and moved between his lair and the bathroom you shared. I didn't want any encounters with him so I waited a while longer, half enjoying the peace, and then, when all was clear, took myself off to bed.

9

"Another walk?" your mum said the next morning, amused and frowning all at once.

"Oh Morsa, you know I love the woods. And at least it's nice!"

"You're besotted with the place!"

"We've packed our breakfast and we're going," you said, patting a bag I knew to be empty.

It was a cold day, blue and bright. I ached for it to be ours, and ours alone. I didn't want to think about the muddied ugliness of the previous afternoon, or having to go home later to a house full of anger and unbreathable air. And I didn't want to see Manus again.

But where to even begin with those feelings? I knew I was being unrealistic. So I said nothing and slowly we walked in the direction of the cottages.

"How did you sleep?" This was the first chance I'd had to ask.

"You mean after my disgrace of yesterday?"

"No, that's not what I meant. But after the mushrooms, yes."

"I slept alright. Well, my body did. But my mind seemed to be going crazy."

"Weird dreams?"

"Mm. In the one I remember best, I was dressed in this heavy robe with huge sleeves and I was walking barefoot along some kind of stone channel. It was cold on the soles of my feet and it had high, steep sides, also made of stone. I think I was underground. Anyway, it was dark, but I was carrying a burning torch, and ahead of me I could make out, in the shadows, thousands and thousands of rats running down the channel."

"Ah. Rodents again. Were they laughing, the rats?"

"No. Quite the opposite. They were terrified of me. They were shrieking as they ran. I had the feeling I was driving them to their deaths. I seemed to know in the dream that they were all going to plunge down some great hole in the earth. I kept just catching glimpses of them, swarming about in a great mass, up the sides and along the bottom, tails flickering."

"Lovely."

"I know."

"What do you think it means?"

"No idea. It definitely doesn't mean that I want to kill loads of rats though."

We eked out that walk, stopping by the river for a while, watching the swollen waters surge. After we'd stood in silence for a while, you surprised me by saying, "I'd laugh if the old village flooded and all their schemes came to nothing."

"Really?"

You shrugged.

"Because we don't have to go –"

"No, Alex, we do. I need to know what they're up to, and what they reckon my part in it might be. We've been wondering for ages. Both of us have. And now we're really close to finding out."

I nodded, a barely-there sort of nod.

"Hey," you said. "Hey! It doesn't mean I'll be interested in doing what Manus wants. It doesn't mean that I think *they're* the most important thing."

"Okay."

"Anyhow, how important can it be, whatever it is they're doing?"

"Yeah, I suppose."

"No, I'm serious. It can't matter that much, can it? Hardly anything does." You turned and slipped your arms around me, chased after my eyes with yours, and

smiled when you caught them. "Except you. You matter."
We kissed, but I wasn't convinced.

When we broke apart you said: "And please don't think I've lost perspective. I know they're probably all raving mad."

I managed a small laugh.

"Loonies, the lot of them."

We knocked at the door of Manus's cottage. But it wasn't Manus who answered, it was Helen, the "Brother" from the night before. Dressed in wellies, trousers, a baggy black jumper, and with tousled boy's hair, she might, with the briefest of glimpses, have passed for a man, but, no, she was a woman, a woman with dark eyes and crinkles when she smiled.

Writing this, I wonder where Helen is now.

I never stop wondering where you are, Christa.

"Oh, hello again," you said. "We were looking for Manus. He asked us over for breakfast."

"Yes," said Helen. "Please come in, both of you."

We stepped inside. A classical music LP was playing on the record player. Glancing into the kitchen, I saw the table there was set for a meal.

"Manus is sorry," Helen began, "but he's been called over to the church. He asked me to give you a little breakfast and then take you to see him afterwards. Is that okay?"

We nodded and said it was and Helen took our coats and guided us to the small, round table. We took our seats, frowning at one another without Helen noticing.

"I've just got back from the farm, actually," Helen said, her back turned towards us as she busied herself at the kitchen worktop. "The bread couldn't be fresher."

"Farm?"

"Yes." She turned to face us. "Hasn't Manus mentioned it?"

"No," you said. "We barely know Manus. And he hasn't told us much about anything yet."

Helen seemed amused and nodded. "Well then, let me be the one to tell you that, yes, we have a small farm. I suppose smallholding would be more a more accurate description, really. But we always call it the farm. It's not far from here, a few fields and a pair of old stone buildings. We bought it a few years ago."

Helen looked down at us both. You said nothing, so, picturing something like Jay's father's set-up, I asked, "What is it that you rear?"

"Oh no, it's not a livestock operation. Not anymore. We grow fruit and vegetables for ourselves, and we've created a small bakery there. That's where this bread came from. We do keep hens. But the hens aren't laying at this time of year, so no eggs I'm afraid."

Helen went into the other room to flip over the LP. When she returned, she finished her preparations. Breakfast was simple, but delicious – thickly-sliced, crusty bread for toast, jam made from fruit grown on the farm, black coffee.

For a few minutes we ate more or less without speaking. Perhaps it was awkward, at least a little bit, but that's not how I remember it, not during the meal itself. I remember the lovely bready and coffee smells, Helen's smile, and the music playing on the turntable. I remember you sitting back in your chair, almost as if you were content. All traces of the ordeal of yesterday were gone from your face. Eventually, you said, "What's this music, Helen?"

"Do you like it?"

"Yes."

"It's one of my favourites: *Quartet for the End of Time* by Messiaen. Have you heard of it?"

Neither of us had, so Helen told us all about it's composition. Messiaen, she said, was French and had been taken as a prisoner of war by the Germans in 1940. Imprisoned in a stalag, Messiaen had been helped by a guard to obtain paper, a pencil, and a barrack in which it was peaceful enough to work. Messiaen had scored the quartet for piano, which he played, and for cello, violin, and clarinet because these were the instruments played by the three other professional musicians in the camp. The piece was premiered in freezing-cold surroundings, on second-rate instruments, in January 1941. The audience was made up of Messiaen's fellow prisoners and the German officers of the stalag. Reading from the album sleeve that she had brought through to the kitchen, Helen listed the names, in English, of the quartet's eight movements. Jesus was mentioned as Eternal and Immortal, and an angel was mentioned twice who announces the end of time. For once, the name of Jesus didn't make you go all tense, not so far as I could tell anyway.

Helen began to clear the breakfast things away. I wanted to say something in response to the story she'd just told us. I knew so little about classical music, so I chose to say something about "fortitude". That was the word I used, a word I'd learned and liked: *fortitude in wartime*. Maybe I was thinking of stoical stories I'd been told when I was young of landmines, incendiaries and bombs. Explosives dropped on Lancashire, of houses blown apart and people killed, of a V1 rocket landing in a village where relatives of mine had lived. And maybe I was thinking of my grandfather, a young man then, never having been much further than Manchester, carrying top secret intelligence across India alone by train.

For a moment, Helen said nothing. She carried on dealing with coffee grounds, placing cups and plates in the sink. Then she stopped, leaned back and looked at you. "Christa," she said, "you're half Swedish aren't you?"

You nodded and I'm sure we were both wondering how she knew that.

But before we had the chance to ask, she said. "As it happens, I'm half French. On my father's side." And I thought, yes she does have an accent. In fact, it seemed to be getting stronger as breakfast wore on. "Perhaps it partly accounts for my love of Messiaen. France surrendered and was occupied. France collaborated. But, in Stalag VIII-A, it was this visionary Frenchman who brought about a remarkable triumph, aided by a German in awe of his talent. You see?"

"Yes, I see."

"Then again, I'm not much of a patriot, so perhaps not. What about you, Alex? Are you English through and through?"

"I think so. Might be a little Irish too. Or so I've been told."

She smiled. "I think some would feel Christa and I haven't too much to be proud of, country-wise, when it comes to the Second World War. Unlike the English, of course: Dunkirk, the Blitz, the Battle of Britain. Such extraordinary courage and endurance. Such defiance, undaunted by odds."

"Do you mean it?" I said, a question that just slipped out. Her smile was all slanted now, her eyes ... was that mockery I could see in their depths?

"Sure, I mean it. Everyone knows it to be true, don't they? British fortitude, as you put it. But history is full of curious details. Contradictions. Things that don't quite fit." She shrugged and turned towards the sink.

I was perplexed. Why would she be needling me over such a thing? It just seemed so random and obscure. And even if she was, why would I care? The war ended nearly thirty years before I was born.

But I couldn't resist. "What kind of things? What kind of things don't fit?"

"And, I'd just like to say," you interjected, "that I'm only half Swedish. I'm half British too."

Helen was facing us again. "Do you know that when war was declared in 1939 one of the very first things the British did was to massacre their pets?"

"What!" you cried. "That can't be right."

"I assure you it is." Helen set down the knife she was holding and came to sit with us once more at the table.

I said, "It doesn't sound like the kind of thing that would happen here."

Helen smiled ruefully and made a gesture with her hands, as though to say, "Nonetheless, it did." I sensed that if she had been playing a game with us for the past minute or so, then the game was over now. She seemed sincere again.

"Animals," she said, "have always been the helpless casualties of human history. Just look at the Siege of Paris. That was the Germans too, well, the Prussians. In 1870 the Prussians laid siege to Paris and the city began to starve. Pretty soon restaurants were offering all kinds of treats: soups and puddings made with horse meat, dogs' livers served on skewers, cats, and even rats, cooked up in stews. And that's before we get to what they did with the animals from the zoo."

"The zoo?"

She grinned. "Oh, yes. Camels, antelopes, kangaroos, wolves – all went in the pot. Even, famously, the elephants, were eaten. Castor and Pollux they were called. It's said that they were rather tough and tasteless."

"Good!"

"But," I said, "people were starving. So it's not that surprising. Let's go back to what you were just saying about the war."

"Yes. It really is true. As soon as war was declared, without delay, hundreds of thousands of animals were destroyed by their owners. Hundreds of thousands. They queued to do it, queues half a mile long. Very British. Or they did it themselves. Even before the first shot had been fired, or the first bomb dropped. And remember, the Blitz didn't begin until a year after the War had commenced. The Blitz didn't begin until September 1940. But by then countless animals had been killed. And for what? The government didn't tell them to do it, not directly. There wasn't any shortage of food yet. But still ... this curious massacre of animals, dogs and cats, that were no doubt loved. Cherished! Because, after all, the British are animal lovers. Isn't that correct?"

Her eyes widened with the question and I found myself thinking how this was all so odd, stuck in that small kitchen with her, not knowing who she was, where she was from, and why she was telling us these peculiar things.

You said, "So, they didn't eat their pets or anything like that? It wasn't like in Paris?"

"No no, not at all. The bodies were buried or cremated."

"Then why?"

Helen shrugged. "Who can say? There are various theories: quiet panic, memories of animals starving during the First World War. Perhaps the British imagined that later on they would have to do the same to their children, kill them, put them down, rather than live under German occupation. People do what they must, even if to others, and perhaps even to themselves, it remains impossible to explain." She glanced at the clock and, with a shockingly loud scrape, pushed back her chair. "We should go. Manus will be waiting."

*

In silence, we walked to the church, or, anyway, the building that'd once been a church. I was thinking about Helen. She was intriguing of course, but I found her kind of alarming too. The night before she'd appeared friendly and still pretty young. Thirty or thirty five tops. I wasn't sure, but younger – or younger seeming – than our parents, and much younger than Manus. And then, when we'd arrived for breakfast, she was basically the same. A little bit punky, I'd thought, with her great hair cut, a little bit new wave. A person you could relate to.

The more we talked, though, the more my impression of her changed. It wasn't just her accent coming through. I'd started to get the idea that she was a person from the black-and-white era, from the time of black-and-white photographs and black-and-white films. It was even there in her colouring, dark hair, dark eyes, pale skin. In library books, I'd seen pictures of glamorous women in the twenties and thirties with short, tomboyish hair, women who would go on to live through the Second World War. From the forties, I'd seen pictures of land girls. Helen was like a combination of the two. I remember sitting at the table in the cottage and thinking that Helen was much, much older than she appeared to be, and that she'd actually lived through war in Europe. And yet, stealing glances at her now in the bright December light, she looked younger and fresher than ever.

The door of the church's porch was closed. Helen rapped out a pattern of knocks on the wood with her fist and a few seconds later a lock was turned and it opened slowly.

We stepped inside. A "Brother" in grey peered at us curiously. Helen gestured for us to keep going. I saw you smile up at the man and step forward. I followed, producing a sort of half nod as I passed him. Behind me, the man moved to close the door.

It was like a scene from *Prince of Darkness*. It's what I thought of, straight away: researchers in a church.

Dotted along both aisles were computer stations. Some were occupied, some vacant. I saw mice, colour monitors, and you could hear the hard drives whirring and clicking. We paused a moment, taking it all in. Then a printer burst into life and we both jumped. In that old, sombre building the effect was strange.

Helen led us into the nave and headed towards the chancel. We walked as slowly as we could, short of outright dawdling, both of us scanning our surroundings. There were shelving units crammed with books, there were pinboards, charts and maps. There were machines I didn't understand, panels of switches and dials. A young man, distracted by some papers he was holding, almost collided with us as he headed in the opposite direction. Glancing up to apologise, he looked directly at you, blushed, and hurried away. You grabbed my arm and whispered, "He was one of the ones that stopped me and asked about my black eye."

The smell of coffee was in the air. People – men and women, I saw – were moving around, sitting alone, or gathered in small groups. Some were glancing at us, some were preoccupied with work. I caught sight of Walter, standing erect beneath an archway, following with his eyes as we passed by.

In the chancel, Helen turned and said, "Please wait here while I go and fetch Manus." She headed towards a heavy-looking wooden door in a side wall leaving us standing before a table, draped in a white cloth, beneath the east window.

"Isn't this an altar?" you asked, pointing.

"School project?"

"Sorry?"

"Didn't you do a school project about the layout of a church when you were young?"

You pulled a face. "*Nej.*"

"Oh. Well, anyway, yes. Or rather, no, because they don't hold communion services. That's what an altar is, where the bread and wine is consecrated. But it's where the altar would've been."

"So what do you think this is?" And this time you pointed at the object that stood upright in the middle of the table.

We both looked. It was made of wood and was in two sections with a hinge in the middle. Both panels were painted with foliage and figures. On the left side there were four women. Three were standing and one lay, apparently dead, beneath their feet. The three women who were alive had features that were very similar, though one seemed significantly older than the other two. In their hands they held what I thought then were tools of the textile industry.

On the right panel, the original dead woman had disappeared, only the three sisterly figures remained. But now it was the turn of the two younger women to meet their fate. With daubs of blood on their dresses, they lay murdered on the floor, the victims, presumably, of the one who was older. She was gazing down at their bodies, an inscrutable expression upon her face.

"I see you've found our diptych."

We turned around. Manus was standing there and smiling at us. "All purely symbolic of course."

"What does it mean?"

He gestured, showing us the palms of his hands. "You might say it means that nothing can go on forever. Even myths must have an end."

"Which myths?" you said.

"All of them."

Neither of us responded to that.

"Come on," Manus said. "Follow me through to what was once the vestry. I have Christmas gifts for the both of you."

We did as we were told, trailing him across the tiles and through the side doorway. He ushered us inside, gestured for us to sit, and pushed the door closed, securing it with a big black latch.

Manus had made the old vestry his private study. I'd never been in a room like it. It looked like the lair of a genius, but what kind of genius it was hard to tell. Neither of us could stop looking around.

It was the opposite of his bare little cottage. It might have been quite spacious in there, but he'd filled it with so much stuff that instead it was cramped. The ceiling was high and one of the walls was covered from top to bottom with books – there must have been more than a thousand of them. Lots of the volumes looked very old, with leather bindings and gold lettering on their spines. Books were heaped on the floor, on chairs and a battered wooden chest, and spread across a red patterned rug. In front of us was a small pile of books that, I guessed, were, in Latin. I still remember some of the words from their titles: *avibus*, *herbis*, *inferni*. There were many modern books as well, in several different languages: English, German, Italian, French, and languages I didn't recognise. There were books about religion, mythology, history, the occult, whole sections of works on philosophy, medicine, animals, and plants. There were scores and scores of books about birds. It was an amazing collection, and intimidating too. A great wall, a great stack, of knowledge. It made my own small collection of paperbacks at home seem unbelievably pitiful.

Manus had settled himself into a high-backed chair on the other side of his desk. He was obviously amused by our gawpings, but when we stopped and tried to compose ourselves he made a gesture that said: "By all means, carry on."

There was an open fire that had just been lit, with crackling logs still uncharred in parts. Everywhere we looked there were striking objects. He had an antique globe, an oil painting of a snake – a mountain adder, Manus told us later – and something called an astrolabe. He had an old brass telescope. "Ah, but there's a much bigger, modern one in the belfry," Manus said. Hung on a wooden stand was his black waterproof from the day before and a crisp white lab coat. Beside them was a large robe, made of thick, rich material, green and trimmed with gold. Various pieces of camera equipment lay about the room. And beneath the narrow window, on a small ebony table, there was a neat row of notebooks and a microscope that looked expensive and up to date.

There was another ebony table in Manus's room. On it was a glass case. Inside the case, mounted on a perch, was a stuffed bird. It was partly grey, with black-spotted wings, and a bronze neck and breast.

"That's Jacques, my passenger pigeon," Manus said. "Do you know the story of that particular species of bird?"

We shook our heads.

"No? And yet I believe I once overhead the two of you in the woods discussing the songs of birds, and you, Christa, seemed very knowledgeable indeed."

We stared.

"After all, I am a nemophilist like yourselves."

"A what?"

He smiled. "A haunter of the woods." He reached down and opened a drawer in his desk. "As for Jacques and his kin, from what I understand, you've had enough such stories for one day."

Manus lifted his long arms and carefully placed before us two small black boxes, wrapped with red ribbon. "Your gifts," he said.

"I thought you were going to answer my questions? About your work and what you want me to do."

The pleased and playful expression left Manus's face. I saw him wince, as though he was fighting with feelings of annoyance. Fixing us with stern eyes he said, "It's not something I can just lay out for you, nakedly, without preliminaries, without any initiation whatsoever. There is the question of trust. More importantly, there is the question of understanding." He tugged at his iron-coloured beard. "Already I have taken enormous risks showing you both this much, though I confess the risk was always going to be taken." He frowned and then his features darkened still further. "You do understand the need for secrecy, both of you, don't you? After all, you *are* a secretive pair. You wouldn't be in here if you weren't. Surely it does not need to be said? Nonetheless, I shall say it. I must *insist* on secrecy. Absolute secrecy!" With a great thud he brought down the palm of his hand on the top of the desk.

We both jumped. I think Manus was about to apologise, or reassure us, but you cut him off. "Look, we don't really like anyone. All the adults in our lives are utter idiots. We don't tell them anything. Speaking for myself, I never have. Well, not since my dad died anyway. I don't mind if you threaten to pull my arms out my sockets or make me disappear. I don't mind what you say. But there's really no need. We'll never say a thing."

You turned to look at me. I nodded. "Yep," I said.

Manus fell back in his chair. "Forgive my outburst. In fact, I've been, mostly, steady in my belief that I am right to place my faith in you both, and Christa especially. My instincts are rarely off."

Someone knocked softly at the vestry door. Manus closed his eyes and held them like that for a moment. Then he thundered in the door's direction, "I am not to be disturbed!" It was becoming ever more obvious that Manus had heavy responsibilities and a great deal on his mind.

Turning to us again, he gestured towards the boxes. "These gifts come with a grave warning. Listen to me, both of you. Listen.

"Inside you'll find chocolates. Handmade. A festive treat. At least, that's how they will appear should anyone else discover them. But they are not what they seem.

"You must not gorge yourselves on the contents of these boxes. If you are feeling greedy over Christmas then you must stuff yourselves with sweets other than these. Do you understand?"

We both nodded.

"Say it aloud."

So we both said that we understood, no gorging on the chocolates.

"Good. Do not eat more than one every twenty four hours. Do you hear me? No more than one a day."

"What's so special about them?" you said.

"They contain The Flowers of Bologna, a compound – or, rather, series of compounds – I developed some years ago. I must warn you that the effects will be dramatic and not exactly pleasant, though you should suffer no lasting bodily harm."

"Then why would we eat them?" I wanted to know.

"Are you interested in moving closer to the truth about life or not?"

"I'm not sure."

"Hm!" Manus seemed to find this amusing. "Well, what about the truth about what we are up to here?" And he gestured to his surroundings with his hands.

"Yes!" you said.

"Then I suggest you consider sampling these chocolates. The experience will be infinitely more meaningful than your sensory derangements of yesterday. You will not lose control of yourselves as the result of delusions or hallucinations. In fact, quite the opposite. Which is to say, that you may indeed lose control of yourselves, but it will not be as a result of fantasy. Think of the drugs as a short cut to insight, which is the kind of thing that is sometimes said of mushrooms and LSD, is it not. Though such claims, I think, are dubious."

We looked at one another.

Manus pushed back his chair and stood up. "I can see you are uncertain. It's hardly surprising. The problem is, there's so little time. Time is continually pressing upon us, never letting us take a breath." Again he gestured around the room, drawing our eyes to his books. "Here is a sliver of a long lifetime of learning. And some of what I have learned must be imparted to you in the next few weeks. But, in truth, with so little time, with taskmaster Time cracking his whip, we must skip to the end of the lesson. It is not knowledge per se that you need to obtain to help us with our work. What you must come to grasp, and quickly, is the *weight of knowledge*, the burden of all knowledge worth having. It is the heaviness of knowledge, the pain of experience and understanding, of which you must learn. Think of it as mere acceleration."

We were silent. Manus looked down at us, frowning, obviously dissatisfied, but whether that was with himself or with me and you I couldn't say. At last, he reached forward and with thick fingers and thumbs pulled at the red ribbon on the black cardboard boxes, one after the other. Once the ribbons were removed he lifted the flaps and held the boxes up for us to see. Sure enough, there were chocolates, not quite perfect looking, nestled inside.

"What will they do to us?" you asked. "You need to tell us a bit more. Be more specific."

Manus strode away from his desk and went and stood by the case holding Jacques. He ignored us for a moment, staring down at his bird. Then, with his back still turned, he said:

"I'm not prepared to discuss their effects until you've tried The Flowers for yourselves. But nor am I here to compel you do anything against your wishes. The chocolates are a gift. The promise of this gift is new awareness. You may take the chocolates or leave them here. You may take them and decide not to eat them. All I ask is that you keep them secret, even if you are caught acting strangely. Some things must be left to chance, but the pair of you are skilled at eluding adult authority. I must trust you to cover your tracks. And mine too. If you accept the gifts then we are co-conspirators."

After this last remark Manus fell silent. It was maybe a minute before you stood up, and the sound you made caused Manus to face us again.

You reached for a box of the chocolates and, fumbling a little, attempted to fold down the flaps. "We'll take them," you said. "When will we see you again?"

"I'm not sure. Certainly not for three weeks or so. I've people to visit far from here."

I got to my feet also and picked up my box.

Manus led us towards the door. With his hand on the latch, he paused. "Remember," he said, regarding us severely, "'Whoso keepeth his mouth and his tongue keepeth his soul from trouble.'" He tilted his massive head. "In truth, if you choose to eat the chocolates then your souls *will* be troubled. But please, no talebearing. All that you have seen, all that we have spoken of today: *be discreet and keep it secret.*" With a startlingly loud sound, he undid the latch and swung open the door.

"Someone will see you out." And I saw him gesture over our heads.

Outside the church, holding our boxes of chocolates, we weren't sure where to put ourselves. We didn't want to go into the woods or back to your house. We ended up down by the river again. The chocolates went into your bag.

At one time, I think we would have been elated just to have managed a glimpse inside the church. But, having had the tour, sort of, we were both disappointed. Your questions hadn't been answered, your curiosity hadn't been satisfied. And I was sorry for you, but I was sorry for myself as well. Because I knew now for certain that we were bound to have further involvement with the Brotherhood.

We didn't even bother to go over the many startling details. It was only later that we talked about all the things we'd seen, and began to speculate about what they meant. I remember those minutes standing by the water as being horrible, dead. We couldn't sit down, it was too cold and wet and muddy. We wanted to be totally on our own, but had nowhere to go. We just milled about, churning the sodden bank with our feet.

Manus acted as though he'd entrusted us with a great secret, but boxes of trippy chocolates didn't excite us, especially after the fiasco of the day before. What, really, could drugs reveal about Manus and his plans? Why couldn't he just explain, especially about what he wanted from you? Instead, he'd sent us away, sent us away with homework, and it sounded like it was going to be hard.

It didn't help that now the appointment with Manus was over there was nothing standing between me and my miserable fate. All I could think was, "I'll have to go home soon. I'll have to face my parents." When I mentioned this, you looked despairing and sick.

"What do you think will happen? Oh God, it's all too much! I can't stand to think of you having to go back there."

I watched the water flowing and toed the mud. It was amazing how little brain space I'd given over to all this since Friday afternoon. Just three nights earlier I'd run all the way to your house in the freezing dark with bare arms and nothing on my feet. Bizarre.

"Alex, I'm really worried about it. I'm worried about what your dad might do." Drawing close, you slipped your arm around my waist.

"Yeah, it is a bit scary."

"And your mum's no use."

"No ..." And that's when I thought of it, my plan for dealing with my dad. It just popped in there. I didn't tell you, standing by the river. I'm sorry. I let you worry, so that when you saw me off late that afternoon it was with a blanched, despondent face. I felt I shouldn't rehearse it. I held the idea at the back of my mind. If I'd thought about too much or discussed it with you I might not have had the guts. It was only on the phone, after dinner that evening, that I let you in on my scheme. And by then I knew it'd worked.

When I walked into the house there were no civilities, and no sense that they'd done anything wrong. I supposed I'd hoped I might get away with being subjected to the silent treatment, but no such luck. Within seconds, they pounced. My mum was brandishing the note I'd left, my dad was yelling, t-shirt tucked in, fag smoke surging like something out of *Poltergeist*. Expressions of anger, disgust, and lists of punishments. I listened until they said, inevitably, that you and I were not allowed to see each other anymore, not while I was under their roof. (They actually used that phrase!) Yeah, right. That's when I went for it:

"Okay, but this is what *I'm* going to do. I'm going to go to my room and I'm going to ring my Grandma up." I meant my dad's mum, of course, my farmor. It was my dad I was talking to now. "I'm going to tell her that you're drunk all the time and a gambler as well. Obsessed with the 'gee-gees. All the stuff you hide from her, I'm going to tell her everything. I'm going to tell her about the debts and the stress and the shouting whenever I need something basic. I'll go over to her house – no, no, I'll ask her to come and pick me up – and I'll show her the sorry state of my plastic school shoes. I'll tell her how embarrassing it is and I'll tell her that my teenage girlfriend is buying my clothes for me now, even my socks and underwear. I'll tell her all about your rages and your dodgy, idiot mates. I'll tell her about your Chubby Brown tapes which I have to listen to through the floor when I'm trying to get to sleep on a Tuesday night with Games the next morning. I'll tell her about the piss-ups and the language and the threats and the fear. I'll tell her how you drive to work still over the limit stinking of booze. I'll tell her I've thought of suicide. And I'll tell her that you both hate me and I don't know why!"

I was great! I amazed myself. My sunbed-baked father had gone pale. They tried to come back at me, but they had *nothing*. A quick repeat of my threats and that was enough. I actually started to grin. I might even have laughed at them a bit. They looked at me like I was possessed. And I sort of felt I was. If only I could have turned my head around 360 degrees. That, Christa, would've been sweet.

There was some storming about and some tumult in the kitchen. I was upstairs by then. But we ate together, as we almost always did, weirdly. By the end of the meal I could tell that a bitter truce had been called, at least for the Christmas holidays, which was my dad's main focus now, what with all the drinking he planned to do.

After the meal, I called you up. You couldn't believe it and I basked in your delight and admiration. As I said to you that night, I was only following your philosophy: if someone hurts you, hurt them back. Hard.

Min lärare Christa.

10

My parents had broken up for a fortnight's holiday. They were in a good mood, which was always hideous. The box room was filled with booze. The tree was up and had to be cooed over, as though it'd just been born, not killed.

It wasn't Christmas until the snow globe was placed on top of the telly. It wasn't Christmas until the plastic robins were standing in the soil of the pot plants. It wasn't Christmas until the window sills were dotted with fluffy reindeer and smiling sheep.

And it wouldn't be any kind of Christmas if I *pulled my face*. My father made this plain. He took me aside and with special gravity and painful eye contact explained that he and my mum didn't want Christmas spoilt by me "having a cob on". Would I agree to make an effort? Would I agree to refrain from being a misery? It was a man-to-man moment of sorts. I did agree, bearing in mind, Christa, that this seemed to me yet another sign of returning normality in our household. No fury or threats, no blackmail on either side. Just a regular chiding, albeit before I'd done anything wrong.

Christmas kept us apart, even though we both despised it. We needed to play the role of people's offspring, just for a short while. Your mum took a few days off, my parents mellowed, or, worse, became sentimental. The headlocks happened more often. Dad would grab me and assault my scalp with his scrubbing knuckles, bellowing beerily, crushing my face into his gut.

I hadn't been fair to him. He didn't hate me. This was love.

*

There was always the phone, and we were on it a good deal.

"How is it at yours?"

"Mum's doing her best, which isn't very good, but I think I'm expected to show gratitude. Mats is wearing his family-man mask, prowling about the place in fancy dress, pretending to be a loving son and a civil brother. It's unbelievably creepy. I nearly painted a big black eye on with make-up. Do you think it's the weather?"

It'd grown even colder and, after a few wintry showers, the sky stayed clear. The hilltops were white and the lawns were crispy with frost. It certainly *looked* Christmasy, but of course it wasn't, and never would be again.

"Yeah, I think that's part of it. They're really in the spirit here as well."

"God. I dread to think."

"Yep."

"So ... have you tried one yet?" You meant one of Manus's chocolates, obviously.

"No. Have you?"

"No. I keep chickening out. Boxing Day, I reckon."

Christmas itself wasn't so bad. Late morning my dad achieved that perfect point of drunkenness, the one where he wanted to start plying me with festive drinks, peace offerings I thought they were. And so when my grandparents arrived for lunch we were on good form and nothing went wrong because my dad had to behave himself.

While my parents slept it off, my dad sprawled and snoring on the green leather sofa, I went out for a walk. I found myself heading towards the moors, and so called in to see Jay. His dad gave us a couple of beers and we smoked some weed with Carl behind the lambing shed. After that we all ended up in Jay's room watching the last part of *Back to the Future*.

At home, they were awake and my dad was laughing too loudly at *Only Fools and Horses*. I sat down and flipped through the *Radio Times*: Rolf Harris, Jimmy Savile, Bruce Forsyth and Ronnie Corbett. I drew a big black square around *The Maltese Falcon*, which the BBC were showing on Boxing Day at six, and went upstairs.

I was so bored I almost ate a chocolate then. I could hear Manus's warnings in my head, but I thought: well, what does he expect? Where does he imagine we'll be when we try them? We can't spend our whole lives in the woods. We don't have houses of our own. I thought of Kathy White, the rock chick in our class, who'd told me a story about how she'd dropped acid for the first time over the summer and ended up watching Wimbledon with her mum, the two of them on the sofa, her mum oblivious, involved in the tennis, whilst Kathy was, as she put it, "tripping my tits off".

In the end, though, I waited until the next morning, after breakfast. I knew my parents would be occupied and wouldn't mind that much if I ended up having to leave the house. My plan, if I started to lose it, was to head into the hills or up onto the moors.

Another thought occurred to me as I selected a chocolate to eat on Boxing Day morning, sitting on the floor in my room. If it all went wrong then there was only one person to blame. And that person was Manus. That's what I'd say to you, and you'd be forced to agree.

It was surprising how fast the drug worked, but then that was in keeping with what the drug did. None of this is easy to describe, Christa. I don't think I ever did that good a job of it at the time. But I'll give it a try. It should be easier now that I'm older, and you'll know what I'm talking about in any case.

The chocolate I chose contained the death drug, the one that took you on a death trip in two distinct phases: knowledge first, and then experience. Phase one brought the end of life rushing towards you at top speed. It wasn't anything specific about our dying that was revealed to us when we took the drug, but simply the sheer *certainty* of our own deaths. And it was this overwhelming certainty that gave the experience its power.

I was amazed. I thought I knew about death. My little sister had died. I'd watched my grandfather die slowly of cancer. I thought I was a child prodigy when it came to death. But no, until then I knew nothing about it at all. That gesture, just before a car collides with the fatal wall or tree, and the driver's arm is thrown up in terror, that's what I felt my mind was doing over and over again. I sensed the blackest blackness hurtling towards me: *now* and then *now* and then *now*, and it was this repetition that seemed to produce the steady state of certainty that *I was going to die, I was going to die, I was going to die.* The vague awareness of it made utterly solid.

It must be said that it wasn't as though you felt you were going to die then, at that very moment, at least not in the trip's opening stage. It was more that the span of your life, short or long, suddenly seemed irrelevant. The very idea of a "lifetime" was a trick, a con, something to distract you from the unbroken blackness that would arrive very soon, *very soon*, whether you lived for another day or another century.

But Manus was smart. He knew that no one could take these initial effects of the drug for long. I lay on my bed the whole time I was experiencing them, the certainty of death looping, with barely a glitch, in my brain. I doubt I was actually paralysed, but I was so trapped inside my head it seemed that way.

And yet when the effects started to abate it was still morning. True, my music had stopped, but it was still early, and I could tell that my parents' friends, who were coming round for Boxing Day drinks, hadn't yet arrived. And very quickly, as the worst faded, I began to understand something. I began to grasp that Manus wasn't trying to fill those who took his drug with a horror of death, but instead to make them really believe in it, for themselves, for the very first time. As a result, it was life, and *not* death, that seemed odd now and out of keeping with the order of things. Death was a certainty, life was not. And this was a comforting thought. Because *normality*, non-existence, would soon be restored.

Alone in my room, I started to laugh. I felt relieved and free. The transformation was astonishing. I bounced up off my bed, put a single on, and moved about. But it didn't last. The second phase started to kick in. I caught a glimpse of myself in the mirror and was brought to a standstill by what I saw.

My wardrobe was old, a hand-me-down from my dad's side of the family. It had sliding mirror panels in a section at head height. These were removable. I lifted one out and sat on the edge of my bed and looked at myself. Something was different. Something was wrong.

I sat there for ages, staring. It was strange what I started to think as I gazed at myself. But my body seemed to agree, agree with my strange thought, I mean. My body was growing numb. Something was leaving me, had left me, in fact, and now the next stage could commence, the decay would begin. There was no feeling of panic. How could there be? The dead don't panic and that's what I'd realised about myself as I examined my reflection: *I was already dead.*

While I was coming to the realisation that I'd died, and trying to work out when it'd happened, my parents' friends had arrived. Music and voices, cans cracking open and the pop of corks being pulled: all these sounds were travelling up the open-plan stairs. And then my mum was calling me. Would I like a drink? And there was plenty of food as well. I should come down and show my face.

But I was dead. So what was the point?

I lay on my bed for a period. I wasn't mourning myself. I just couldn't understand why I was still in my room when I was dead. How long had I been here? I looked at the clock, but it must have been wrong because I knew I'd been lying on my bed for a long time now. None of the things around me, my old books, my old records, were mine anymore. They'd have to be given away. I felt a flicker of anger at the thought of someone else getting my music collection. Yet it wasn't something I could control. How long my parents would keep my stuff I didn't know. They hadn't got rid of my body yet, so maybe quite a while.

That thought, the notion that I would be kept in here, rotting, made me anxious. Everything else may have changed, but I still didn't like my parents' attitude. They were mistreating me even after I'd died. Again, the anger I felt about this was only faint. I knew, though, that I needed to get out. This was the first real impulse that I'd had since my death: escape, escape from the place I used to live. It was cruel to keep me laid out in here. This room couldn't be my resting place. After all, it wasn't as though they had the corpse of my sister stashed away somewhere inside the house.

Slowly, I manoeuvred myself up and went over to the window. Beyond the roofs, stark against the white shapes of the hills, I could see the dark spire of St Thomas's church. I kept my eyes fixed on it and didn't move for minutes, standing by the window, seeing the blue sky, but thinking of things that lay below, not above. The sight of the spire connected me to a particular patch of ground, to headstones and graves, to the hard earth and the bodies it contained. I shifted my feet. At last, I understood. I needed now to be with my kind: the dead. I didn't belong anywhere else. I needed to go to the churchyard.

There was an automatic quality to the things I did next. I pulled on trainers and a scarf and coat, actions remembered from being alive. Walking down the stairs, I gave no thought to what my parents would say. There was Tania, one of my parents' less grotesque friends. I'd once quite liked her. Now she was a wraith. They all were.

Perhaps something about my appearance alarmed them. Their chatter and laughter subsided. My mother appeared with a plate of food and a glass of beer. "I was just bringing this up to you," she said.

I didn't respond for a moment. I didn't want to speak. And I wanted to eat and drink even less. Showing me food just seemed vile. Why would you want to feed a corpse? A dead tongue can't taste, a dead stomach can't digest. My organs were defunct. I felt empty inside, but not hungry. I'd never be hungry again.

Barely moving my mouth, I murmured that I was going out for a walk. My mother turned to look at my father who was standing behind her, framed in the kitchen doorway. He shrugged and I backed away from the food and left the house.

The avenue was empty of humans, the road free of traffic. The living were ghosts, bound to their homes, haunting themselves. Magpies and crows were dotted here and there, on lawns, on roofs, croaking, screeching, hurling moss from gutters. Their lives were nothing but seizures, a flurry of spasms between birth and death. As though it were a very long time ago, I remembered how I would sometimes leave the house with a pocket full of peanuts and toss them to the birds as I headed away from home. It was unthinkable now. I didn't belong in the world of struggling creatures anymore. Or so I thought.

I walked on slowly. Time was meaningless. Huddled in a long scarf and a thick coat – more to keep from view than for reasons of warmth – I drifted towards the church.

I kept my eyes on the spire. I knew where I was going, but I felt some confusion nevertheless. Death isn't doubtful. Death is the seal that can't be broken. And yet ... It nagged at me dimly: I was still *fretting*, fretting about death. I was fretting about where the *best* place to be dead was. And I shouldn't be fretting about *anything*, should I? I shouldn't *be* anything at all.

I was on the main road now. The houses here had wooden doors hung with Christmas wreaths. Through big bay windows I glimpsed the movements of dim, mortal shapes. I flinched from their sickly living world. I didn't want to be seen. I didn't want to see breathing things, things with heartbeats. More stupid fretting. My faint thoughts, faint fears, were not yet faint enough. But the blankness would come, of that I was sure. There was still some dawdling to do it seemed. It would be over soon. Maybe once I reached the graveyard.

The place was deserted, as it tended to be six-and-three-quarter days of the week. There were no colours but grey and green. Bare, grey trees bent over thinning grass and grey ground. Grey steps and a grey flagged path led up to the grey church. Crooked grey headstones were growing green with age.

I threaded my way through the graves. A crow flapped up from behind a wind-bitten monument. I turned away and covered my head with my hands, although, spooked, it'd flown in the opposite direction. Again I felt that dull, distant anger and fear. I wanted to be wholly alone with the dead. I wanted the birds gone. I wanted the worms in the earth to stop their writhings. I wanted the soil itself to die, to be incapable of sustaining life.

Surrounded now on all sides by crosses and slabs and upright stones, I sat on the grass. Beneath me were the dead-at-peace, the dead who didn't want anything anymore. I shuffled forwards and lowered myself to the ground.

Inside my veins, the blood had frozen. I had no heartbeat. My ragged breathing was redundant. I was dead, but my body's response to my end was patchy. It was bewildering, not how I'd imagined it at all. But perhaps it wasn't so strange that death should turn out to be surprising ... and even an anticlimax.

Why did I have to go through this? The journey, the seeking after slumber, the need for companions who were deceased. Why was being dead such a task? I was tired, tired of death. It required too much effort. Death was work, an assignment. I pressed myself down, pushing harder, with real force, into the earth. Death wouldn't stop. It just kept going, a flatlining without end. Grim monotony. Dissatisfaction. And always something else to do.

In need of comfort, I hugged the frigid earth. Still lying on my front, I kicked and jiggled about. Inscriptions on the headstones spoke of rest, sleep, peace. Trustworthy tablets making promises of a proper end. But not for me. For me there was no repose. The frustration was immense.

I pushed myself up onto my knees and began to tear at the grass with fingers so stiff they barely worked. Rigor mortis, I supposed. Ripping at the turf and then clawing at the soil, I began to dig down into the grave, without success. More drudgery. Death was dirty. Death was ugly and rough. Anger flared, stronger than any feeling since I'd died. Fury! I hacked at the earth with my dead, filthy hands. I was clawing at the resting place of a man named Beddoes; he didn't appear to have been anyone's beloved husband or son. How long had he lingered a century ago, straining, striving to perfect his death? I would whisper my question to his earless remains.

I craved fulfilment, but the frozen soil wouldn't yield. The desire to be underground with the still and silent dead was overwhelming. I was lifeless, and yet fixated. Something drove me on, to dig where digging couldn't be done, to burrow deeper into death, to obtain an end that was more complete. I wanted so much death in me that I would be entirely free of it. I'd thrown away my life. And now I wanted to get rid of my death. Forever.

It was at this point that I began trying to eat the gravesoil. At first, I simply scooped up the bitter blades of grass and black crumbs and and placed them in my mouth. But after a few handfuls I lowered myself face down onto the ground and began to gnaw the dirt. My teeth scraped at cold, crusty earth. I made little impression so I tried harder, raking at it with my mouth. Nothing happened, but still this didn't deter me. Again and again I rasped at the hard surface – tongue, lips, teeth – until at last I felt a stab of pain. I jerked upwards. Fumbling in my coat pocket, I produced a crushed white tissue and pressed it to my mouth. When I pulled it away there was a shocking amount of blood.

Crawling forwards, I slumped into a sitting position with my back against Beddoes' headstone. I was puzzled. Why had I felt pain in my mouth? And why was I bleeding fresh-looking blood? This wasn't the behaviour of mere remains.

I closed my eyes and squeezed the lids. My senses were unbecoming for a corpse. My unbecoming was being thwarted by my senses – they hadn't fully died.

For a long time I sat there in unsatisfactory darkness. When, at last, I opened my eyes to the obscene light, I found myself staring down at the tattered, gouged surface of Beddoes' grave. Something was taking shape in the murk of my mind. A memory was rising, resurrected. I could hear my mother's voice. She was telling me – my father was out, she'd been drinking gin – that shortly after my sister had died my father had been found down at the cemetery, weeping and grief-stricken. He was in the middle of a nervous breakdown and had been trying to unearth her coffin. He'd had to be led away.

I felt a throb of horror that I should be in any manner like my dad, mauling a person's resting place. And after that I began to wonder again why I was feeling anything at all, especially about my old life, my shady parents. Surely that couldn't be right? It was hardly consistent with being dead. I was fretting again: and the signs of life were starting to smother the signs of death.

I sat there stiffly, trying not to breathe, trying to resist. But the comedown came, and once it was underway it was pretty quick. The numbness that'd masked the cold started to fade. My body began to feel horrible, somehow defrosted and freezing all at once. I was shaking, my hands were raw, rigid claws, and my tongue was pulsing with pain. I turned and lowered my head to spit on the ground. There was blood and saliva and dirt. A foul taste seemed to be growing worse by the second.

I wasn't dead after all. It was bleak to realise it, Christa, bleak and disturbing. And for the first time since the whole hideous episode began I thought of you.

I clutched at the headstone, struggling to make my fingers flex, and hauled myself to my feet. All I wanted was to be clean and warm in bed, skin still glowing from a bath. No chance of that.

An instinct was working within me, telling me I would be in trouble if I didn't sort myself out before going back home. But my brain, like a mummy, had been swathed in bandages and needed to be unwrapped. I wasn't yet able to form a plan.

It was still light, and I supposed that was good, as long as I could make it out of the churchyard unseen. This I managed. Glancing down at myself I saw that my clothes were grubby, but since I was mostly wearing black they'd probably pass. My hands, though, were in a bad state: grazed, grass stained, torn around the fingernails. In the wing mirror of a car, I checked my face. It was streaked with earth and blood.

I weaved my way up the road, limbs resuscitating, but not in a pleasant way. Meanwhile, my mind seemed to stagger even more than my body. It took me some time to remember it was Boxing Day and what that meant. But doing so gave me an idea. *Boxing Day: everything is closed. Except for the Asian grocers at the rear of the village parade.* At least, I thought so. I was sure that was what my dad had said. It had to be open. I needed supplies. Cold, aching, I headed as fast as I could in direction of the shops.

A few minutes later, I reached the place. Part way down the line of shuttered premises, I saw light. I could have sobbed with relief. But then I thought for the first time of money. How could I have forgotten? I patted through the pockets of my coat. *Nothing. Nothing.* I kept looking. And at last I pulled out a rumpled fiver and felt I deserved it, this bit of luck.

Inside, I grabbed water, baby wipes and two Yorkie bars. I was famished! The guy behind the counter, who I'd only seen once or twice before, was looking at me with frowning severity.

"Yeah," I said. "I've just come off my bike. Got it for Christmas."

He handed over my purchases with a single nod and nothing more.

Outside, away from the shop, standing by a litter bin, I got to work. Using the water sparingly and the wet wipes freely, I cleaned myself up as best I could. Hands and face: I splashed and scrubbed, removing blood and dirt, doing what I could with my clothes too. I took my time, examining myself in the wing mirror and windows of another parked car. I rinsed out my mouth and spat and saw the the bleeding had mostly stopped. At the end of my efforts I was certain I looked much better, though my tell-tale hands might give rise to questions, depending on how much they'd had to drink. Thinking of a story, I set off home. They didn't have to believe me necessarily. They often didn't believe the stories I told them. It needed to be just good enough so that they could say they'd asked.

Back at the house there was music on and the Boxing Day gathering of large men in v-neck jumpers and their heavily made-up wives was still going strong. No one seemed especially bothered about where I'd been or alarmed by my appearance. I grabbed a beer and a plate of food and went up to my room.

I had to have a shower. I couldn't stand not to. This *did* cause my parents some annoyance because none of the guests could get in to use the loo and my dad ended up knocking irritably on the door, shouting at me to be quick.

I ignored him and took my time. Finally clean enough and back in my bedroom, I put on *Permanent Sleep* by Lowlife and called your house. Your mum answered. You'd gone out on your bike, been out for hours she said. I was a bit surprised. You'd decided I was right, basically, about the Dutchie being no good for hilly terrain and hadn't been riding it lately. I left a message with Svea for you to call me back and drank my beer and ate sandwiches and pickled onions and crisps.

I'd dozed off when the phone rang. Things were a little quieter downstairs. *Diamond Life* was on the stereo. It was pushing six and dark outside.

"Hi. I hear you've been out on your bike."

"Mm."

"You sound funny. Distant. Are you okay?"

"Sorry ... I'm just trying to get back to normal. Except –"

"Oh God, you've not been in a graveyard have you?"

"What? No."

"But you did eat one of the chocolates?"

"Yes."

"What did it do?"

There was a lengthy silence. Then you said: "I think I'm starting to feel better ... It's not easy to talk. I've been so trapped inside my head."

"What happened? You're not hurt?"

"No, no. Nothing like that. Like you say, I've been out on the bike. I've been trying to escape my thoughts." Then, tutting, you said, "No, that's not it."

I waited.

"Well, maybe that's what I was attempting to do at first. But soon it was that I couldn't stay still even if I wanted to. I really had to keep moving. Fast. It was just easier."

"Okay."

"It actually works on the mind though. It does what it does to the mind, not the body. At least, I think so. And then the body sort of panics in response. I think that's what happened. I mean, it might be different for you."

"I don't follow."

You started to try and explain, to describe what the drug had done to you, picking up speed as you spoke. At first, I wasn't sure what you meant or why it was such a big deal. Not much seemed to have happened. There was nothing so striking in your story as: "Well, I thought I was dead and then I tried to gnaw my way into someone's grave." You said the drug had made your mind too busy, too full of thoughts. When I said that didn't sound so bad and started recounting my experience you interrupted and told me I didn't understand.

"It *was* bad. Because when all these thoughts started to crowd in I began to realise what they were. They were *intruders. Invaders.* I didn't invite them in, but they came in anyway. I mean, they were familiar thoughts. They were the kind of thoughts I have all the time. And that was the problem. Because my mind was racing so much, I started to think – there's that word again – about where all these thoughts were coming from. So many thoughts, so many thoughts I didn't want to have. And that's when I realised I wasn't in control of them and maybe I hardly ever am. They just arrive, unwanted, unwelcome. My dad. Cutting myself. Cutting other people. Imagining my mum dead, and Mats. Especially Mats. Me dead. You. Seeing myself hanging up in an abattoir. I picture that all the time. Your dad would probably like it. Myra Hindley. Why do I think about her? I do, though, far too much. Being old and ill. Or dying suddenly. My body rotting in the ground. Every day I think about things like this. And sex. Having sex with all kinds of awful people. Having awful things done to me. Being murdered. Stabbed. Strangled. That girl Frankie who went to our school. Do you remember? She was doing some babysitting and the woman's boyfriend came round. They had sex and then he found out she was only thirteen and killed her. I got given a copy of a Geography textbook that she'd written her name in at school and now I think about her every single day. Every day. Why? These are not *my* thoughts at all. But then they are, even though I don't choose them. They're just there. They make me think of parasites squirming in my brain. And is that something you want to think about when you think about your own thoughts? No. Which kind of proves my point. Or Manus's point anyway."

"Yeah. That does sound horrible. Which other people do you think about having sex with?"

"Oh, stop it. As if you don't."

"Hm. Anyway, it's quite the gift from Manus."

"Yes. God knows what other treats he's got in store for us."

I was about to provide part of the answer when you started talking again about what the drug had done to your mind and what you thought it all meant. I listened and didn't say much. I pictured your manic pedalling. It was obvious you were still feeling the effects of whatever it was you'd taken. You were repeating yourself.

At last you paused and said, "Sorry. I've been going on for ages. I'm feeling a bit light headed. I think I need to eat something. It's your turn. What happened to you?"

By now, though, I wasn't as keen to share the events of my afternoon. While you'd been flying down lanes with a hyperactive mind, I'd been drifting about in a haze of death. Then I'd put all my effort into getting cleaned up, drunk a beer, and gone to sleep. So far, I'd given it all very little thought. I'd no ideas about meaning. And you were being so overbearing on the phone.

"I went and hung out in the churchyard. St Thomas's."

"Oh, right. Why?"

"I don't know. I just had to go there. I spent some time sitting on a grave, got really cold, and then came home."

"Okay. It doesn't seem like such a big thing. Was that even the drug do you think? Maybe it didn't work."

"No, it worked. I felt it. I felt a strong urge to go there. I needed to be with the dead."

"Hm. Well, I guess they can't all be so powerful as mine today. I suppose it's a sort of *memento mori* type experience. Very goth of Manus. I don't know, though. It seems a bit underwhelming. Maybe it'll act differently on me."

"Haven't you had enough of bad trips?"

"That's not how I'd describe today. Not even close. Anyway, no – I want to try again."

"But not tomorrow? I was supposed to be coming down to yours tomorrow."

"We can wait another day can't we? We see each other all the time. Let's both have a chocolate tomorrow morning and then I'll call you tomorrow night."

This wasn't what I wanted, but I didn't argue much. I could tell you were determined and I was feeling angry and stung. I looked around at my boxy room and thought about your house in its rich, quiet setting, the woods behind deepening the evening darkness. Manus was winning. We agreed to meet in two days and I hung up the phone.

11

The next morning I was still thinking about questions you'd raised the night before. Your thoughts, you'd said, were parasites, invaders, not yours at all. What did it mean, you wondered, if even a person's regular thoughts were not their own? What was left of you or me then? Who were we, we who were infested?

I held a chocolate in my fingers and stared at it. I didn't have the answers, but I was beginning to get some kind of idea of what to expect from these compounds of Manus's. One of them had given your mind a jolt sufficient to make you a stranger to yourself. Another had caused me to believe I was dead, which was something you didn't know yet. They were not, these drugs, going to inspire us to do the jig of life. That wasn't where this would end.

I popped the chocolate in my mouth and let it melt. Sliding off my bed and onto the floor, I flipped through my records and picked out *Only Theatre of Pain*, one of my favourite presents from you.

"Cavity – First Communion" started up and I looked around my room. I looked at the hand-me-down wardrobe and the bed in which my grandad had died. I looked at the fake pine chest of drawers with the digital clock on it and the flimsy lamp. And then I looked at the stuff I'd saved up for when I was doing my paper round or mowing lawns and washing cars – my records and books. Only these seemed to be really mine. None of my clothes were right, apart from the things you'd bought me in recent months. My stereo was old and temperamental, obtained from a mysterious someone second-hand. The carpet and curtains were thin and cheap, the duvet cover faded. Their patterns had been chosen for a ten-year-old boy.

It was still my room though, even if it was filled with unlovable objects. I'd spent so many hours in here, hiding, dreaming, always listening to music. I'd danced in here, and blubbed. I'd read James Herbert and *Nineteen Eighty-Four*. I'd found plays on the radio, watched the rain and the snow come down, eaten toast and crisps, had sneaky drinks, and rehearsed the speech where I told my dad I was giving up meat. I'd talked to myself a lot, talked to phantoms, and done everything I could to ignore the emanations rising up the stairs: the drunken rows, the drunken laughter, the bad tunes, and the smoke.

I'd been satisfied to stay in here for many hours at a time. I was never one for hanging about in parks or out on the streets like so many kids. I never enjoyed going to school. If it'd been up to me, I'd have remained in my room and neglected my education. And it was my refuge from my parents. I much preferred to be alone in here than downstairs with them. In here, with albums and library books, I could eliminate the world. An apple or a bag of peanuts, my headphones on and *The Metamorphosis* to read: there was a time when this was all I needed.

But now everything had changed. Now, always, something was nagging away at me, a craving, a craving for us to connect intensely, and for us to stay intensely connected. I wanted you to be inside me, an eternal mood, and I wanted for me to be inside you in just the same way, like we'd swapped our hearts. And so I couldn't be content any longer to simply stay on my own in my room. It would never be enough.

I turned over the record and began to move about restlessly, albeit in a space that was cramped. I would, I knew, never be free from you, and this longing for connection. I'd never be free of the hollow feeling I had when we were apart. Even when we were together, and you were distracted, or things between us were bad, then the hollow feeling was there. And when we were happy – which wasn't that often – despite the joy I felt, I was always worried about what came next: tension, disagreement, one of those drab afternoons where we sat through the silence in your black room, or walked sullenly through the woods.

And always: what were you thinking? Always, I'd want to know. And did you care what I thought? Did you want to hear? The endless revealing and concealing, not just with words, but with eyes and smiles, gestures and skin. The world getting lighter or the darkness coming in. And always: what was the mood?

But then: if I could release myself from all of this, release myself from my fixation with you, is that what I'd go for? If I could be content to sit in my room again, stay in here alone, is that what I'd choose?

I'd never dreamt of asking these last two questions before, and as soon as I did so my agitation began to increase. Manus's drug was in me, working. My movements, my pacing, became more rapid. A feeling of horror was building. We shouldn't be apart. Not today. Not any day. Again and again, I heard you say it, the soft blow hard enough to hurt this morning: *We see each other all the time. We see each other all the time.* Your words on the phone the last night.

Do we, though? Do we see each other all the time? It doesn't seem that way to me. I was expecting to see you today and yet here I am freaking out on my own in my room. Freaking out because we're separated, separated by Manus's schemes. Freaking out, too, because this drug isn't only making me miss you, making me crave your company. It's causing me to question everything, making me feel trapped, claustrophobic.

Anyway, I think it was the drug. It was having a double, exaggerating effect. I was agitated about us being separated, but I was agitated about my attachment to you as well. I'd never been so aware of it, never been so aware that I didn't really have a choice. I wanted to be with you; but did I *want* to want it? Did I want to want it so very much? Wouldn't I rather be free? Wouldn't I rather have more control at least? Because all I could feel was need, a terrible, gnawing need. It never stopped, not even when we were together, like a permanent hunger that wouldn't go away no matter how much I ate. Dominating my life.

And so I found myself asking: *If I could be content to sit in my room again, remain in here alone, is that what I'd choose?*

But as you know, Christa, it became impossible for me to stay where I was, trying to formulate some ruminative response. The answer came in the form of a rush of actions. The next thing I knew, I was scrambling for shoes, trainers, boots, anything. I was grabbing my coat, I was grabbing my keys, and I was bounding down the stairs.

The day before I'd been dead and had drifted down the road at a walking corpse's pace. Now I was running in a fever of longing. Even as I tore past gardens and houses, I could hardly believe what I was doing. I'd no idea where you were and I knew you didn't want to see me. The thought of turning up unwanted filled me with disgust. And yet I couldn't stop myself, the desire to be with you was so great. Manus was mocking me. That's what I said to myself as I ran, showing me that I was filled with needs I couldn't control, just as he'd shown you that your thoughts were not your own. I was like a character in an arcade game: programmed behaviour, stuck in a maze, my pathways set.

The estate was behind me now and I was pelting up towards the school. Someone drove past and pipped their horn and I glimpsed a long, jeering face through the window on the passenger side. An idiot from our year no doubt. I knew there were those who laughed at us. Round the back way and towards the start of Inkle Lane, and once I hit that I somehow managed to speed up. My running was crazed. Even in the winter cold, my breath freezing, I was drenched in sweat.

Now the hawthorn hedgerows were streaking by. Above the desolate fields a flock of blackbirds whirled. A car approached and I had to give way, halting a moment by a gate and almost screaming with impatience. As I waited, I saw fieldfares hopping on the grass. Then off I went again, down, down the bending, narrow lane. The syllables of your name were in the beat of my boots on the road. I reached the end, turned and tore past the abandoned clearfelling site and pressed on towards the humpback bridge and the village. I was running without form, breathing in great gulps, and my speed had dropped, but I kept on going. I had to see you, I had to see you because ... It was all emotion. I wouldn't have been able to tell you why.

I pounded by the cottages, glimpsing a pair of grey figures lurking on Clewkin. Then I was past the old village and surrounded by the good homes. I saw a bald man in his window wearing yellow knitwear. There were kids out on bikes, weaving around in the sharp winter sunshine. The river was glinting white and gold. Everything looked perfect, but I wanted it gone. It was all just in my way.

Finally, the end of your driveway came into view. I reached it and there was your house, the last in the village. Somehow, it looked forbidding that day, big and blank, like a tall man with square shoulders and an empty face. I didn't stop though. I sprinted up to the front door and, resisting the urge to hammer on it, knocked normally and tried to make myself presentable and recover my breath.

No one answered. I looked around and noticed that Svea's car wasn't there. I walked to the side, still breathing hard, and peered in through the large bay window. The long living room was dim, no lights, no TV, no sign of anyone at home. I hadn't forgotten about Mats. I didn't want to encounter him, especially if you weren't in. But I couldn't stop now, I had to track you down. So I knocked on the door again, and this time I really went for it.

When still no one appeared, I began to wonder if you were in your room listening to loud music. At least, that's what I hoped. So I scrambled over the fence and dropped down into your back garden. There were no lights on at the rear of the house either. It was a bright winter's day, but your house was screened at the front by conifers and the woods rose up behind it. Natural light was limited; the squares of dark grey beyond the panes of glass were not encouraging. Even now, though, I didn't give up. And this time, unlike the night I ran to your house in my pyjamas, I did lob a couple of stones up at your window, desperate for you to throw it open and cry out my name. But of course, as you know Christa, you didn't, and I was left standing there, horribly disappointed.

It was then that Manus's strange word popped into my head. *Nemophilist*: haunter of the woods. In an instant I'd convinced myself that that's where I'd find you. It made perfect sense – you were always in there, besotted with the place, as your mum had said. I ran to the end of your garden and climbed the fence. Seconds later, I was threading my way among the trees.

I was so intent on finding you that I didn't really think too much about what state you would be in if I succeeded. I knew you would probably have eaten a chocolate as well, but I was convinced somehow that we could harmonise ourselves. The drug I'd taken left me feeling that the drug you'd taken couldn't possibly matter. The mood between us, that was all that counted, and it was going to be better than ever before.

I moved through the woods at a brisk walking pace. Above me, in the branches, small birds flitted about, or they darted up from the ground. I imagined us spending the rest of the day together, moving with silent understanding through the trees, settling to wait for different species to show themselves. I tried to guess what it was you'd most like to see: siskins, maybe, and lesser redpolls.

I followed all the familiar trails, seeing no one. I resisted the urge to call out your name. I had the feeling that once I'd started I wouldn't be able to stop. I paused often, turning, watching, in all directions, hoping for a glimpse of you. And I listened carefully for any human sound.

When, at last, I heard something, I was elated, certain you were approaching. It was a twig, cracking underfoot in the stillness of the winter afternoon. Birds called and stirred. I started to rush forward, but immediately I caught something else: the sound of voices. I halted a moment and then, ahead, on higher ground, I saw two figures moving in my direction. Without further hesitation, I darted from the track and down a leaf-strewn slope. I crossed a patch of frozen mud and positioned myself behind the trunk of an oak, thick and old. Doing my best to stay hidden, I peeked out and waited to see who would pass. If it's Christa, I remember thinking, I want to know who she's walking with.

Their voices – one voice, mainly – grew louder. Slowly, they came into view, and I was left in such a state of confusion. It was Helen, and she was doing most of the talking, gesturing at the girl beside her who was taller and strikingly straight-backed. I couldn't help making a sound, a too-loud, startled release of breath, and for a moment I thought they'd heard me. They slowed a little and Helen glanced around and down in the direction of the oak. But she carried on speaking and they walked on, in no hurry at all.

The girl with Helen looked too much like you. That is, she looked too much like you for it to be a coincidence. She had your height, your posture, your long limbs. Her hair was dark blonde, with a full, heavy fringe. I glimpsed, above the collar of her coat, a pale, serious face, perhaps a little older than yours. I glimpsed her beauty and the drug inside me sharpened the pangs. I watched her evoke your presence and it made your absence worse. Did she have your long-lashed, hazy green eyes? I couldn't tell, not from my hiding place. But I'd seen enough. If she wasn't quite your twin, then she was without doubt in the sisterly mould.

Through my shock, I'd been trying to follow what Helen was saying. Her accent was strong that day, stronger than the morning she'd given us breakfast. She was talking about birds. They'll "billow up", she was saying. It seemed an odd word to choose, "billow". But she said it more than once: "The birds will billow up and fill the sky." And something about Manus – I caught his name. And "here, right here in the woods". The low, murmuring comments of the girl I couldn't catch, though I watched her nod as Helen spoke.

When they'd passed out of view, I turned around and with my back to the tree crouched down, trying to think. I didn't get very far. I was so preoccupied with finding you that my mind wouldn't work. Just staying still was a struggle. At some point though, maybe then, maybe when I'd set off again, I decided not to tell you about your lookalike in the woods. I knew for sure you'd be upset.

I searched for at least another hour. I couldn't find you and by the end of that hour I was throughly demoralised. I began to wander, rather than following the trails and heading for specific spots. I was watchful still, but weary, lacking all conviction. I felt sick. I don't mean only in my stomach, though there was that as well. I felt soul-sick. I wanted to give up, to give up searching for you, to give up caring where you were, but my body wouldn't let me. A part of me said: *it's hopeless, there's no point, she doesn't even want to be found*. Yet my legs kept going. I was trapped inside of it, sick of looking, sick at the prospect of going home, sick of myself. And, Christa, I was sick of you too. Sick of the hold you had over me. Sick of your spectre.

On my knees, in a clearing, I ended up vomiting. Afterwards I felt calmer, less full of poisonous thoughts. I found a stream and washed out my mouth with the icy water. I stood there a while, listening to the water run, drinking a little and splashing my face. The drug, I think, had left my system. I still wanted to see you, but there was no reason any longer for me to believe it was going happen, or that it was wise. I was glad I hadn't found you. *We see each other all the time*, you'd said. *We see each other all the time*. And so, with one last mouthful from the stream, I set off for home.

I was just leaving the old part of the village, having passed Manus's cottages, when I saw you in the distance, coming towards the humpback bridge.

You were approaching strangely. You moved, I remember, with these long, prowling steps and your posture was odd. Your back, normally so straight, was bent forwards, your shoulders hunched. You were pressing yourself against the wall separating the road from the steep drop down to the river and you were turning your head, as though you were fearful of being watched. For the briefest moment I was dismayed to see you, but curiosity swiftly took over, curiosity about the state you were in. I stopped and raised my arm in greeting and you paused too, staring rigidly, as though on high alert. A moment passed and I saw you relax a little and set off again, slinking and skulking all at once.

We met in the middle of the bridge. You were looking extremely ragged. Your hair was tangled and wild, your clothes were damp and dirty, your face bore dark streaks. And then there was the smell: the odour of cold skin and sweat and ... something else.

"What's been going on?" I said.

You twitched your head, and regarded me mutely for what seemed far too long. Then, as though the words were foreign to your mouth, you said: "I'm starving."

"Oh, okay. Lets –"

"I'm starving."

I took your hand and led you back to the house. I've no idea what we would've done if Svea or Mats had been there. At the door, I extracted your key from your jeans pocket and let us in. You darted into the kitchen and I heard water running. By the time I'd got my coat and footwear off and followed you through, the fridge door was open and you were standing by the breakfast bar pulling at something with your blackened fingers, cramming pieces into your mouth. Drawing closer, I couldn't believe what I was seeing. It was a raw rib-eye steak.

"Christa, stop!" I cried.

You huddled over, arching your shoulders, holding the flesh to your middle. Tearing off another chunk, pink and marbled with fat, you wolfed it down.

"Christa!" I reached to try and take the meat from your hands.

Springing away, you lifted the steak and took a big bite, showing your teeth. And then another. And in that fashion, standing in the corner of the kitchen, you devoured the whole thing.

In truth, the horror I felt was fleeting and my protests faded quickly. I remembered that the day before I'd tried to gnaw my way into someone's grave.

After you'd eaten the meat, I asked you if you wanted something else. You nodded and so, hurriedly, I made us both a sandwich and ushered you upstairs, bringing the food with me. Liv the cat followed us. We ate in your room, both of us gobbling, and then I said: "You need to take a shower now, before someone comes home."

"Smell like a human again," you said.

"What? You already smell like a human – just not a very clean one."

I began to help you undress. You peeled off your jeans and I spotted the problem. "Christa, did you ... go to the toilet outside today?"

A pause and then: "Yes. I went. In a field."

"Well, you've got some on yourself, and on here. I need to wash these things."

I guided you to the bathroom and then dashed downstairs to the machine. Button and dials. I stared at them for too long, peered at labels, realised I was being ridiculous, and finally chose a setting. The machine was full of damp clothes: sock and shirts, Mats' stuff. I piled them in a basket and looked through the bottles of detergent and softener. It was a simple task – put some clothes on to wash – but it seemed to be taking forever. And the thought of Svea coming home and catching me standing there with your honking 501s was not a good one.

At last, the machine was filling. I dashed back upstairs and waited on the beanbag in your room, listening to Coil. You were gone for another forty minutes. When you came in, towelling your hair, I could see immediately you were much more your normal self. You came and sat on the floor between my legs and as it grew dark outside we exchanged stories.

We were both embarrassed. You were still regaining your composure, so I went first. I had to admit how the morning's drug had made me feel, how I was overwhelmed with the need to see you and how I went blazing along roads and stalking through the woods, all in the hope of tracking you down. You kept squeezing my hand as I told the story, making sounds to let me know you were sympathetic. The person who'd said the night before that we saw each other enough was nowhere to be found now. I felt there was this new, grown-up tenderness between us, and I wished we could take ourselves off, away from our homes and our school and our parents. Away from Manus and his influence. And live in total seclusion.

I told you, too, much more about my experiences of the previous day, about how I'd come to believe I was dead, and how I'd gone to the churchyard and tried to dig my way through the frozen ground into a grave.

"But what was it like when you thought you were dead?" you asked. "How did it feel?"

"It felt kind of like today, only without the feeling."

"What?"

"I know. I know it sounds odd. So, today I really wanted something to happen. I wanted to see you. And I had this burning need for it, you know? This red-hot longing. I felt like I was running through fire to find you."

"Mm."

"But yesterday, I just wanted nothing to happen ever again. I didn't want to see anyone or feel anything and so I just got on, grimly, with what I believed I needed to do. Clawing at the cold, grey earth. And now, thinking about it, they seem like the same thing."

"Wait, so wanting to be with me is like being dead?"

"No! You seem to forget – I wasn't *actually* dead."

So we bickered about this for a while until, at last, you were ready to share with me what you'd been up to. I'll do my best to tell it how you told it, but it'll be hard for me to get it right, even if I do seem to hear your voice in my head:

"I woke up really early, just after five, and none of my usual tricks were helping me get back to sleep, thinking about floating in a dingy in the freezing North Sea and such. Besides, I wasn't tired. I was alert. I got out of bed and put on some Kate Bush, quietly, and wondered what to do.

"I realised I had a craving to eat another of the chocolates. Did you have that? An actual craving to eat one?"

"What, this morning? No. I just did it because I thought that's what we were doing."

"Well, for whatever reason, I *really* wanted another one. So into my mouth it went. I hardly gave it a thought. I was determined not to think too much about anything after the day before. It was foolish, really. It was so early in the morning and I could have ended up in any old state, rampaging around the house, waking everybody up, completely off my face. Anyway, that didn't happen. I ate the thing and calmly got dressed while I waited for it to work.

"It kicked in pretty quickly. The first thing was I started to feel trapped. So I grabbed my stuff, snuck downstairs, and went out of the front door. I stood on the drive for a short while, just breathing the fresh, cold air. Everything was still and quiet, no one was about, but something was bothering me. I wasn't sure what it was. All I knew was that I felt uneasy, wary. I had this growing sense that I shouldn't linger, that I was in the wrong place.

"So I did what I always do and set off towards the woods. But two things happened. The first was that not long after I reached the woods I saw those lights again, and I didn't like that at all. They were moving towards me, like someone was coming out of the trees, back towards the houses. I found it very startling. The second thing was that my senses were getting keener and keener. And I picked up a scent, or scents I suppose, scents that made me afraid."

"A scent? What scent?"

"The scent of human beings."

"Oh. Really? The scent of human beings?"

"Yes. So I changed my course, but I detected it again, right away – people scent. It was everywhere, although it was just one set of smells among many. I seemed to be able to smell all kinds of things: animals, vegetation, the earth itself. I remember I could smell exhaust fumes off in the distance. The air was full of musky smells, sharp smells, land smells. But only one smell was making me worry. *Human.* I knew exactly what it was and it was woven through the whole of the woods. We think of it as our place, but really there's hikers, dog walkers passing through. And Manus's followers. So I swerved off the path and began to run, zig-zagging through the trees, leaving the woods behind, crossing the road, into fields, heading for higher ground. I realise now that I was taking it for granted that I could see my way in the morning dark. I could smell everything. See well. Hear well. I felt strong and fast. But I was still frightened.

"I kept going. The heavy scent was growing less intense. It's like the blanket of human smell was being unwoven until there were only individual threads. In a sheep-farmer's lane, I smelled the B.O. of a man who'd gone by recently. I knew he was a man even though I didn't see or hear him. Only his smell remained. I don't know what I would've done if we'd met.

"I did some serious trespassing. Jill would've been proud. Jumping over fences and dry-stone walls, climbing into the hills. I kept going and going. Getting away from humans and all their stink. Until, at last, I stopped and crouched and looked down into the valley.

"Everywhere there were lights. Street lights. A car's headlights. A few house lights coming on. Human lights. Not the lights of the sky. Danger. But not near.

"I just crouched there and watched. Thought faded away. There were no words in my head at all. I can't tell you how right that felt, especially after the day before. No thoughts wriggling in my brain. I was just heartbeat and muscle and breath. I watched and listened and smelled. I kept lifting my head, my nose, to catch the currents of the air. I was completely alone. I seemed to settle into myself in a whole new way.

"I'm not sure how long I stayed, but it still wasn't dawn when I moved. I was hungry and thirsty. At first, I went higher, the instinct to get away from humans was strongest, but I needed food too. I paused and crouched again. There would be nothing for me up here. The hill was bare. It seemed lifeless to me. Down there it was dangerous. But I had to eat. I longed to keep climbing, to flee from people. Instead, I started to descend, back to the world of human lights, human noise, human smell. My heart thumped, but my belly was growling.

"I'd no idea what I was doing. I kept seeing images of mice and rabbits in my head. I think I was dreaming I was a hunter, a druggy waking dream. I did my best to stay out of sight. I dreaded contact with people. I had no curiosity about them at all. The sun came up and I was down from the hills and following the courses of hedgerows in the fields, creeping along, doubled over. I don't really know why. These drugs seem to make us obsessed. At one point I had to go to the toilet, but I got confused and tangled up and made a mess of myself. Of course, I found no food. By now, I was filled with a bitter hunger. And I was horribly tired. I felt like howling! There was nothing to eat, and nowhere free from fear. Humans were everywhere. They could never be trusted. It was like one had hurt me in the past, wounded me with a weapon. I ended up in a copse of trees in a field not too far from our school. I've often looked over at those trees and wondered if anyone goes there. Instinct must have drawn me to them. Well, there wasn't as much of a human smell so I stayed. I found an old foxhole and curled up and went to sleep. I didn't seem to feel the cold very much at all. When I woke up I had the idea to come back to village and scavenge for some food. I was scared, but so hungry. That's when you met me."

In your wild state, you'd gorged yourself on raw meat. This freaked us both out and we agreed to have a rest from the drugs that Manus had given us. When we did try them again it was after New Year, and then throughout the period that led up to Easter, when so much was happening. Neither of us ate a whole chocolate again; it was too much to take. We reduced the dose. Even so, by the end of it all we were well schooled in Manus's philosophy. The empathy and compassion so strong it left us heart-wrung and suffocating. For you it was the animals being factory farmed, abused and slaughtered all over the country. You imagined yourself being herded and stunned, the flow of your blood onto the floor. For me, it was my sister's death. I couldn't stop thinking, over and over again, about the fear and panic she must have felt during those final moments when she couldn't take a breath. Did she know? Did she understand what was happening to her? I could feel an actual tightness in my chest. Something was gripping and squeezing. I ached for my sister and was angry for days afterwards. But when I took the drug of grief it was my grandfather I thought about and I ended up catching two buses to visit his grave. I could hear his voice in my head, the voice he used when he taught me to read. In the cemetery, I cried so hard that a elderly woman stopped and came over and tried to offer me comfort, though I just pushed her away. And with you, it was your dad. You had an identical compulsion and ended up in the same graveyard, alone. It was a dismal day and in the low light you glimpsed a tall figure striding amongst the stones. It was your dad, you knew it, though you never saw his face. You didn't give chase. You found yourself balled up on the wet ground, weeping. You felt terrified. And for the only time, after that particular episode, you said to me, "What are we doing to ourselves?"

But we kept on going. One drug just gave us pain! For me it was my tooth, for you it was your head. Horrible aching that lasted for hours, a pain that couldn't be pushed away, even on a smaller dose. Nothing else mattered, not music, not food, not even you, Christa. All I cared about was that the pain would stop.

Then there was the drug that, when you took it, made you feel you loved your family and that they loved you. You said you wandered around the rooms of your house, just looking at things, fondly, gratefully, enjoying the peace and the space. You walked in the garden, played with Liv. You felt at home. When Svea came out of the office, she found to her surprise that you'd been baking and that you were preparing dinner for the two of you. Sat at the breakfast bar, you even started a letter to

Mats. You could hardly believe it afterwards. "But I was happy," you said. "Not ecstatic or anything, but I did feel warmly towards them both and wanted to be with mum. I'm quite sad it was only the drug."

Fortunately, my experience with that drug was different. Getting cosy with my parents would have been a trip too far and I would have hated Manus for it. Once again, I felt the lure of the churchyard. I'd never dared to tell you, but when I was small I did believe in God. Now I went and sat on the steps of St. Thomas's and thought that, after all, maybe you and I were part of God's plan. There must be some basis to religion, I reasoned, especially since my father and I had seen a ghost long before I'd ever taken one of Manus's drugs. The more I thought about it the more certain I became that God loved us, loved me and loved you, Christa. I saw that for God we were a kind of new Adam and Eve, eating apple after apple, only for this final "apple", the chocolate I'd eaten that morning, to reveal His plan: He was going to let us back into paradise. We would be together forever and our happiness would transform the world. I'd never felt so glad about anything. I just sat there and smiled and smiled. When my belief in the idea faded, I tried so hard not to let it go, but soon I could hardly make sense of it, and I was left to walk home disgusted and bitter, and well aware that I'd better not tell you that I'd temporarily gone back to God.

The only time we split a chocolate and ate it together we had strange fits of giggles, and yet everything seemed disgusting and wrong. We ran through the house laughing and saying: "This. And this. And this. This pillow. This shelf. And this chair. This lamp is definitely evil. This picture is evil. This fire. These shoes. The scissors are really evil. The chopping board." You held up a figurine. "Evil," I said. You held up a book. I nodded. "Evil, without a doubt."

Outside, in the woods, you said, "Everything will die. All the trees are dying. Everything deserves to die. Everything sucks the life out of everything else. Plants, insects, animals, birds. The earth itself. Every living thing is a monster." You made monster claws with your hands.

I grinned. "So you're a monster then," I said.

"Yes, I am. And so are you."

12

I remember, Christa, that before Manus came back from his travels we took our own walk in the woods with Helen. We both had the feeling she'd been instructed to keep watch over us, over you in particular, and you'd been invited to her cottage several times. When the walk was proposed, I was tempted to reveal my secret. In the end, I stuck with my original decision and said nothing to you of that other woodland walk I'd seen Helen taking, the one with girl who resembled you so much.

Once again, before very long, Helen brought the conversation around to the Second World War. And once again her story touched on the subject of music. This time Helen told us about *Brundibár*, the children's opera by Hans Krása. *Brundibár*, Helen said, was about a poor brother and sister who must raise the money to buy some milk for their mother who is ill. They go to the marketplace and try busking, but their efforts are thwarted by Brundibár, a malevolent organ grinder with a moustache. Brundibár chases the brother and sister away. Three animals arrive to help: a cat, a dog, and a sparrow. The siblings and the animals enlist help in the form of a group of children from the town. The children and the animals sing to earn the money for the milk and together they defeat the wicked organ grinder who tries to steal their takings.

It was raining, a grey, dank day, even danker in the woods. Helen drew to a halt beneath a lime tree and with wet faces we turned to look in her direction. Then she told us about Theresienstadt ghetto, where *Brundibár* was performed by a cast of captive Jewish children more than fifty times. In 1944, Helen said, the children performed the opera for a committee of the Red Cross whom the Nazis wanted to fool into thinking that conditions at Theresienstadt were humane. The children were also filmed performing *Brundibár* for a propaganda film. Helen said she'd watched this film countless times, staring at the sombre faces of the dark-eyed children who were singing in unison on the stage. "They were murdered," said Helen, "immediately afterwards. I always notice in the film how the curtain comes down on them with a terrible swiftness. Straight away they were forced onto cattle trucks and deported to Auschwitz. The composer, the musicians, almost all of the children – gassed as soon as they arrived."

We looked at one another. No one spoke. Together, we walked on in silence.

I didn't get to have my secret for long. When Manus came back he introduced you to your sisters, both of them, not just the girl I'd seen walking in the woods with Helen. For a brief spell, you were angry and intensely jealous. You said you'd been misled and that you felt betrayed. You shouted at Manus that you didn't want any sisters, not even of the "symbolic" kind. One shitty brother was quite enough, thank you very much. Manus expected all this and knew exactly what to do. He spent time alone with you. He told you that you were the most important one, more important than ever now your sisters had arrived. Only at the end, Manus said, would you understand just *how* important you were. Everything depended on you. It was a clichéd line to take, but you liked it, and as we found out, just weeks later, Manus wasn't lying, wasn't even exaggerating. Not at all. Meanwhile, I was off at the side, if only for a few days, jealous of your jealousy, wondering if there was anything *I* could ever do to make you behave in such a demanding and possessive way. You never did notice, Christa, how I was feeling then.

The commotion caused by the appearance of your sisters died down soon enough. It helped that Manus was now much more ready to talk, to lay things out, and even give us things to do. This readiness, he said, was because the three of you, the three sisters, were together at last. He made this point more than once.

Manus listened with great interest to our ongoing experiences with his compounds, The Flowers of Bologna. He praised our courage and our managing to keep the whole business a secret. He was willing to answer at least some of our questions. We spent many hours in his study. Often your sisters were in there with us. Manus turned it all around, and before too long it looked like the three of you were enjoying yourselves.

But at home the situation for me had deteriorated terribly.

We were back at school. One day, skipping double games, I darted home, got changed, and then ran for three miles and caught the direct bus to Manchester. There were a couple of albums I really needed to buy, as in suddenly obsessed. It was strange how the lie you'd told the previous year came kind of true that winter's afternoon, though it was me, not you, who was attacked in the bus station.

Then again, nothing about that mugging was normal. I remember how at the time the details fascinated you, and Manus too.

I'd bought my records and was waiting for the bus home in the sallow light of a long, almost empty shelter. It was always bleak at Chorlton Street and especially so in the freezing January weather. The partly open concourse had been designed, it seemed, to entrap and enrage the slicing wind. All you could do in such a place was huddle and hope your bus wouldn't be too late arriving.

So I was drawn within myself and not making eye contact with anyone else. Why we had to catch our bus in an intercity coach station I'll never understand. It made the valley where we lived seem even more remote. At that time of day, at that time of year, there were very few travellers about. Most of those who were roaming about the place were neither passengers nor staff.

He must have come into the shelter from one of the side entrances and approached me while my back was turned. The first I knew of him was when I felt someone jab me sharply in the spine. Alarmed, I span around.

He was around my height, perhaps slightly shorter. He wore a dark top with a hood and the hood was up. His sleeve was pulled down over the fingers of his right hand and from it a stubby knife blade protruded level with my stomach. He had no face, none at all. There was pink-grey flesh over bone, but a total absence of features, not even the barest contours. I might have said the head inside the hood was as blank and smooth as an egg. But there was something, just about where his upper lip should have been. A blister, yellow and crusted. A cold sore, though he had no mouth.

He made a gesture with the fingers of his other hand. It meant: "Give it to me." For a second, I didn't move and he jerked the knife. I fished in my jeans and pulled out some change and a five-pound note. I held out my hand and he grabbed the money and it disappeared into a pocket at the front of his top. Then he twitched the blade again and made the same greedy, impatient gesture as before. I lifted the bag of records and he shook his faceless head once. That wasn't what he wanted. With immense reluctance, I pulled my wallet from the inside pocket of my coat. This was the only time I tried to speak. Very quietly, holding it up in my fingers, I began to say I wanted to take out my bus ticket before passing it to him. That's when he hit me. A fist flashed and I smacked into the shelter wall and slid to the floor. He stooped, grabbed my wallet, and ran.

No one came to help. As I pulled myself to my feet, I saw a couple of people looking in my direction, but they remained at the opposite end of the shelter.

I was shocked and groggy. I'd grazed my hand badly as I'd fallen, and my jaw was numb (soon to be throbbing) where my attacker's knuckles had connected. Leaning against a barrier, I closed my eyes and, feeling the spread of an inner cold, started to shiver.

I was more distressed to have been mugged than to have met a faceless man. I'd had some strange experiences in recent weeks. I'd taken a lot of substances. And lately I'd seen some startling *demonstrations* in Manus's study, some dramatic manifestations, locked in there with you and your sisters. Oddness was in abundance. What I *was* struggling to cope with, though, was the theft of my bus ticket. Still shaking, I searched through all of my pockets already knowing they were empty. All my money was gone. I was stuck in Manchester with no means of travelling home. It was this miserable fact that filled me with dread.

And I was right to feel it, dread, doom. I was going to have to phone my parents. The consequences would be grim. Dad's wrath. His leathery rage. I considered ringing the police, but I didn't think I should. Manus hated the police. My dad hated the police. I wasn't keen either. And I knew I would have to lie to them. I could hardly describe my assailant, the "mugger with no mug", as Manus would call him later.

With a pulsing jaw, I left the concourse and trudged over to a phone box. Inevitably, it stank of human piss. I had one of those moments where I thought: "Yes, Manus is right about everything." Then I lifted the greasy receiver and dialled 100. I was going to have to reverse the charges.

My mum accepted the call, but the tone of her voice when she came on the line was sour and cross, devoid of concern.

As I say, Christa: dread, doom.

I explained where I was and what had happened, leaving out the weird bits. My dad came on the phone and I explained it again. His every response was curt and cold, but, yes, they would turn off the tea that they'd just started cooking and come and pick me up. They didn't really have a choice, did they?

It took over an hour for them to arrive. As I waited, in pain, propped up back inside the shelter, I remembered something I'd overhead Manus say when speaking to a man in grey. He said that he'd started "tinkering with things in preparation". And he'd added: "It doesn't happen, in its entirety, on one day alone. Already, I've begun making certain changes ... Those around the world who are observant might begin to suspect that something is going on."

What to make of these grand statements of his? I was stuck between two provinces. One where a reverse charge phone call was a calamitous disruption. And one where the plan was to thrust all of humanity into a new world of turmoil and grief. For this is what Manus had revealed to us in his study. I'd not been certain he meant it. Part of me of had continued to think that all of us, even Manus, were pretending, running around in the hills and woods of the valley, playing a kind of elaborate D&D. But now I'd had an encounter miles away in Manchester with a faceless man and his far-from-fantastical fist. This was sobering. Suddenly, it was the notion that our adventures were just village games that seemed make-believe.

When, at last, I saw my dad enter the concourse, it struck me that here was a man who had altogether *too much* face. Because he was bald, his features had to fend for themselves, and they did so ferociously. His nose had bulk, like a shrunken boxing glove, and was growing dimpled. The ridge of his brow was heavy over colourless eyes, and his jaw was thick. The brownness of his head seemed to have less to do with the garden in summer, or top-ups on the sunbed, and more to do with what goes on in a tannery. In the midst of all this, his thin lips were white, and especially so then.

I was marched to the car under orders delivered in the form of a scalding look. I don't remember the first part of the drive that well. I huddled in the corner of the back seat while my mum let rip. Fortunately, they never figured out that I skived off school. Mum was just fixated on the utter stupidity of my coming to Manchester on a weekday. She didn't seem too concerned about the mugging or my injuries, except that they were inconvenient and shameful. It was more that the evening was ruined. And then there were the petrol costs. My dad kept quiet as we threaded through the city-centre traffic and joined the motorway. This wasn't his terrain. For several miles he just drove. He hated Manchester. He hated cities. He found them intimidating. He wasn't ready yet to make his feelings plain.

But my mum kept going, his unwitting warm-up act. She just wouldn't stop. Her ability to repeat herself was amazing. In time, the traffic started to thin and the silhouettes of hills began to rise up on either side of us. The motorway changed to an A road. We were approaching home.

He'd been in the fast lane almost the whole time, travelling as speedily as traffic would allow. Now, on his home patch, with far fewer cars about, my dad really put his foot down. At first, my mum carried on berating me, but soon she shut up. Even she began to realise my dad was driving recklessly.

We were on a two-lane dual carriageway. I stopped looking at the speedometer when he hit 105. Still pressing the accelerator, he began to blast his horn and cut from one lane to another, hurtling past and around the other vehicles with limitless aggression. By now my mum's arms were braced against the dashboard. For the first time in the back, I slipped on my seatbelt. "CUNT!" he screamed at a driver he thought was in his way. "CUNT!" he screamed at every idiot who dared to be out on the road. "CUNT!" he screamed at the clock ticking down the minutes of his evening. "CUNT!" he screamed at a world that had given him such a disappointing son. And still he picked up speed. And gave someone the finger, though there was no chance they would see it. All in the winter dark.

At home, intact, somehow not dead, the rampage continued. I was hiding in my room. I didn't need to be visible to arouse or suffer his demented fury and hate. Doors were smashed shut, repeatedly – SMASH! SMASH! SMASH! The cheaply-made house shook. Curses and threats flew up the open-plan stairs. Stuff was hurled about in the kitchen. On and on it went, his inexhaustible anger. At one point, when I thought I couldn't take it any more, I launched myself off the bed with every intention of running downstairs and sinking a knife into my throat right there in front of them. Spray them both with my sullying blood. The thought that stopped me was that it would only serve to make my dad more like himself.

Eventually, with much slamming about, he charged out of the house, swearing at the cat as he went, and roared away in the car.

The moment he'd gone I went down and confronted my mother:

"What *is* all this? What is he *doing*?"

"I don't know."

"Why did he drive like that? He could have killed us all!"

"I don't know," she said again.

"Why is he like this? Why do you let him treat us this way?"

She shook her head.

"Are we even safe here?"

"I am," she said. "I don't know about you."

Back upstairs, I called you up and told you some of what'd happened, and what my mum had just said.

"Oh, fuck. Just grab some stuff and come down here."

"What about Svea?"

"*Svea*," you said, pronouncing her name as though she was someone you'd just heard of for the first time. "Last night, she told me that she *is* seeing someone else, just like I've suspected all along."

"Oh, really? Why didn't you tell me today?"

"I hardly saw you today. I didn't have chance. Anyway, he's called Brian, if you can believe it. Apparently, he's loaded. So predictable."

"*Brian?*"

"Yes."

"I can't see Svea with anyone called Brian."

"You can't, and I don't want to. See him, I mean. See them together. God, no."

"But what does it mean? Should I stay away or come?"

"You should definitely come. Morsa feels sorry for you about your dad. And she's being nice to me, in a somewhat creepy way. I've been totally blank over this Brian situation, and I can tell she's worried. Start getting your stuff together and I'll call you back after I've checked. But I'm sure it'll be all right."

That night, sleeping in the guest room at your house, I dreamt that my parents were lying outside on the landing. Under the closed door they whispered, over and over again: "We've clothed you. We've fed you. We've put a roof over your head." It seemed to go on for hours and in the dream I was convinced that I was awake, trapped in bed, which was my grandfather's death bed, transported to your house, unable to make them stop or go away.

A day or two later, in the vestry, we told Manus all about what'd happened, including my dream. He wanted to know more about my relationship with my parents. He listened and absorbed all of my outbursts. At one point he said grimly, quoting: "'Or what man is there of you, whom if his son ask bread, will he give him a stone? Or if he ask a fish, will he give him a serpent?' Well now we know what man, don't we." And he shook his head.

Later, I remember he looked at me intently and said: "Now with all this going on, I wonder if you are still able to give Christa the support she needs?"

"Oh, yes," I said. "More than ever. She's all the matters."

He studied me and tugged his beard: "You're helping her with the diet? And the recitations?"

"Yes. I'm on the diet too when I'm down here. And I sit through all the recitations when I'm around."

He nodded. "And no foolish notions of running away together or anything like that?"

"No. That would just be stupid. Where would we go? Our money would soon run out. We're staying until it's over. Then we'll see. Don't worry. We won't let you down."

He nodded. "And the other matter we discussed?"

I don't think I blushed. "We're doing exactly as you asked."

"Good," he said, and looked at peace.

"Yes, good," you added, and squeezed my hand.

But Manus's tranquility didn't last long. We were just readying ourselves to leave when the door to the vestry burst open. It was Walter, tall, gaunt, and out of breath.

"Forgive me," he gasped. "I can hardly believe it. A Gilder! Fleeing now towards the woods."

"It can't be!" Manus was on his feet and across the room with near-unnatural speed. "We dealt with them! All of them. Years ago!"

"I saw him myself."

"Was he alone?"

"I do not know. I saw no other, but –"

Manus charged from the vestry and the three of us followed him.

In the nave, everyone had gathered. They were silent with worried faces.

Manus spoke to them with urgency: "Somehow, a Gilder, still active, has found us. Walter is certain and that is all the verification we need. The Gilder has a head start and has fled towards the woods. But he will not, he *must* not, escape!"

"A few are after him already," said Walter, who was standing behind us.

"Those who are able, come with me now," said Manus. "Remember, there may be others."

A crowd of us poured out of the church and into the darkness of the evening. It was only later that I realised you'd been held back. Walter and one or two others had prevented you from leaving. No one paid any attention to me.

Through the village we ran and soon began to stretch out. Manus was at the front of the group and I was amazed how fast he could go. The others swiftly fell behind and even I began to struggle to keep pace with him. I'll never forget the sight of Manus tearing through the winter gloom. There was a frenzy in his running, a violence, like he was hurling aside obstacles I couldn't see. As the trees grew closer he began to disappear from view. But before he vanished, I saw him throw back his huge head and into the darkness he cast a long, rhythmic cry, high-pitched and urgent. I've no idea what he said, or even what language it was in, if any. All I know is it rose up into the sky with incredible power and must have been heard deep in the heart of the wood.

And then Manus was gone. I kept sprinting too. I reached your house, glimpsing Svea through an upstairs window. I skirted around the conifers and the high garden fence and pushed on, my feet hitting muddy ground. It'd all been oddly exciting; but moments later I'd come to a halt. Away from the village, there was too little light to run. Now I found myself alone, surrounded by looming tree trunks. My eyes were adjusting somewhat, but, still, I had no idea what I was doing. Should I be going for speed or stealth? What was a Gilder anyway? Did I want to encounter one, and what would I do if I did? I turned about, trying to locate Manus, or one of the others. Trying to locate you. For long seconds, nothing. Too late, it occurred to me that perhaps I should have stayed behind at the church.

Several things happened at once. From behind me, I heard other people arriving. Ahead, lights began to glow amidst the trees. And then there rose up into the night a burst of barks and hootings. I jumped and I must have have exclaimed in fear. A hand touched my shoulder.

"Alex –"

I whirled on the spot.

"There's no need to be frightened. It's only the foxes and owls. They are on our side." It was Helen, with a young man beside her.

Again, there came a series of cries: short, piercing shrieks and, as if in response, though it hardly seemed possible, a series of hoo-hooing hollers.

"Listen to them calling out," Helen said, obviously thrilled. "This Gilder will not get away."

A number of figures approached. They bore tied bundles of sticks, rather like ice-cream cornets in shape, with shining orbs mounted at the top. I had no idea how this could be. But a more pressing question occurred to me.

"What's a Gilder?" I asked, turning to Helen.

She smiled in the eerie orb light. "It is a nickname. They are really called something else. We call them 'Gilders' because they place a thin layer of gold over everything. Philosophically speaking. Not literally. But it is easily scraped away."

"And then they belong to the Guild," said Helen's companion.

"Yes, that's 'Guild' with a 'u' though." Helen gestured to be given one of the strange torches. "You don't need to know this, Alex. It's not for you to worry about. Nor Christa. In any case, we'll soon have everything under control."

I must have looked hurt. Helen put a hand on my arm: "But do come, please. You'll be safe with us."

We advanced into the woods, the group fanning out as we walked. I remained with Helen. For a time things would be quiet, and then the screeches of the foxes and the hootings of the owls would begin again, together and separately. It was impossible to tell how many there were and whether they were close by or far away. The directions from which the sounds reached us seemed always to change, and so did the volume of their calls. I had the sense that the creatures were moving rapidly through their terrain: running, flying, searching.

Above us, grey, ghostly branches swayed in the cold breeze. I stumbled, taking too little notice of the ground, entranced by glimpses of shadowy figures stealing between the tree trunks, carrying their mysterious lights aloft. Helen turned to check on me and gave me a sly smile as I indicated I was able to carry on.

And then I saw an owl. It landed in a tree just ahead of us. The owl, a tawny, arrived in silence, and perched stockily. For a moment, it seemed to be at rest. A few breathless seconds later, it rose up on its feet, its talons scraping the bark, its body angling forward, and flew away.

"It will move from tree to tree until it finds its prey," said Helen in a whisper.

On we went, never hurrying, not hidden, yet somehow in pursuit of this Gilder with the help of hidden creatures and a feeling, a mood, of stealth.

At last we heard a sound that was neither fox nor owl – it was a tortured human cry. And then another, and another still. All together, we started running. Moments later I made out the dark forms of three or four foxes streaking through the trees. They overtook us, heading in the direction of the human screams. But when we arrived at the scene ourselves the foxes weren't there. They must have seen they were no longer needed and peeled away.

A cluster of lights held up high led us to the base of an ancient oak. There, slumped on the ground, was a man in dark clothes with a mass of blond hair. He was groaning and pressing his hands to his right eye socket. As the lights swayed, I saw that blood was flowing through his fingers. Standing over him, with others, was the enormous figure of Manus. As our group arrived, he turned to Helen and said simply, gesturing down at the stricken man, "Owl."

Seeing me, Manus frowned. Helen didn't need to be asked. She took my arm and tried to steer me from the scene. I resisted a little until she grew more firm: "Come on, Alex! We must go back and leave them to it. In any case, we need to find Christa."

Returning through the woods, I was full of questions:

"How was that possible? Owls and foxes hunting jointly? Hunting with humans, and hunting a human too? Was Manus somehow in command?"

Helen, leading the way, carrying an orb light, said: "He wasn't in command. And the effect was temporary. He has simply reminded the animals in these woods of their strength and has showed them the secret and the power of being in league together. When we needed their help today ... well, the rest followed." She stopped and turned, her face floating in the darkness as she dropped her arm a moment. "This was something we toyed with for our bigger plan. Years ago now. We imagined teaching the animals to fight a bitter war against their ancient masters. But it was swiftly rejected as too violent and narrow and impractical."

She resumed walking, leading us back in the direction of the village.

I thought about what she'd said. The thought of a badger clawing angrily at my father's face appealed to me, despite its impracticalities

"What will happen to the Gilder?"

"Him? Nothing. Well, no further harm will come to him if that's what you mean. He'll be patched up as best we can, though it looked to me like he'd lost an eye. And he'll be held until everything is complete, which, as you know, won't be long now. Then we'll let him go."

"Will others come?"

"That is what we don't know. I'm sure Manus will want to find out."

When we reached the church I found you cavorting with your sisters. Your bond was growing all the time, or so I thought. The three of you were passing a cat's cradle one to another and whispering, laughing and dancing about. "I haven't done one of these in years!" you cried. I could hardly recognise you then. The news of the Gilder's capture had already reached those of you who'd stayed behind and for some there was a giddy mood. It took you a while to notice I'd returned.

Later, back at your house, with Svea now out for the night, you decided for the first time in ages that you wanted to go into your dad's den. You fetched the key and we switched on lamps, put a Tangerine Dream LP on the turntable, and finished off the last of the Glengoyne whisky.

"She'll get rid of all this soon, now Brian's on the scene," you said, sweeping your arm around the room.

"You think so?"

"Yeah."

"Do you mind?"

You sipped your drink and thought for a moment. Then you shook your head.

"How come?"

"I've got to let it go, haven't I? We've got to let everything go now, so ..."

"Do you feel sad?"

"Sometimes. But then I feel excited too."

"You think they're doing the right thing? That we are?"

You shrugged, and a moment later you said, "We can't know can we? I can't really imagine it. All I know is it feels right. I just think about some of the things Manus has asked us to think about – some of them I used to think about anyway – and it feels right. That's why Manus likes us. He's says we understand as well as anyone he's ever met. Do you feel sad?"

"Well, we'll still be together, otherwise I'd be rebelling. So only really when I think about music. About how soon all that'll come to an end."

"Yes, I've thought about that too. But then I think that there's no reason why music would go on being so good forever anyway. I mean, films aren't. Look at the films my dad loved." You gestured around the room again. "Bergman, Hitchcock, or whatever. There's nothing that good now."

You went downstairs to get some red wine, and when you returned you said, "And besides we've seen what life is. We'd already guessed bits anyway and now Manus has shown us. Everything is evil, especially humans, and our minds are full of lies."

I started laughing, it was so off-hand. I couldn't stop and it only got worse when you joined in.

13

For a short time we fell into a pattern. During the school week, I would sleep at my parent's house. At the weekends, I stayed down at yours. This arrangement kept appearances up and meant my parents got their house vacuumed and dusted, which was one of the things they cared about the most. It all came to an end one night in February when my dad, even drunker than usual, slurred out the following phrase right to my face: "– that slag Christa." I've no idea how his vile sentence began, I just know that it ended with those unforgivable words.

"What did you say?" I yelled and shoved him hard in the chest, though without much effect. That's when he grabbed the scotch bottle and swung it at my head. I jerked myself away, but he caught me with the bottom end. I can still recall the crack of the impact. The glass didn't break, but I ended up on the kitchen lino, dazed and shocked. My dad was moving in for more. For the first time ever, my mother intervened. All she did was cry out his name. It was enough to make him hesitate. I pulled myself up, pushed past him, and walked slowly upstairs, no doubt nursing my head. My dad bellowed after me. "Don't you dare phone your grandma!" and I heard him go behind the TV and tear the extension from the wall.

This time there was no frantic exit. I packed a bag of clothes and another of school books, taking my time, fighting through the horrible throbbing in my temple area and the flurry of confusion in my mind, gathering up everything I thought I would need. And then I simply walked out the front door, leaving the two of them sitting at the kitchen table smoking smuggled cigarettes. They didn't call me back.

I walked slowly to your house. I knew you would save me. Svea's car wasn't there so I came up to the front door with both my bags and we sat at the bottom of your large wooden staircase and I told you what had happened. You were pale with rage, contorted by it – your mouth, your hands. After I'd finished telling you everything, not just what'd happened, but also how desperate I felt, we sat quietly for a time. Then, slowly, you pulled yourself up from the stairs, made me a cup of sweet tea, and asked me to wait in the kitchen. You said you wouldn't be long. This needed to be sorted, you said, once and for all. I was too exhausted to ask what it was you planned to do.

About half an hour later you were back. You'd been to see Manus. You'd insisted that he help. Some rearranging had been agreed upon and I would get a cottage in the village to myself. Svea need know nothing and we could carry on as before, only now with extra time together in the week. You would slip out and visit me in my own place. We were elated.

And so began what were the happiest few weeks of my life. It's true we weren't entirely free. There was still school to go to (but at least we could walk there and back together) and Manus's instructions to you had to be followed – the diet and other restrictions, the recitations that needed to be done every day. But for hours and hours we could do almost anything we liked. On occasion we helped out with the preparations, and you needed to be with your sisters from time to time. Mostly, though, we just mooned around being content. It was all so simple. In your room or – more and more – at my cottage, we'd cook and eat and listen to music and talk and laugh. We went for walks in the woods and watched the birds. We played with Liv. We gossiped and speculated, but in the main we avoided serious topics. Everything was decided now and I needed nothing at all from my parents. Helen or one of the others brought supplies to the cottage and anyway you always had masses of money. My father was a fallen ogre. What could he matter when placed alongside Manus and his crowd? For the first time since we got together we were almost always carefree, light hearted. You said you'd started dreaming the same dream night after night, that you were sleepwalking through the village, walking from your house to the cottages. You were tired in the mornings and complained of heavy limbs and a blurry brain. But you soon livened up and then the mood was as close as it could be to bliss.

For Easter Sunday was approaching, and we weren't at all sure about how things would be after. Manus refused to entertain a single question about what lay beyond that late-March day. We knew nothing of his plans and the plans of those around him, or whether the cottage would still be mine in April. And so this tinged the brightness of that time with just a touch of darkness. But we were both excited (although nervous too) about the ceremony to come and the new world Manus said it would make.

Everyone had to remain alert in case more Gilders stole into the village in the build-up to Easter. None did. Things had never been more peaceful. The standard of our school work hadn't ever slipped that badly, but now, in both our cases, it improved. The weather grew warmer and more settled. On certain days the grey skies cleared. Snowdrops bloomed and then, in gardens throughout the new part of the village, daffodils appeared. Just before we broke up for the holidays, we saw the first swallow of the year. A day later, the fortnight off arrived.

We spent a week moving between the vestry, the woods, and my cottage. Manus, Helen, Walter, your sisters: we visited each of them and they visited us. I kept in the background, but I was always allowed to watch, even when Manus directed a final rehearsal with the three of you amidst the trees. I saw things then few others had so far been permitted to see. I think Manus knew it made you happy and cooperative. At night, we had time to ourselves and often we went out walking alone. The darkness was unusually full of the cries of foxes and owls.

At last it was Easter. On Good Friday we all assembled in the church. Much of the equipment had now been removed, or at least packed away. Where pews would once have been there were rows of wooden chairs. We sat with your sisters near the front. Someone handed out chocolates. We waited. After a while, no one spoke. The world beyond the old stone walls – the village, the woods, the whole valley – seemed to grow impossible, doubtful and remote. But there was no feeling of company inside the church. Everyone had grown withdrawn and separate. I became obsessed with looking at the details of things, the mouldings of stone archways, the timberwork of the ceiling. When a heavy door banged it was a shock. It was Manus. The time had come for his big address.

He arrived like a conjurer with a large object hidden beneath a square of black cloth. He placed this hidden thing on a table that also displayed the diptych – the hinged painting of the two groups of women, both alive and dead. Suspended above this table, or rather just behind it, was something white and rolled up. Now Manus reached up and with a tug released it. A simple white sheet unwound to hang plainly behind the table. There was no design of any kind. I turned in my seat, trying to locate a projector behind us, but there wasn't one so far as I could see.

Manus surveyed us all. He wore a shirt of clean grey linen with the sleeves rolled up to reveal powerful, hefty forearms. His beard was a solid iron mass, his brow was dark and his eyes darker still. The bulk of him with his huge sculptural head was shocking all over again.

He began to speak and as he did so, as the sentences unfurled, I thought I heard hints of accents from across the world. More than ever, it seemed futile to try and guess where Manus was really from. Maybe the effect was nothing more than an hallucination, an altering of the ear. Certainly the tape I have of Manus speaking doesn't capture my memory of his delivery, though the words are recorded for me to transcribe here. But there, in the moment, his utterances were so startlingly at odds with his colossal presence in the room. The more he spoke, the more the reality of Manus Ainger, a particular man from a particular place, melted away. His ever-changing voice called out to us from many countries and many eras all at once.

He began by whisking away the black cloth. Beneath it was a kind of simple bird cage, made of wood and wire mesh and furnished with a stand of six or seven bare branches. Some in the room exclaimed with surprise – they are audible on the tape. Perched on a branch was a pigeon, a single slender bird. It looked to me exactly like Jacques, the mounted specimen Manus had kept beside him in a glass case in the vestry. But if it was Jacques then something amazing was happening. Because the bird before us today was moving. Jacques the pigeon appeared to be alive.

"Observe," said Manus softly. "The world's loneliest creature." We did as we were instructed. Several of us got to our feet and walked forward for a closer look. More soon joined in. Others, perhaps those who had assisted

Manus with this astonishing feat, remained in their chairs. There was much murmuring, though neither you nor I said anything. In fact, when I glanced at you, I saw that you seemed dazed. Your expression was strange, wide-eyed, but unseeing, like you were somewhere else. I touched your arm but you didn't respond.

Jacques was restless. He dropped from his perch and paced the floor of his cage, bobbing his head. He stirred his wings and turned about in every direction. Manus had supplied him with acorns and other nuts to eat and water to drink. But for now he ignored the food. We pressed around the cage for several minutes. Eventually, Manus gestured that we should return to our seats. I remember that you'd already done so. Jacques fluttered up to his highest perch, relieved, perhaps, that we humans were no longer crowding him.

In motion – *alive* – I could see him so much more clearly than I ever could when he stood there stuffed in Manus's study. He was narrow with a rosy, red-bronze breast and feathers that changed from grey to brown to bluish-grey down the length of his body. There were whitish feathers too, on his lower parts, and black spots on his wings and tail. His legs and feet were pinky-red and his irises were redder still. He was lovely to look at. And yet as we all stared at him, a poor, startled, lonely bird, he made a sound that I remember was far from beautiful. It was a single raw shriek. Perhaps he was scared. Perhaps he was trying to warn other pigeons, or attract their attention, draw them to him. But none would answer and none would arrive. The passenger pigeon was extinct. It had been extinct for seventy-five years.

"No one can be sure how many of these birds were here on Earth when their numbers were at their height," said Manus. "Perhaps it was five billion, perhaps ten. What we do know is that they were once the most numerous bird in the world. No small achievement given that their terrain was confined to the eastern part of the North American continent.

"But what a terrain that must have been. A land of vast, bountiful forests, filled with beech and oak and chestnut, all producing the mast on which these birds loved to feast. For the passenger pigeon was a forest bird, migrating across miles and miles of open sky, only to come down and feed and roost and nest in colossal colonies amidst the innumerable trees of America. Millions and millions of birds flying through the forest looking for a temporary home.

"Of course, the native tribes caught them and ate them, for millennia, but did little damage to their numbers. They took their share sustainably. And then the Europeans arrived.

"What they saw, those early interlopers of the sixteenth and seventeenth centuries, what they saw of the passenger pigeon in flight, must have left them awe struck. Flocks of birds miles and miles in length and greater than a mile wide. Hundreds of millions of birds, perhaps even one or two billion, flocking together. Nothing in Europe could compare."

"I've seen it!" you cried out. Almost everyone in the room jumped at the shock of your voice. There were mutterings of astonishment that you'd interrupted Manus, but he just turned his gaze in your direction and smiled.

"I've seen the forests and I've seen the flocks!"

"Nonsense!" calls out someone on the tape.

"Not at all," Manus says. "Please, Christa. Please go on."

"I can't explain it. I've been having dreams. Dreams that I go walking at night through the village."

"Yes."

"That's all I could remember until just now, when you brought out Jacques. It's like it was blocked. But it's starting to come back."

"Good. That is as it should be. Can you tell us more?"

"Every dream, I think, starts the same. It's midnight and and I've walked from my house to yours, Manus. To your cottage, I mean."

"And then?"

"You greet me at the front door and guide me through to the back. It seems to take a while, which is weird because your cottage is so small. I step outside again, but I'm not here anymore."

"Where are you?"

"I'm walking alone through a forest. It's filled with so many birds. They're everywhere. I mean, *everywhere*. I've never seen anything like it. I don't think anyone has. The branches are laden with them. The trees are crammed with nests. The pigeons are fluttering, cooing. The forest is full of their noise. It's like the whole world belongs to them. It's amazing."

On the tape, I can hear several people gasp. I know very well why. Across the white linen sheet a moving image had spread, clear, but with muted colours. We could see: the roughest of tracks; a glimpse of boots; a look upwards. There were trees all around, heavy with nests and birds. Nests side by side in the branches, hundreds in each tree. Young pigeons and adults flapped about everywhere. A look down: many were feeding on the forest floor. Great mounds of droppings. So many birds. Thousands taken in with every glance of yours.

"Is this your dream?" asks Manus sternly.

"Yes. I –"

"And this?" Manus interrupts.

The image changed. The colours brightened a little and then still more. Green foliage, a blue sky, and light rippling in running water. There was a wide river, with a small island of trees and grasses. Close to the river bank began the forest's edge. It seemed you were crouching or sitting by the water. We couldn't see you, of course, only what you were seeing: a fresh and tranquil place. Peaceful. I glanced at your face. It was peaceful too. Your eyes were closed. On the white sheet you were still in the same spot. Suddenly the image dimmed and you looked upwards sharply. Silently, in a great unbroken front, the pigeons swept in. It was hard to believe their numbers. They engulfed the sky utterly. Even in those bizarre circumstances, it was wondrous to behold. In the dream, you leapt to your feet and threw your arms into the air. Above you, the countless, countless birds streamed across the sky. Everyone in the church sat and stared. For several minutes the image barely altered. The pigeons just kept coming and coming, until, at last, the colours faded completely and the sheet returned to white.

"Was that your dream too?" Manus asks, gently this time.

"Yes."

"What we have just seen is something no one alive today has witnessed. The pigeons would storm across the sky, in the fashion of Christa's dream, from dawn until dusk. A native writer, looking back at his youth, spoke of birds flying in 'unbroken lines from the horizon, one line succeeding another, from morning until night'. And of birds sweeping in 'one unbroken column for hours across the sky, like some great river, ever varying in hue'. This, too, is what the first European arrivals must have witnessed. The blocking out of the sun, the darkening of the sky, the heavens filled with an endless torrent of speeding birds."

Manus pauses. He sniffs (audible on the tape) and glanced, I remember, at Jacques, who was perched and jerking his head.

"Let us leap forward a little. Throughout much of the nineteenth century the birds were still, it seemed, massively abundant, with nesting sites hundreds of square miles in size containing hundred of millions of birds. And yet. And yet! On September 1st 1914, around lunchtime, the last passenger pigeon on the planet died. Her name was Martha. She'd been bred in captivity and it was in a state of captivity that she lived out the thirty or so years of her life. By 1910 she was the very last of her kind, an endling attraction at the Cincinnati Zoo, the only one left of countless billions. The torrents in the heavens, the Mississippi in the sky, had been reduced to a solitary droplet. And then even that droplet was gone, like an evaporated tear.

"How? How did it happen? How could this have ever come to pass, and so rapidly too? The answer is complicated. And the answer is simple: *humans.*

"We tore down their forests, depriving them of shelter and food. We shot them in their countless millions. We captured them in nets. We smashed them from the sky with sticks. We baited them. We orphaned their young and left them to starve. We blasted them for sport. We industrialised their flesh. It's known as *progress.* Barrels full of dead birds racing across the youthful nation, taken to market on the newly-built railroads. And then, when they were gone, we erected monuments to their passing and put Martha in a museum."

Manus looked at the floor. For a moment I thought he was going to spit. When he looked up again he said to you: "And have you any other dreams to share with us, Christa? Dreams not so ... Edenic?"

I turned my head. You were white and rigid and your eyes were closed. You didn't look like yourself anymore. Your face was that of someone much, much older. I started to get to my feet but Manus gestured emphatically for me to sit back down.

"Through the village to your front door. You guide me through to the back."

On the sheet a scene appeared. It was a factory. A textile mill.

"The noise," you say on the tape, "the noise is terrible."

You walked past machines. You walked quickly. It was hard to see. A dark, enclosed place. We glimpsed yarn, bobbins, wheels and bands. Cotton waste on the floor: wetness and smudged, bare feet. Lines of frames for spinning. There were people in rough, ill-fitting clothes: adults and children. A view up close of a teenage boy with a pale, pinched face. He mouthed words at you but you don't report what he says. Perhaps you couldn't hear him.

"It's hot and dusty. It's hard to breathe."

You were still walking, even faster than before. You entered a dim, narrow corridor. As you passed, a swift glance out of a small lattice window revealed trees and a river and a wooden water wheel. You walked into a new room. Plainly dressed workers were everywhere: caps, aprons, shawls, dirty shirts. There were many children. Exhausted, pallid faces, shadows beneath their eyes. The movements of a boy caught your attention. He was on the floor, crawling. He disappeared beneath one of the great machines. Still you walked, and only stopped when you saw it: another child, a small girl, who'd been working wool, snatched up right in front of you, caught and hoisted up by a pulley belt. For the briefest of moments she was held there for you to see, struggling in vain. Thin limbs and a loose, filthy blouse. And then she was carried away, all in a tangle, into the machinery. The machine didn't stop its motions, remorselessly it drew her in, tighter and tighter into the works, slicing and smashing her body, blood splashing its parts.

In the silence of the church, you screamed.

The sheet faded to white.

"Here," Manus calls out. I reached for you, but Helen had appeared behind me and restrained my arm. "Here in this very village, all across this valley, throughout the whole county, and beyond: children beaten with straps and sticks, their fingers bruised, broken, and severed by the machines. Children half-starved and freezing, or else sick in the stifling air, forced to work for a pittance sixteen hours a day. Children humiliated and driven past the point of endurance. Hideous punishments: hair hacked off, bodies shackled in irons, weights attached to scrawny necks, drenchings, floggings, beatings that drove them to the threshold of madness. Their childhoods stolen, their adult lives ended before they had barely begun. Maimed, crippled, killed. A yarn of advancement being spun. Progress!"

"Through the village to your front door. You guide me through to the back."

"Manus!" I cry. And I must have jumped up.

"Sit down!" he bellows in response.

On the sheet a scene of green and brown appeared. It's hard to believe, even now, Christa. All this pouring out of you, with more to come. There were trees, bare earth, simple thatched buildings. An African village. In the distance, the edges of a rainforest. You walked forward swiftly. Almost all the people there were black and wore few clothes. I – you – glimpsed one white man in a white uniform and a pith helmet, his back turned.

"I can hear screaming!"

You started to run. You ran in a confused manner. You didn't know where to go.

Abruptly, a little girl appeared in front of you. You stopped running. She was different from the others. She was wearing a simple white skirt and a short-sleeved top. She lifted her arm to point. She had no hand. Her hand was gone. You looked down at her. Her small face was solemn and sad. You reached out your own hand towards her face, but then withdrew it. Unmoved, she gestured again with her arm and you set off in the direction she'd indicated. Ahead, another figure appeared. You paused. It was a small boy, with a questioning look on his face. His middle was wrapped in a length of white cloth.

"Which way?" you say on the tape.

He lifted his arm to point. He too had no hand. You ran on, only to encounter a tall, spare teenage boy. He was covered by the same white cloth as the other. His expression seemed to contain an impossible number of emotions. Or perhaps none at all. He lifted his handless arm to show you where to go.

So it was that you ran to a place near a group of huts where villagers and some men with rifles were standing. The men with guns wore blue uniforms with a red trim and red fezzes on their heads. Baskets containing a whitish-brown stuff lay about. A man was pleading with one of the soldiers who snarled in anger and smashed the butt of his rifle into the desperate man's bare chest. A young girl, almost naked, was dragged forward and thrown to the ground by one of the soldiers. He stamped down viciously on her small arm, pinning it to the ground. The girl didn't put up much of a struggle. Another soldier stepped forward. Raising a machete, he began to hack off the young girl's hand.

The images faded from the sheet.

"It was the king of my country who was responsible for these terrible things," says a shaky, slightly accented voice on the tape.

"Indeed," Manus replies. "Leopold II of Belgium. The Congo Free State, where human hands became a kind of currency and were piled up by the basketful. As for Christa's dream, many children had their hands cut off because their parents had not made their quota of rubber. Some children were murdered, dismembered, and, it's said, cannibalised. But still, the industrial world got its rubber and progress continued apace."

"Through the village to your front door. You guide me through to the back."

"That's it!" I shrugged off Helen's hand from my shoulder. When it returned I twisted in my chair and gave her a furious shove, throwing her off balance. I grabbed you under the arm and tried to make you stand. Your face had aged so much. You were thinner. Your hair was limp. But you were tough. I couldn't move you from the chair. Your stiff body seemed to have a new-found sinewy strength. Suddenly hands were grabbing at me. It was your sisters. And they too were surprisingly strong. I was hauled down the row of seats and held at the side of the church. They both resembled you, of course. But they were still young. They gripped my arms tightly. You were beyond my help.

In your dream you were following a shambling crowd across a muddy field. As the crowd slowed and bunched, you forced your way through towards the front, past figures in baggy clothes. There was a large hole in the ground. Beside it stood a cart that had been drawn to the spot by a gaunt grey horse. It looked exhausted, its head drooping. You pushed to the edge of the hole, jostled angrily by others. In the hole lay another horse, or the carcass of one, with a chestnut coat, dirty now. It was wasted away, its ribs and pelvis protruding, it's face eroded by hunger. There was so little flesh. The skin, it seemed, should have been sliced open by the sharp ridges and bulges of the bones beneath.

Two workers were climbing out of the hole. As they left, the men and women of the crowd began to clamber down into the pit. Everyone you could see was hideously thin. I remember hollow eyes, famished faces. There was confusion. Blades were raised by skeletal arms. The people hacked at the body of the horse with cleavers and knives, though there was almost no flesh left to take. Hair, skin, and muscle were chopped from bone. Tongues lapped at sluggish blood. Starving humans scavenging from a starved animal's open grave.

Someone pushed you from behind and you stumbled and fell forwards into the hole. In the church you cried out. On the sheet there was a moment of darkness and the scene shifted. You were in a dim room, a small, dim house. You moved about. We saw white walls, pictures on the walls, wooden beams above your head. There was simple furniture, fabric, clay pots on shelves, and, hanging up, cooking utensils. On a table there lay the body of young girl, scrawny, with rigid, twisted limbs. She was naked. Her throat was cut. You stood by the table and looked at the corpse for a period of time – seconds, perhaps, but it seemed like minutes. Then we saw you raise your thin arm, a knife in your hand. With the greatest of care you began to cut a slice of flesh from the young girl's thigh ...

In the church, you were hunched over in your chair, shaking in a way I found extremely disturbing.

"The Holodomor," Manus says on the tape. "Stalin's terror-famine of the 1930s. Millions of Ukrainians died of starvation and disease. Perhaps the dead girl's fate is to be turned into sausages. Certainly such things occurred."

Maybe he intended to say more, but you interrupted him. It's barely audible on the recording, but I remember it clearly. It was merely a murmur this time. Once again you said: "Through the village to your front door. You guide me through to the back."

I fought so hard to get free! I really struggled. It's not easy, Christa, to admit that your sisters were stronger, but it's true. They were *much* stronger than me. Their fingers seemed not so much to be gripping my arms as crushing them. I couldn't shake them off.

"Christa!" I shout on the tape. "Christa, stop! Just get up and go outside!"

On the sheet you were lying on a table. We could just about see that the table was made of metal, perhaps stainless steel. You were naked, looking down the length of your body to your swollen belly. You were pregnant. Shadows stirred in the room. Glimpses of people moving. Your view darkened. A masked figure in a surgical gown loomed over you, and then another, this one wearing spectacles. He held up a scalpel. You were still conscious. I don't know why you couldn't get off the table. The man with the scalpel repositioned himself and began to cut you below your bump. And still you were awake. In the church you began to scream like an animal in a trap. On the sheet you struggled, but to little effect. Something held you down. The skin, the flesh and muscles of your bulging belly were being sliced open and were coming apart. We – you – could see the emergence of your baby's hand, your baby's bottom and foot, perfectly formed. The man continued to draw the scalpel up your body, along your chest. The blood was running freely and now a second figure was pushing his hand into you, wrist deep. He pulled back his arm and some part of your insides came spilling out. And still the scalpel came, cutting you open, finally, from your pelvis to your neck. Before the image faded, we saw your baby move amidst the mess ...

On the tape Manus says: "Unit 731, a Japanese research facility in Northern China. Prisoners, including children and pregnant women, were vivisected while awake, infected with diseases, exposed to frostbite, raped, burned, buried alive. Many of the scientists who worked there had backgrounds in animal experimentation. Their research led to the publication of papers in scientific journals. There are reports that Shirō Ishii, who ran Unit 731, established a benevolent clinic after the war and converted to Christianity not long before his death."

There is a long pause before Manus resumes. No one came to help you. I was still pinned at the side of the nave. Jacques was pecking at the contents of the floor of his cage. You were doubled over and trembling.

At last, Manus begins again. "It seems to me that Christa could have spent a great many of her nights enduring such dreams, dreams of the suffering of children. *Children*: those of whom we say, at least when it suits us: 'We care about them the most.' She might have dreamt of Cherokee children being marched along the Trail of Tears, of slave children separated from their families in the antebellum South. She might have dreamt of children being mutilated, assaulted, killed during the Rape of Nanking. And she might have dreamt of the children waiting to be gassed at Treblinka, naked in the Polish winter, their freezing feet sticking to the ground, so that finally, when their turn came, they had to be torn free. These are merely a sample of those of whom she might have dreamt.

"Child chimney sweeps, child miners, the child soldiers of the Khmer Rouge. She might have dreamt of these too. Or she might have dreamt simply of children scared of their fathers and mothers, scared of their teachers and priests."

With this, Manus turned to your sisters and said: "Thank you. Please allow Alex to return to his seat."

I was released, my upper arms throbbing, and made my way back to where you were sitting. You didn't respond or even acknowledge me when I tried to comfort you. Your body didn't feel like yours – it was so hard and cold, and the shaking wouldn't stop. I couldn't do anything but stay by your side.

"What we've done to children, what, even now, we do to them, and what we do to animals as well, isn't merely a measure of our hypocrisy. After all, that's such a limited and all-too-human way of looking at things. Nor are our crimes against them just adverse outbreaks of history, though that is what certain historians would have you believe. How they love, these historians, to explain everything away with ingenious specifics: singular circumstances, the economy, politics, ideology, power. Complex, contingent causes it takes a donnish lifetime to understand. Whole shelves of books written to explain how each set of atrocities are, in effect, aberrations, utterly unique." Here Manus paused, his jaw working beneath the beard. Almost to himself, he said, "Well, perhaps that's not quite fair. But I am so *weary* of history. Weary of events and weary of the study of those events." I glanced at Helen. She was nodding. Manus collected himself and said more forcefully: "Too few historians concern themselves with the essence of things, believing that it's not their job. The essence is this: what we do to the innocent, what we do to each other, we do because it is an irrepressible expression of who we are. The endless episodes of cruelty are not serial aberrations, not exercises in historical distinctiveness. We are not, primarily, historical beings. We are, first and foremost, creatures of nature, and in the realm of nature it is *we* who have become the grimmest of aberrations. The passing of historical time has revealed a dire truth, that human beings are *deviants*, deviants of nature.

"Now, the state of nature is itself cruel. At least, that's commonly how we see it. The will-to-live, simple biology, fills every sentient being with the need to eat and procreate and almost all animals find themselves the potential prey of other beasts. Food is scarce, the winter is cold, shelter is hard to come by. But cruelty in animals, if that is what we must call it, is instinctive, not *imaginative*, not ceaselessly *inventive*. Humans have made inventive, gratuitous cruelty the crux of things, the most arresting and alarming element of life. Ever more so, it has become the meaning of our story."

I didn't hear you say anything, but, while Manus was speaking, another dream had formed. You were inside a poorly-lit pig farm. In narrow metal crates, pigs lay trapped on their sides, covered in sores. Pigs caked in excrement were crammed into filthy pens. A piglet trembled, it's foot caught in a broken floor grill. You moved from section to section. It was an absolute hell. Dead pigs lay everywhere. There were pigs with open wounds and horrible swellings. You saw piglets suffering spasms, pigs gnawing at the bars of their cages, pigs gone lame. Live pigs nudged at the bodies of the dead with their snouts. Outside, in the rain, there were more dead pigs discarded on the ground, half buried in manure, and open bins with the bodies of piglets mixed in with the trash.

Meanwhile, calmly, Manus pressed on: "All living things are subject to the will-to-live. All living things suffer from a litany of needs or wants about which they have little choice. But desire has become limitless and deviant in the human being, with its grotesquely swollen consciousness, its overdeveloped mind. We have become, at once, nature's apex and its caricature. It is not, chiefly, an infatuation with viciousness and death that drives us to torture and kill. It is our compulsive drive to survive, and survive well. We conquer because we believe in the idea of home and we murder because we love our rich and complex lives. And our ingenuity is excessive.

"For some our cleverness is a sure sign of progress. But technological improvements are progress of a very limited type, and in the end they will prove environmentally and biologically ruinous. The notion that we are progressing, morally, politically, to a more advanced condition is a lie. The Holocaust was a uniquely monstrous crime; and yet there will be further genocides. The world will do nothing and historians will gorge on the particulars. Besides, what do we, what *can* we, measure progress against? Only our own appalling failures. The question should not be how do we compare to our ancestors, but how do we compare to other species? The answer, needless to say, is badly. And that answer will never change. The truth is, even if redemption were possible once, it is now far too late. Our crimes have been too many and too great to ever rehabilitate ourselves. Our history would be our damnation, even if our determining nature were not. But our nature *is* our damnation, and the world is an inferno for the beings we eat or who stand in our way.

"Now, I'm no misanthrope." Here Manus paused, and even smiled, and almost everybody tittered. They were hardier than me. I couldn't laugh. On the sheet another, final, scene had appeared. You were in some kind of large metal shed. It swirled with white down. You were sat on the floor watching women ripping feathers from the bodies and wings of live geese. As she worked, the woman beside you stepped on the neck of a struggling bird and your eyes alighted on its feet which were bound with twine. Where the goose had already been plucked, its skin was inflamed and raw and the wounds it'd sustained bled freely. Before they faded, the images blurred. In your dream, you were crying.

"On the contrary, I recognise that human beings have some excellent qualities. And chief among them is not reason, but *compassion*. Compassion is the basis of ethics. On that we are all agreed. But I would add that even an ethical impulse is a form of suffering. Our minds torment us uniquely. An animal in the wild lives not only without an abstract sense of time, without foreknowledge of its inevitable death, but also without reflecting on the suffering it causes to its prey. The Komodo dragon is not conflicted as it eats the buffalo alive. Humans inflict much suffering, but they are capable as well of being *afflicted* by it, even when it does not directly affect them. We weep for those we love. But we weep, too, for those long dead, for those we have never met, for those in a country far away. Even as we lay waste to the world, we worry for those not yet born. And this expansive sense of pity burdens us with a moral responsibility that animals can never possess. It is this responsibility that years ago we pledged jointly to face. It is time, my friends. It is time for us to perform the ultimate moral act, the ultimate act of compassion, empathy, and sacrifice. We have travelled so far together, but now we have arrived. On the morning of Easter Sunday, we will gather one last time. On Easter Sunday, there will be a resurrection, and our compassion will wrap itself around the world." And Manus picked up the black cloth and draped it back over Jacques' wooden cage.

They'd obviously been listening to every word of the speech, and understood it was at an end, because, as the black covering went back on, that was the exact moment the Gilders burst into the church.

My first thought was how ridiculous they looked. No doubt they were serious people. After all, they'd tracked Manus down and were apparently determined to stop him. But as they clustered there with their golden knives, certain they were the good guys, they only proved how right Manus was about everything. Their plan, it seemed, was to stab us to death in the name of humankind. The last Gilder to enter closed the church doors.

Their leader stepped forward. He was a tall man, perhaps about 40, with wavy blonde hair. It was bizarre. Hardly anyone had got up off their chairs. We just sat there, twisting around to see what was going on. Walter had made his way to Manus's side. You remained bent over on your seat. The Gilder at the front spoke first. He addressed Manus in a way that seemed to suggest they were picking up a recent conversation.

Softly, he said: "Will you surrender?"

"Of course not," Manus replied.

"We cannot permit you to proceed." The man spoke English with an accent. I thought he must be from somewhere in Scandinavia.

"You're embarrassing yourselves," Manus said. "I remember when Gilders were something to be contended with. You're nothing but the rump."

The blonde man snorted bitterly. "You can insult us if you wish. History is on our side. We have always prevented people like you from getting their way."

"History? History isn't on anyone's side. History is a horror story. And not one of you will be a named character. You're far too late."

The Gilders began to fan out at the back of the church. Their leader was probably the oldest among them. They were mostly men, a few women too. There were perhaps twenty-five of them, although maybe that's an exaggeration. They were dressed in dark outdoor clothing and sturdy leather boots. Every one of them gripped a golden knife with an upwards-curving blade. Their weapons looked so strange held in soft hands emerging from the cuffs of waterproof coats. I can't really recall their faces. Some of Manus's people were rather odd-looking I suppose, but far more memorable.

The head Gilder stepped forward and those behind him followed his lead. It was only now that one by one we started standing up. Were they really going to attack us? It hardly seemed real. I caught Helen's eye and she shook her head and made an exasperated gesture.

"Everyone move behind me," Manus called out, his voice perfectly steady. "I'm their main target, together with Jacques."

People didn't run. They stepped slowly out from the rows of chairs, turning their backs to Manus as they went, facing the Gilders in case they came on with their blades.

There was one exception. You remained hunched over in your chair near the chancel arch. When I saw that you had no intention of following me I tried to go back, but again one of your sisters held on to my arm. Into my ear she whispered: "There's nothing to fear. No one is going to be able to hurt her now." And when she said it I believed her.

With extreme caution, the Gilders crept towards us. I reckon they were more frightened than we were. The whole place was heavy with disbelief. Their movements were stiff and tense. Still, they were the ones with cruel-looking knives. I remember thinking that we should've picked up chairs as weapons or shields. But, in the oddness of the moment, no one had done so and now we had no means of protecting ourselves.

I guess I expected Manus to produce a surprise attack or defence. And yet, other than the night we'd chased after the first Gilder to arrive in the village, and Manus had called out to the foxes and owls, I'd never seen Manus *in action*. His big plan had involved many years of patient and meticulous preparation. Even the demonstrations in his study, put on for you and your sisters, were carefully designed. Manus was methodical, a man of instruments and books. Thinking about it now, I find it hard to imagine what he would've done. Maybe something extraordinary. Maybe nothing more than swinging his fists.

But of course, Christa, Manus wasn't the one who dealt with the Gilders. That was you.

As they drew near, their knives began to shine. Later, I heard someone call this the "Aureate Glow". The gleaming knives of the Gilders made them more resolute. Now they stepped towards us in perfect unison. They came partly side-on, like fencers. On the face of their leader, I caught the flicker of a grim smile.

And then you stood up, straightening slowly as you raised yourself off the chair. Slowly you turned your aged body to face the Gilders and slowly the whole church began to grow dark. The blackening air thickened and stirred. It's hard to describe. It was uncomfortable to breathe. The temperature dropped. There was a cold, clogging sensation in my nose and throat. When I tried to move I felt a resistance in the atmosphere. Our group remained mostly still. The lights in the church were smothered. The gleaming blades of the Gilders' knives were hidden or extinguished. So much for the Aureate Glow. I heard movements. Stumbling feet, chairs scraping and being tipped over, collisions and confusion. I'm sure we all snatched at the sound of metal clattering as it hit the stone floor. They were dropping their blades. The Gilders began to cry out and we could hear them trying, and failing, to open the doors. "Please!" someone shouted, and there were shouts in other tongues. I caught a "No!" and a brief, panicked gasp. And then a scream came, raw and agonised. And after that another noise, closer to a groan. And then nothing but the rasp of one knife after another being picked up, which took two or three long minutes. The air thinned and the church grew lighter. The body of their leader lay on the floor, and protruding from every part of it were the Gilders' knives, sunk handle deep. Twenty or more bits of golden metal sticking out of him, messily.

As the light returned, the surviving Gilders gathered together at the end of the south aisle of the church. Some had to crawl to join their fellows. You were standing facing them, their dead leader behind you. Your hands were bloody. I noticed how hunched your back looked.

Immediately, Manus took charge. With Walter and another man by his side, he strode to the corpse of the head Gilder. Each of them pulled a knife from the body. Manus chose the one that had been plunged into his throat. He yanked it out with force.

In moments, being threatened by their own blades, the Gilders were moved up the aisle, away from the tower and the south porch, into the chancel.

Meanwhile, Helen and your sisters had rushed to offer you help. With a sharp gesture of her hand, Helen made it clear I wasn't to join them. Surrounding you, murmuring close to your ear, they held you round the middle, and keeping your face hidden from view, led you from the church.

I could do nothing but watch you leave.

Others were gazing in your direction. "She is almost ready," said a youngish man standing beside me. "Ready to take the shape of Fate."

I turned my head and must've given him a murderous look because, flushing, he lowered his gaze and sidled away.

I'd had enough. I was disgusted, scared, and full of rage. It wasn't all the death and suffering we'd witnessed. All I could think about was your lovely body looking bent and old. They'd done something vile to you and they'd wrenched us apart, just as I always knew they would. I left the church and ran back to my cottage. I bolted the door and pulled the curtains closed. I was certain they'd keep you hidden, and I wanted to hide away too. I'd have to wait until Easter Sunday to see you again.

14

Even when Manus started letting the Gilders go, one by one, having forced them to eat quantities of his chocolates, and even when some of them could be seen wandering through the woods and village in a confused state, even then no one in the new-build houses woke up to what was going on where they lived. It was a rainy Saturday and they stayed indoors, bar the odd dog walker. They had their televisions on, they had their silky blouses to wear, their sporty v-necks, yellow and pale blue. They had no pub or shop or post office to visit. If they wanted something for the Easter weekend, they got into their expensive cars and drove off to the supermarket. The BBC showed *Grandstand*, *Jim'll Fix It*, and films about Jesus. Manus and his machinations remained hidden in plain sight.

Walking in the woods on Saturday afternoon, I found one of the Gilders trying to dig his own grave. He was a man, maybe in his late twenties, with fair hair. He had no tools, but the earth was wet and soft enough for him to have made some progress with his hands. Still, he was a long way from being finished. There were the ragged beginnings of a human-length hole in the ground where he toiled away, but it had nothing like the correct depth, nothing like the depth I knew he craved.

He flinched pitifully when he saw me approaching. Of course, he believed he was dead. He tried to hide his face from me. He couldn't flee – the dead don't run. So he just stayed there, on his knees in the shallow pit that he'd made, desperate for me to go.

I knew he was a prisoner of the dungeon of his mind, and how dark it was in there. I should have left him alone. But I couldn't pass by. Here was somebody having a worse time than me. No one would envy my life, I thought: basically homeless, and with you, Christa, off in an unknown place and an unknown state. But, right now, they would envy this Gilder's life even less.

I stood at the edge of his resting place. The rain was coming down heavily. The Gilder was soaked and filthy with wet, black earth.

"It's horrible, isn't it, how much work death is?" I said in a matey tone I'd hardly ever used before. "Don't you find it's a massive hassle?"

The Gilder was much further gone than I had been. He began to writhe and whimper softly beneath the sound of my voice. I should've had more sympathy for him. I remembered how I'd wanted to lie at peace in wormless dirt. How I wanted my death to be perfect and undisturbed.

"They don't tell you," I went on, "how much there is to think about once you've crossed over. All the worry and trouble. I wouldn't wish it on anybody. But it's not as though you have a choice. It just gets handed out – like homework. Today's assignment: being dead."

I shrugged. "And then you've just got to get on with it. This enormous chore. I know all about chores. My parents make me do the dusting and the vacuuming every single day."

I exhaled, wearily, to show him I knew how dreadful chores could be. He clawed feebly in his hole. And then, evidently, he had an idea. Slowly raising his hands, he began to push bits of soil into his ears. I watched him for a while, packing more and more in. When he started on his grave again, I left him to his task. Some time later, I checked. He hadn't made a success of it. There was no body under the earth.

I soon felt bad about what I'd done, so I kept watch for other Gilders as I walked, planning on being kinder.

Eventually, I left the woods and the village. I remembered where you said you'd gone when you were scared of all humans, the copse of trees not too far from our school, the place with the foxhole where you'd slept. I trudged up Inkle Lane (it was still raining) and crossed the sodden field, wondering if I might find a Gilder full of fear. There was no one. From my pockets, I laid out some peanuts and an apple on the fallen trunk of a dead tree. A Gilder, in an animal state, might find their way there, just as you had, in need of food.

At last, I faced up to the necessity of going back to the cottage to eat something myself. But, before I went inside, I walked through the village again and found myself going up your driveway and standing outside your front door. I knew it was useless. The house was dark. Svea was away in London meeting relatives who were over from Sweden. Mats was staying with university friends. And you were with Helen and Manus, probably up on their mysterious farm. Still, I stood there for a long time, trying to sort through everything that had happened since that first journey down here with Jay. I couldn't do it. The events wouldn't unfold in any kind of order in my mind. It was only your face that would come. Your face in a certain light, in the dimness of your room. Your mouth, your cheeks, your eyes looking me up at me as you sat on your beanbag. It was all I could see.

I was just leaving, when I heard the phone in the hallway of your empty house start to ring. I waited and listened. It rang a long time. Maybe it was your mum, calling to check up on you, calling for the second or third time that day. The thing is, though, I had the strangest feeling that it wasn't your mum, but your dad who was calling. I had the feeling he wanted to say that he loved you very much. I had the feeling he wanted to beg you to stop.

*

I slept on the sofa that night. The knock on the cottage door came very early and it was still dark when we gathered in the street. Each of us was handed an orb light and we walked in a loose procession in the direction the woods, moving through the new part of the village, past the family homes, brazenly, ahead of the dawn.

I knew we were about to change everything, but all I could think of was seeing you.

We went swiftly along the road. No one spoke. I was near the back, walking alone. Soon we were amidst the trees, going more slowly now and spreading out. The air, damp and cold, seemed to cling about me, though the rain had stopped some hours earlier and the sky was clear. Once again I found myself glimpsing, by the dreamlike light of the orbs, dark figures threading their way through the wood, weaving between the trunks of ash and oak.

We kept on for many minutes. Steadily, the way grew trickier, more so than ever as we all converged where the trees grew at their thickest and there was no footway to be found. Reaching the place where all the others were gathering, I saw that two men were standing with their torches up high, holding out their hands to guide each newcomer over the edge of a slope. We were deep into the heart of the wood, at a spot you and I had often described as a secret place. It was a great sunken feature, a plunging, crater-like hollow, perfect, I realised, for the kind of thing Manus had in mind. Steep-sided and with few trees at the bottom, it would be his very own amphitheatre for this unique ritual at sunrise.

Waiting for my turn to descend, I heard the cry of a tawny owl. And, from another direction, a second owl answered the call. We were being watched, I thought. Hidden creatures had come to witness the transformation of their world. Manus had been whispering to them, imparting the good news.

Sidewise, careful to grip with my feet, I dashed down the slope to join the others. Some were stood in small groups, some alone, and some paced about, still using their orbs to light their way.

I never wore a watch and so I approached a young man standing by himself. "What time is it?" I asked.

He held out his arm to catch the dial in the glow of his torch. "The sun's about to come up," he replied. And I could see his face well enough to notice his eyebrows lift. "This is it," his expression said.

And so it was. As the light crept into the hollow, where all of us were at last assembled, Manus strode towards the centre of that place and began to speak. It wasn't us he addressed. Instead, he reached out to the remotest of deities, the most distant of goddesses, daring to invoke Lady Necessity. He did it in verse. I can't remember the lines exactly. Perhaps that's just as well. The poem was mesmerising, repetitious, highly patterned, full of clever rhymes. It needed to be utterly irresistible. I recall that he described her as she who holds the spindle, she who bears the torch. He named her winged Ananke, who coiled about the cosmos in bodiless serpent form with her consort Chronos. It was they, cried Manus, who had crushed the egg to make the heavens, the Earth, the oceans. All now despoiled! He denounced the false and subtle serpent, he said that the day of the subtle serpent was drawing to an end. And when he had honoured stern Ananke with many titles and acknowledged her primal power, he implored this merciless Lady, who had never once granted a prayer, to send forth her detested daughters. It was time, Manus cried, for these terrible daughters to bring to an end what could no longer be borne.

It seemed the implacable Lady agreed. From the shadows the three of you emerged, dressed in white robes. Everyone moved forwards a few steps. I felt so angry that I wasn't given any special place from which to see you. Crowding together, we formed a circle in the centre of the hollow, surrounding Manus and you and your uncanny sisters. There was a squeeze and I found myself jostling to get a good look at your face.

You were a *crone*. It was your word, from a few months before. Your sisters were upright, two young women beautiful in the light of dawn. But you were old and ugly, your back and shoulders bowed. I remembered your horror in these same woods when we took mushrooms and you became convinced you'd shrivelled up with age. A *hag*, you'd called yourself, a *witch*. I remembered how panicked you'd been. Yet here you stood, for all to see, with sunken cheeks, dead-looking flesh, and a bent body, supported on the arm of your second sister. But now there was no fear in your face. Yours was the face of Fate and it was we who were afraid.

Manus was dressed in the green and gold robe we'd seen so often in the vestry. He lifted his arms and called you by your immemorial names. The three of you separated. Your first sister held her distaff and spindle, your second her measuring rod, and you your abhorred shears. You didn't look at your sisters. It was us you regarded. Later, someone said that it was with an expression "as frigid as the cold spring of the Scamander". I didn't know what that meant. I just found the whole thing devastating. What had they done to you, my poor Christa?

At a point in the circle some distance from where I was standing the people suddenly made way. A young woman I had never seen before came walking slowly into the centre and stood before the three of you, full of trepidation. She was not much more than twenty. She had long, straight red hair and a round face. In her arms, wrapped in a blanket, she held a tiny baby, only a few days old. She knelt and Manus placed a huge, heavy hand upon her head.

No one spoke. Everyone grew unusually still. Deftly, yarn was spun from the cloud of whitish fibre at the top of the distaff. The thread was drawn out and held up. Your second sister measured it. Turning at last from the crowd, you shuffled to the side and lifted up your shears. The child started to cry. But I knew that now was not the time to cut the thread of life. If you did so, the baby would never grow up. That was the story. It would die right away, here in the woods. It would be a violation of your second sister's domain. And this had never occurred, not once in all of time. It was against the inevitable order of things.

And yet a violation, a breach in nature, had to happen. It was at the heart of Manus's plan. But it was only supposed to be make-believe, that was what Manus had always said. "Strictly symbolic, of course!" he'd remind us all at every rehearsal.

Moving, suddenly, with incredible speed, you rounded on your sisters. I saw their lovely faces turn rigid with terror. Oh Christa, they looked so much like you! It's hard to think about what your own face must have looked like then. Some final change had taken place. I could tell from your sisters' paralysed eyes. Such depths of cold as you stared at your doubles and opposites, the spinner and the apportioner of life, destined to die. How much you must have wanted it, an end to these incarnations of your once and future selves. Again the amazing quickness as you slashed open the throat of one sister and plunged your shears into the heart of the other. In unison, our circle let out its sighs – and screams. I can still hear that collective cry. It contained horror, elation, anguish, ecstasy.

Both sisters fell to the ground, their white robes filthy with blood. Your second sister clutched ferociously at her throat as the blood leaked around her fingers. She sunk first to her knees and then fully down, making sounds all the time. Your first sister seemed to die almost instantly. Nothing came from out of her mouth as she hit the earth with a short, soft thud.

Manus started to call out, to declaim again in verse. I heard words in ancient languages. I've learnt enough in the libraries of London since to know he was chanting of light, lamps, darkness. There were a few moments of turmoil. Some of us seemed to have purpose, some did not. I was in the second group and was pushed aside, ejected as the circle rearranged itself and closed in on you. Meanwhile, as in the church on Good Friday, the air grew cold and disturbed, and gloom began to smother us.

But this time it was different. All those that were part of the plan had kept their orb lights in their hands. Now they lifted them up high and joined in with Manus's cries. The torches began to glow with different colours. There were orbs that were crimson, emerald orbs, white, greyish blue. At a certain point, maybe when they'd all clasped hands, the swirling darkness outside of their circle swiftly dispersed and the morning light returned. Inside the ring, the darkness remained, a great column of roiling night with you hidden at the heart of it. The torch bearers held it there, bellowing Manus's hymn, while Manus himself rushed over to the bodies of your fallen sisters.

I saw what he did. He collected blood from both of them inside a phial of some kind. This he hurled into your pillar of dark with a great ceremonial shout. It was impossible to tell whether it was a plea or a curse.

The black column seemed to flare, to widen, to change colour, hued now with dark red. "Quickly," called Manus, "the bird!" A man handed him an object draped in cloth. Manus unveiled the cage of Jacques the passenger pigeon and held it up in one enormous fist. With his free hand he ripped away the wooden bars at the front and, throwing back his head, let go a great, joyous cry. Jacques seemed to know exactly what was expected of him. Bursting from the cage, he flew up over our heads, the first passenger pigeon to fly free in more than seventy-five years! We all looked at him. He was glorious, hovering there in the new day's light, a shaft of brightness catching his feathers. For a moment, he waited, displaying his fine body and rich, lovely colours. And then, when every one of us had taken a good look at him, Jacques turned about in the air and flew at great speed directly into the pillar of darkness.

I heard Manus screaming in rapture. I heard foxes and owls, nearby in the woods, joining in. There were other voices too. Walter and Helen were reading aloud from ancient, unknown books, their faces fierce with passion. Moments after Jacques had vanished, the blackness began to change. The circle dropped their torches and stepped back. Walter and Helen read on, the pitch of their voices rising, their mysterious verses locking together. In unison, they chanted. The column started to undulate and we glimpsed in its depths all the colours of the orb lights that had helped to hold it in place, iridescent reds, green, white, and blue.

I saw a hand, a pale arm, appear on the ground. Then your head, your shoulders. You were crawling out from the darkness you'd created. It was no longer yours.

I fought my way towards you. They didn't try and stop me. There were no cruel sisters to clasp my arms. I helped you to your feet. You were young again. You were pale and weak and your robe was stained with blood, but you clutched me tightly, smiled, and then kissed me on the mouth. We turned to look as the birds began to take shape, billowing up, just as Helen had said, the column forming into birds, birds of darkness with traces of colour on their black, ghostly feathers. On and on it went, thousands and thousands of them, revenant birds born from your rage and your sisters' sacrifice. Birds of night filling the early morning sky. A resurrection. An extinction. Above the tops of the tallest trees we could see them soaring, spreading out in all directions. Soon they would flock to every corner of the world.

There was a kind of party afterwards, much to my surprise.

The group stood and watched the column for a long time. Manus was circulating, talking to his followers, gesturing, clapping people on the back, laughing, clearly euphoric about his success. But us he left alone, and I was glad. We whispered and kissed and hugged. I kept pressing my fingers to your face, hardly believing you were back to your young self, and my amazement and happiness about it made you smile, and cry a little too. For a good while we lost ourselves in the delight of finding one another again, so much so that neither of us saw them take the bodies of your sisters away.

Eventually we turned to look once more at what you'd helped to make. How long, I wondered, would it go on? How many birds would be born and fly free from this captured darkness of yours? The column showed no sign of dwindling. Above our heads, the birds kept coming into being, so quickly and thickly it was hard to see it happen in any detail. I noticed that everyone else had gone quiet as well and had fallen into contemplation, even Manus. For several minutes we all just stood there and looked, and, I suppose, every one of us was thinking about the astounding change we'd made to the world.

The spell was broken when we glimpsed a stranger, a man with a English Pointer by his side, watching us from above. It was obvious that the endless uprush of dark birds had drawn him to the spot. He wouldn't be the last. We left immediately and began a lengthy hike out of the woods and into the hills. Someone had clothes for you. We walked slowly, right at the back, with me giving you some support now and then. At a certain point, at the foot of a lane, we were met by a man and woman in a Land Rover who had driven down from the farm. In fact, the farm was where we were headed, but the pair in the Defender had headed down in advance to provide us with coffee from flasks and freshly baked rolls. And I remember how welcome that simple breakfast was – we were famished.

After we'd eaten, I approached Manus and said, "Christa is exhausted. How much further is this farm? She could do with going the rest of the way in the car."

Manus clutched my shoulder and squeezed. "Of course. I was about to suggest it anyway. You go with her, and I'll send Helen along to keep you company."

And so the five of us drove up the lane, onto the moor-top road, and soon after turned off again and bumped our way along a track to the farm. As Helen had said, there were two stone buildings, though they were larger than I'd imagined, and various sheds and barns, one of which, I learned, had been converted into a laboratory. I suspect much of the land once attached to the place had been sold off.

We crossed a cobbled yard and ducked our way into the farmhouse. There were a few people inside. I think they lived on the farm. I'd never seen them before. I remember low ceilings and wooden beams, a scrubbed pine table, tattered thick jumpers, pale young faces turned in your direction.

A curly-haired man said, "We've been outside since dawn. We saw the birds go up and there have been thousands streaking overhead." A pause, and then he added, "It's incredible."

You nodded, nothing more. People were looking tense and uncertain, spooked out even.

Helen said, "Christa, would you like to rest?"

"Yes, please."

She led us into a hallway and up a steep, narrow flight of stairs. At the end of a cramped landing, furnished with bookcases that made it more cramped still, she showed us into a small but immaculate room. It seemed to have been recently painted, the plaster walls white, the wooden window frame black, and the bed had fresh, spotless linen. There were towels, toiletries, a tray with a jug of water and drinking glasses. "There's a bathroom just next door," Helen said.

Neither of us replied. Helen waited, then looked at me. I smiled gratefully, but still she hesitated.

You walked to the open door and gripped the handle. "Thank you, Helen." She nodded, lingered a second more, as though there was something she wanted to say, and then left.

"A shower, or a bath," you said. "Let's have a look."

We went into the bathroom. "Just a bath. Let's have one together."

"Don't you want to sleep?"

"Not yet. Later."

"How do you feel now?"

"It's impossible to explain. I just want a bath."

"Where were you last night?"

"Up here with Manus, in another building. He talked to me all night. I wasn't really me though, so ..."

It was obvious you didn't want to revisit it. So I ran a bath for us both and we climbed in.

"You still have some blood ..."

"Oh, God." I swear I could see you push what you'd done to your sisters out of your mind. You scrubbed, then said, "Let's change the water."

We emptied the bath, I gave it a quick clean, and then we filled it again. "Nice and hot, please." you said.

We steamed in there for about an hour. After a while you fell into a doze and I kept watch. When the water grew too cold I stood up and you opened your eyes and smiled. You stood up too and put your arms around my waist. "Let's go to bed," you said.

"Okay."

"I mean, let's ..."

"Really?"

"Yes. Definitely. We *must*. It needs to be us. The first people in the whole world to do it knowing ... knowing what we know. That I definitely can't ... That it's not about that anymore. And it never will be again."

I smiled, but I must have looked doubtful as well.

"Also, I just really, really want to."

"I like that reason better."

When I woke up, hours later, the party was underway. I got dressed and sat on the side of the bed. I waited for a little while, but you barely stirred. Deciding to let you rest, I unlocked the bedroom door, and padded downstairs. Outside, the light was fading. We'd slept through the whole afternoon.

To my astonishment, when I entered the kitchen a cheer went up. Within seconds someone had handed me a large glass of red wine. Neither Manus nor Walter were there, but the room was crowded and Helen was in the midst of it all, preparing food, drinking and laughing. When she saw me she rushed over with a plate and kissed me on both cheeks.

"Oh, Alex. We did it! Thank you for all your help."

"I didn't do anything."

"Nonsense! Now where is Christa? Is she sleeping still?"

"Yep."

"She's tired. It's hardly surprising. But she must come down soon. She is our heroine!" Helen's eyes were brimming with tears. Lowering her voice, she said, "Such a rare feeling of finality. Utterly unique." She shook her head. "Now, eat and drink. Tomorrow, we will all be separating. But tonight – fun!" And she rushed away, back to the hob.

A man I didn't recognise appeared by my side and leant his mouth towards my ear:

"The birds are still flying," he said.

I nodded.

"Still going up! It's getting too dark to see now, but we were out about an hour ago and you could see them going off every which way. Coming overhead. They don't make a sound," he added.

"I know."

"It's amazing."

I turned towards him. He'd obviously been drinking for much of the afternoon. He was young, pale, with smudgy circles under his eyes. I didn't think he looked very well and his excitement didn't seem to suit him. I felt like it was the first time he'd been fired up about anything in his life and that the emotion would soon wear off.

It was too full in the kitchen and so I drifted away and wandered. Some people wanted to say hello. Some wanted to shake my hand. People kept fetching me drinks. I noticed a certain curiosity about me that'd never been there before. The booze was kicking in, but I was still observant and I noticed something else too. I noticed that there were plenty of people who didn't appear to be especially excited or sociable. Mostly, these people had escaped outside. There were a couple of bonfires burning in the fields behind the farmhouse. By firelight, I saw figures standing alone, sitting alone, or quiet pairs locked in private conversation. There was a woman, I remember, middle-aged, solitary, strumming an acoustic guitar, playing the same doleful tune over and over again. There was a feeling of fragmentation out in those fields. The bonds of Manus's group were already dissolving. His people looked different, more distinct from one another, with different clothes, different faces.

I felt more comfortable outside and I stayed a good while, drinking, chatting now and then, but mostly people watching and staring into the flames. Eventually, pretty far gone, I became aware of an uproar coming from the farmhouse. I headed back. Manus had arrived and was leaning with his back to the big stone sink. This was the last time I ever saw him. His lips were moving, he was murmuring something. Meanwhile, you'd woken up and come downstairs. You were standing on the large pine kitchen table, standing in the middle of it. Your arms were thrown up and you were rotating your wrists, twirling your hands. There was a strange atmosphere in the room. Some people – but not all – were clapping and whooping. Across the plaster walls, across the white ceiling, thousands and thousands of miniature passenger pigeons were flying, their wings flapping, their tiny bodies black. The bad dreams were over and this shadow-lantern display was your celebration, your party piece. With Manus's help.

Everything was despicable. I headed outside again, not very steady on my feet. More drink was what I wanted and I was given some brandy. I slumped down on a milking stool and peered into the flames. I kept taking sips from the bottle, set on getting obliterated, without any concern for tomorrow. When the sun came up, I didn't even know where I'd be living. We'd never projected beyond this point. And I didn't see how anything, anything at all, could go on. It occurred to me that in a few week's time we would be sitting our exams.

The thought of that ridiculous prospect seemed to require some sort of laughter.

You found me passed out in the mud and brought me round. I was cold and confused. I felt hideous. I barely remember, but I know you guided me up to the bedroom and then some time later came up yourself and got into bed beside me.

You were still there when I woke up and went into some kind of attack.

It started as soon as I returned from the bathroom. Dropping back into bed, I found I couldn't stop writhing around. I began to claw frenziedly at various parts of my body and to act as though I was fighting off an invisible assailant, striking at the air above the bed with my hands. By this point you were awake.

Drowsy, your murmured, "What are you doing?"

I couldn't answer. I just carried on battling with the air above the bed.

"Stop it. What's wrong?" You placed your arm across my body, trying to calm me down.

But I wasn't able to stop. Your voice only seemed to make it worse. I threw your arm off, raked my chest with my fingernails, and then began swiping again at empty space, this time even more frenetically.

"Alex!"

You were up on your knees now, trying to grab my arms.

I tumbled out of bed, onto my front. Pushing myself up, I started to crawl around the room. It was dim in there. Everything was grey.

There was such a terrible pressure. I could feel the skull beneath my skin. I felt my insides were putrified. Something was trying to burst out of me.

It started with a howl. It was so raw that some deep and watchful part of me felt surprised. Then another cry, and another. The tears were blurring my vision. I started to gabble. On and on it went. What had we done? How could we have done it? We had no right. Nobody did. It was utterly wicked. I was sick with shame and guilt. It was him, Manus. He'd twisted our relationship. He'd controlled us from the very start. We were young, far too young. He shouldn't have got us involved. We were okay before he came along. I wanted to go back, back to the beginning, and start all over again.

And then I said it. It was unforgivable. I told you that you could never understand the value of a child. I said I'd seen the harm it caused when children were missing. I said it ruined everything.

I was up on my hands and knees, my eyes closed, my face directed into a dark corner of the room. I said I could see my sister, my poor, poor sister. I said, "I know she's dead, I know she's gone, but she's in here with us now, over there. I can see her. I can see her red hair. I'd forgotten it was curly. I can see that her eyes are blue. I can see the buttons on her sleepsuit. It's clean and white. She's standing there and looking at me. She's so incredibly sad. She's crying because of what we've done."

"Stop it!" you shouted.

"My poor, poor sister."

"You bastard!" you screamed. "You shit! I didn't do it for Manus. It was *never* for Manus. I did it for you! I did it for you, Alex!"

"We've taken them all away," I said.

You were down on the floor now, gasping, punching me as hard as you could. You couldn't control yourself. You pushed me over and straddled my chest. I tried to protect my face, but I was weak and you were strong. I deserved it anyway, all the pain. You got several good punches in and then collapsed sobbing on top of me. We cried together for what seemed like hours. Eventually, we fell asleep, close, but not touching, on the floor.

When I woke up later you were gone.

After

I often see faceless people in this city, Christa. We're not so cloistered that we never go out, and the novices have more freedom anyway. Of course, the religious order to which I belong, only a few years old, and entirely wrong about everything, is a joke, but I never let my view of them show. In a way, it's me who has no face.

The faceless ones I see in the streets must be another delusion of mine. We're never free of misbelief, we both know that. I should be more compassionate, inwardly, towards my brothers, but even with delusion there are degrees – and this lot here ... well, they're absolutely cracked.

By the way, we really are a brotherhood. There are no women here. No hidden Helens in the monastery. That was important to me.

Other faces, faces from the past, I can't stop seeing. Helen's face, Manus's. Even my dad's. But yours most of all, most of all by miles.

Oh Christa, to think I'll never be with you again.

I've thought about searching for you of course. But everything is against it. I've no money, no passport, and travel is so extremely difficult in any case. The human world is disintegrating and dangerous. Not that I'm much afraid. But what would be the point of looking when I have no idea where to start? And then there's my belief that you don't want to be found. Not by me. I betrayed you. In that room, up at the farmhouse, I betrayed you. *Rooms*: I've spent so much time thinking about rooms these past few months. That room will always be the last we shared.

We see each other all the time, you once said. I need a lifetime's supply of Manus's desiring drug, the one that made me run from my boxy bedroom and chase after you despite those terrible words. It's everything I want, everything I need. To tear through the world in pursuit of you, never to stop, never to think, until I'm breathless at your door. But the distance between us now is far greater than the length of Inkle Lane.

The writing of all this down is entirely second best, but it's been my way of pulling you close. Now that the story is almost done ... let's just say there's a small flock of dark birds circling overhead. I glimpse them through the skylight in my prize attic room.

It didn't take long at all for people around the world to go into a panic. No children anywhere on the planet were being conceived. Nothing worked, no one could help, not doctors, not scientists, not rabbis, imams, priests.

The authorities were overwhelmed. The pandemonium took many different forms. What's more, everywhere reports were coming in of dark, spectral birds filling the skies. And reports too that small flocks of these same birds were present at every human death. People were kneeling and weeping in the streets. You must have watched it begin as keenly as I did. There were times when I cried along with them, the prayerful and the distraught, but I must admit I found myself laughing too.

In the early days of the ferment, I went to your house for the final time and, at last, persuaded Svea to let me into your room. I took money, I took your broad-brimmed hat, and between the pages of *Dr Glas* I found it: the photograph. A round table with white linen in a restaurant filled with sunlight, obviously not in Britain. Seated at the table: Svea, young and very beautiful, your father, and, at your father's side, Manus. Bearded.

Unmistakable. I guessed the picture had been taken some time in the later 1960s. Everyone in the party looked happy and relaxed.

I stared at it for minutes, but in the end I left the photo between the pages of the book. And I said nothing about what I'd found to Svea as I left. There was no trust between us. If Svea knew anything about your whereabouts, I knew she wouldn't tell me. Manus would've seen to that.

And so I came to London, and lived off your money for a short time. And everything that's happened since means little to me and I won't write it down.

The human race is dwindling, day by day. The wild animals are filled with joy. It brings me comfort here at the end.

I don't know what will happen to this manuscript of mine. The brothers will find it. For the faithful it will be the most shocking revelation, or the most dreadful heresy. Perhaps they will burn every page. It was the writing of it that was important. Readers are not necessary.

It's raining. The birds are circling overhead. I will open the skylight. They always get in anyway.

They're inside now. I'm glad to see them in my room. They carry a part of you, my lost, lovely Christa.

CPSIA information can be obtained
at www.ICGtesting.com
Printed in the USA
BVHW021139061121
620961BV00018B/697